FILTH
M. KING

Dreamspinner Press

Published by
Dreamspinner Press
5032 Capital Circle SW
Suite 2, PMB# 279
Tallahassee, FL 32305-7886
USA
http://www.dreamspinnerpress.com/

This is a work of fiction. Names, characters, places, and incidents either are the product of author imagination or are used fictitiously, and any resemblance to actual persons, living or dead, business establishments, events, or locales is entirely coincidental.

ISBN: 978-1-62798-220-7
Digital ISBN: 978-1-62798-219-1

Printed in the United States of America
First Edition
November 2013

CHAPTER
ONE

"KELVIN JACOBS?"

The woman's voice is clear and calm, but Kel still winces, because nobody ever uses his full name. He packed it away a long time ago, along with the rest of the crap from his aunt and uncle's house. The smell of mildew in the bedroom he had there, the way the rain dried like salt-track tears on the grimy window, the sound of Aunt Gina hollering up the stairs for him to come down *right goddamn now....*

Kel shakes his head, shakes it all away, and goes up to the desk where the receptionist with the nice voice points him to treatment room three, and he walks along there, rubbing his sweaty palms against his jeans.

He hates needles so bad. Really, really bad.

The doctor's brusque and busy and snaps the band on his arm while she's running through her checklist of questions. Kel can't blame her—the waiting room's full, and there are people backed up in the hallways, but then this is a free clinic, so what do they expect? The late afternoon is always busy, anyway. Full of anonymous after-work drop-ins, easy to spot by their nervous, tight-lipped faces and white knuckles.

He keeps his answers concise. No, he hasn't had any problems, any symptoms of anything nasty. No colds, no flu. No nothing. The needle bites—sharp scratch and it's sliding into his arm, cold and hungry, and Kel glances over to see the blood coming out. He taps his heel lightly against the linoleum floor, clears his throat. Hates the smell of disinfectant in here. Way the doctor's looking at him, Kel figures she's noticed he's not nervous about the test, just the needle. She slips it out, he winces again and, where she directs, he clamps the cotton swab to his arm. She looks archly at him as she gives him the spiel about how long the results might take, potential window periods and so forth. He just nods. He knows; he doesn't really care what she thinks. The whole thing takes maybe twenty minutes and after that, he's done, and he wants to go home.

He has to pick up some other results before he can leave, but they're okay. Kel skim-reads the paperwork and smiles tightly to himself. It's a relief, but an expected one. There's a guy in the hallway when Kel walks back out to the front, and he's lighting a cigarette. One of the nurses comes running, clucking at him that he can't smoke here and, with bad grace, the guy puts it out. There's a biohazard tattoo at the top of his right arm.

Kel averts his gaze, and he can't get out of there fast enough.

The light hits him, bright and rich outside, sending blotchy streaks of blue to mottle his vision. Smells of Korean food from someone's open window, burned sunshine on tarmac, and the dirty, gritty breeze all swirl around him, and Kel takes a deep breath. He could walk home blindfolded from here, and he sets off, feeling a little better than he did in the clinic. It's not a good neighborhood, but there are worse. Its most distinguishing feature—aside from the close-pressed rows of dark brick buildings with ironwork veins running across their roofs and walls—is its facelessness. Almost anything can happen here without a single thing being heard or seen. It's a particular kind of dislocation, born of a large number of people all concentrating on not noticing anyone else, being deliberately and decisively blind to everything beyond their own walls. The Projects aren't like this, nor is the heart of town, where everyone knows everyone else's business and has an opinion on it. That's not to say, of course, that the grapevine doesn't run this side of the bus station, but its roots are shallower. This whole part of the city feels less rooted, really. Like a forgotten name, a book pushed to the back of a shelf. Still there, but undusted, unread. Kel's glad they don't live right in the middle of all that shit, though. He doubts Toni could take that kind of hothouse pressure.

Kel worries about that and, just like normal, whenever he worries about anything, Toni is right at the forefront of it. He worries about Toni a lot. More than ever, recently.

Toni is.... *Damn*. Kel turns the corner, idling by the afternoon traffic that clogs the streets, the smell of exhaust layered in fat and greasy slices on the sidewalk. He crosses the road, heading toward the convenience store above which they rent a two-room apartment that, no matter how many windows they open, always stinks of microwave burritos and damp.

What *is* Toni?

He slips by the dumpster at the back of the store and across to the brick-lined stairs that lead up to the apartment. He hops up the steps two at a time, already pulling the key from his pocket.

Toni is everything. Toni is... infuriating and impossible, and totally full of crap, but he's also sweet and funny and he gets under your skin in a thousand of the worst, crazy, stupid ways.

Kel reaches the apartment door. The paint is tagged and peeling. There's an old Madonna album playing inside. It's not that loud, but he can hear it because the door doesn't fit properly. Neither do the window frames, but there isn't much point in complaining.

About six months ago, they had the biggest fight, him and Toni. At the time, Kel thought it would end everything—and sometimes he thinks maybe it should have, because he often secretly thinks things like that, only to feel guilty for it later—but it didn't. It made them stronger, in a way. This thing that Toni's gotten himself into, all these changes... Kel supposes he should have seen it coming. Frankly, he can't believe he didn't see it, but Toni's been fucked up in one way or another ever since Kel met him, so maybe he shouldn't blame himself for not picking one particular fuckup out of a pile of fuckups. Not that it's exactly a fuckup, this thing of Toni's. Not *exactly*, because maybe it is a part of him, or some expression of something he's trying to choke out of himself... but Kel doesn't understand it. No matter how hard he tries, he can't get it to sit right next to the person he knows his honey is. But that doesn't make him the bad guy, does it?

It shouldn't. He doesn't want it to.

The day they met was summer grit and warm, stale air, just like this. The year has gone by really fast, though some days it feels as if it's been a lifetime.

The outreach center closed a few months back. The economy's not great for charity at the moment. It stood a block or so from where

the free clinic is now, just one of the squat, ugly buildings on the way
to the bus station. There used to be a needle exchange on the ground
floor, and upstairs a meeting room with bright-painted walls and hard
plastic chairs. The first time Kel went, he thought it was going to be
stupid—one of those pointless things you do simply to shut people the
fuck up—and he didn't think he'd stick with it, but the guys who ran it
turned out to be nice. They weren't preachy, they handed out free
coffee and sometimes sandwiches along with the condoms, and he
made a couple of friends there. You'd sit around, drink the coffee, swap
the license plate numbers of johns who ought to be avoided, find people
to watch your back when you were working, and that was useful. No
smoking in the building, though, and that was how he met Toni.

This one time, Kel slipped out onto the fire escape—old wrought
iron scaled with rust and overlooking acres of brown brick and
concrete—and he almost trod on this guy, sitting folded in on himself
and looking down at the street below. When Kel apologized, the guy
glanced up, and Kel just saw this perfect crocus of a human being.
Slim, with a face that belonged in an art museum, all soft shadows and
cheekbones, nose like a marble statue's and a mouth made for... well,
the kind of mouth a man could go blind just thinking about. He had the
most beautiful brown eyes, deep-set and shaded with apprehension.
Tight-furled, like a flower in bud. His clothes hung off him, baggy and
faded, almost as if they belonged to someone else—maybe they did—
and his wavy, black hair could have done with a wash.

If Kel believed in love at first sight, he would have called it that.
Instead, he only remembers this weird feeling that pummeled his guts,
nearly knocked his legs out from under him, and made him shoot out a
hand to the rail for support, scratching his palm on the sharp slivers of
rust and peeling paint.

Fuck! He swore at the stab of pain and scowled at the railing like
it was to blame.

Toni just smiled. They ended up sitting there, sharing two smokes
and a bag of Doritos, and he picked the splintered pieces of rust out of
Kel's hand with graceful, slim fingers. He wore dark-blue polish to
hide how yellow his nails were back then.

So, what you doin' out here anyway?

He'd shaken his head at Kel's question, blown smoke at the wind,
and said he didn't like the politics. Even now, Kel thinks this was a lie.

Toni was probably just chickenshit. Ever since they've known each other, he's always been running away from something.

Now, Kel opens the door to their apartment and lets himself in.

He's home. He slides the chain on the door and tosses his keys on the table. You don't run away from home, once you find it. Madonna's bitching on about something in the background, and he rubs absently at the sore patch on the inside of his elbow where the doctor took blood.

"Baby! You okay? I missed you!"

There's a brief blur of movement in the kitchen doorway, but then Kel's arms are full of Toni, wearing nothing but a bathrobe and a smile. He kisses Kel and doesn't seem to want to let him go. Kel's not too bothered about that, because he never quite realizes how much he's missed Toni until he's holding him, and even then it doesn't seem entirely real. He starts to tell Toni about the clinic and how he's got one set of tests back all clear, and it'll be about a week or so to wait for the others, but he's sure everything's fine anyway, and Toni cuts him off.

"I just ran a bath. Wanna share? C'mon."

He's tugging on Kel's arm and pulling the puppy-dog face he does so well, so it's a foregone conclusion even before Kel glances at the clock.

"Yeah, but I have to—"

"You've got *hours*. Come on. Don't you want to?"

Kel sighs. There aren't that many hours, but there's no point arguing. The song on the stereo changes. "Bad Girl" starts playing, Toni's arms slip around his neck, and there's close, swaying dancing and lip-synching. Toni's warm, peppermint-scented breath is tempting, so Kel figures what the hell. He grabs the back of Toni's neck, soft and vulnerable where the black curls—so much longer now than that first day—have been gathered and pinned up, leaving his nape bare, pulls him close and gives him a rough, deep kiss.

"Show you what bad girls get," he mutters into Toni's mouth, and there's delighted laughter and the promise of a whole lot more to come.

The bathroom is tiny—the kind of tiny where you have to sit on an angle to take a shit and the door won't open all the way—but they have candles, and Toni's poured some kind of sweet, flowery oil into the water. He gets in first, and Kel can't help but watch. He's already starting to change, even if it's just the way he holds himself, the way he thinks about his body. Hell, that started when he began growing out his hair, talking about facial electrolysis, and looking up all this crap online. Kel didn't think he'd do it, didn't think for a minute it would come to anything, but he was wrong.

It hasn't been long so far, with the pills. A little over six weeks, maybe. Kel supposes he should be keeping count, but he hasn't. Not properly, anyway. They're the horse piss kind—no prescriptions, and the labels are often in Spanish—and they scare him to death because Toni bought them from some shitty website, sitting there in this cyber café drinking a cinnamon latte and pretending it was just normal shopping. It wasn't. It was a terrible idea. He's self-administering, talking about complicated dosages of estrogen, antiandrogens, and progesterone like he knows what he's doing, but he doesn't. They make him moody as hell—worse even than before he started—and who knows what he's doing to himself in the long term?

Kel figures maybe he'll stop. Maybe Toni will see it's not right for him—because Kel believes so desperately that it isn't—or at least he'll realize, if he *is* going to do it, that he needs to wait and get proper help, and he'll just… stop. Maybe. It's not probable, of course, because this is Toni, and he's a self-absorbed, stubborn little shit who only has room in his head for one idea at a time, on account of the way he believes things with such blazing, incredible intensity, but Kel needs to think it *could* happen.

Because, looking at that body stepping into the water—all long legs and narrow hips, lithe and slim, ripples of muscles and smooth flesh—he doesn't know how much change he can bear.

A perfect crocus, flattened and torn.

Kel can't even begin to imagine that, and he gets dizzy trying. He hates himself for it, obviously, because this is Toni… and whatever else he is, Toni is *his* stubborn little shit. Kel knows he ought to be there for whatever his honey needs, but there are some things he's never even thought about being prepared for, or pictured for a second happening to him, or to *them*.

He climbs in behind Toni, and there's the splashing and wriggling of legs and bodies accustoming themselves to each other, and Toni laughs when Kel tickles him. The water's deliciously warm, lapping up around and between them, and Kel slides his arms around his honey's slender body, wishing he didn't have to go anywhere ever again.

"What'd you do today?" he asks and kisses Toni's nape.

"Not much. Read. Watched some TV. Slept in."

"Hm." Kel pops his lips against the bony curve behind Toni's ear. "You were sleeping when I left. Did you get my note?"

"Uh-huh." Toni leans back into him a little. "You're sweet."

Kel moves away and reaches for the soap so he can wash Toni's back. Toni arches it like a cat and makes a small, soft, happy noise, so Kel takes his time, tracing the hard muscles, the tension, the fleur-de-lis tattoo on the back of Toni's left shoulder... and he tries not to let it matter. Toni is still the same person. His back, so far, remains a man's back, and it's a nice one. Kel kisses it, warm water and warm skin, and he really would much rather stay here than go out, but he has to.

As if Toni's reading his mind—which happens a lot, and Kel thinks proves that, even with all the crap he has to take, Toni is so fucking special—he says:

"So, where are you going?"

"Hmm." Kel cloaks his reluctance with a grin. He knows Toni can't see it, but maybe it'll reflect in his voice. "I shouldn't even be taking a bath."

"Oh, hell, no...."

"Yup."

"The Sherbet Pervert?"

Kel presses another kiss to that smooth back and wonders idly how long it will take before the hinky Mexican pills start changing the way Toni's body feels against his mouth. "Mm-hm."

"Eeww!" Toni squeals, kicking and splashing in the water. "Oh, yuck! Is that why you took those disgusting socks back out of the hamper this morning?"

"Mm-hm," Kel says again, rubbing his hands over Toni's shoulders, still entranced by the landscape of his body and the wet, silky sheen that the imperfectly rinsed soap leaves against his pale-olive skin. "I can't believe you were gonna wash 'em. I spent all week dirtying those puppies up."

"I hate it," Toni declares, and Kel knows there's a pouty face being pulled, though he can't see it. "It's stinky and gross and disgusting. Does he make you call him Daddy?"

"Nn-nn." Kel writes three small, secret words across Toni's shoulders with a soapy finger, then quickly washes them away. "Mr. Petersen. I think that was his eighth-grade phys ed teacher or something. Whack, no?"

"Ick," Toni agrees, melting back against him.

Kel holds him, tickles his ribs. Toni still feels a little thin, he thinks, but he knows it isn't worth saying anything. They'll only fight about it. Toni's scared of the pills making him fat, so he's not eating like he should, and he won't listen to anything anybody says, because he never does. Kel palms his way over his lover's chest, and he doesn't know if the swellings of incipient breasts just starting to bud behind Toni's nipples are in his imagination or not. Not being able to see, like this, it makes Toni's body a shadowed, secret world that he has to learn by touch, memories his only map. Like he *needs* a map. Kel reaches down, strokes the corded flesh of belly and abs, and Toni makes a small back-of-the-throat purr. He pushes Kel's hand away before it reaches his cock, though, twisting fishlike in the water that smells of cheap, synthetic fragrance. Jasmine, Kel thinks.

"Stop it," Toni murmurs, and he does. He'll always do anything Toni asks.

Kel brings his hand out of the water, his skin dripping with the sticky, cloying, fake-flower smell, and puts it to Toni's jaw instead, tilting his face around for a kiss. He feels stubble and remembers Toni's got an electrolysis appointment next week, so he ought to enjoy it while it's there. Kel rubs his chin against Toni's cheek, then comes back to that full, hot mouth and hopes that, whatever happens, Toni will always kiss like a man.

"I love you," he murmurs when they finally part.

A low sigh leaves Toni's throat. "I love you too, baby. Be back later?"

"Yeah, sure. Prolly late. I won't wake you."

"All right."

Toni leans forward, takes up a washcloth and sets to sluicing the perfumed water over his arms. Kel kind of feels he's been dismissed, so he gets out of the tub and leaves Toni sitting there, squeezing out the cloth with a small frown on his face, looking like he's grappling with some intense problem of world macroeconomics.

Kel towels off—rubs away as much of the jasmine smell as he can—wandering into their bedroom as he does it, because he hates it when Toni gets moody. He glances at the clock by Toni's side of the bed, making a mental adjustment for the fact it's always running fast. He isn't sure whether he has enough time to waste, though he really would like to spend a little while with his honey.

Toni doesn't come in, though, so Kel figures he ought to get going.

He dresses slowly, making sure he's remembered everything: dirty briefs, slightly crusty, which he wore four days straight last week, much to Toni's disgust; the aforementioned icky socks; and, finally, athletic shorts a size too small, which go on under his jeans. They ride up on his ass, and he hates it, because it's uncomfortable and they pinch horribly, but he can't mess with it, especially once he has his pants on. A plain white tee with barbecue sauce and sweat stains can be hidden easily enough under his jacket, but Kel still wrinkles his nose at the smell.

Toni's still in the tub. Kel doesn't disturb him with a goodbye. He leaves their apartment, taking the stairs that lead down to the parking lot and the convenience store two at a time, his key and enough change for the bus jangling in his pocket. The light is dying, and a greasy, stale breeze snakes through this little tarmac-and-neon world. Somewhere, a man is shouting and a pounding bass beat plays. The two things may or may not be connected but, either way, Kel doesn't give them much thought. Dogs bark, traffic moves, and a woman is yelling at somebody, just on the edge of hearing. He catches the bus, sits curled in on himself and stares at, rather than through, the grubby window. Kel gets off two stops early, jogging those last few blocks to help work up a sweat, before easing to his customary casual, sloping walk just as he gets near to the house. He knows where it is; he's been here plenty of times before.

Michael is smiling when he opens the door. He's stocky, paunchy, more than a little gray… everything you'd expected from a middle-aged guy in a polo shirt and a semisuburban home. The place is nice: one of those townhouses with the curlicues over the porch. Not big, kind of narrow, but nice. Kel nods, hands in his pockets, weight sliding onto his back foot.

"You'd better come in," Michael says, and he does. It's clean and bright in here, and smells of furniture polish. "How are you keeping?"

"A'ight," Kel says and shakes his head when Michael asks him if he'd like a drink. "No. Thanks."

"You sure?"

"Sure."

Kel wants to ask if they can make this quick, but he knows that might piss Michael off, so he doesn't. Instead, he follows him through to the living room, which has a lot of pictures of Michael on his yacht—he used to sail a lot, apparently, and he won some kind of competition once—and some watercolors that his wife painted. She's on a business trip to Denver. Kel sits on the couch, which is upholstered in off-white leather, and the color reminds him a little bit of the socks he's wearing. He wonders if that's anything to do with why it was chosen, and has a passing but very funny vision of Michael in the furniture store with his wife, hand in his pocket and fumbling with himself as he thinks about boys in dirty gym socks.

Michael gets himself a glass of bourbon, offers Kel one again, and Kel has to choke down a laugh before he repeats his "no, thank you." At least it's not like the first few times he came here. Michael made him sit in the kitchen and eat a bowl of raspberry sherbet while they talked about baseball. *Yes, Mr. Petersen. No, Mr. Petersen.* Kel's never been fond of raspberry-flavored things. He grew even less fond after Michael made him rub the sherbet all over his dick and suck it off. He still likes to do that sometimes, and Kel can't even look at raspberry flavored Jell-O seriously anymore.

So, all in all, he's pretty glad it's just a little bourbon being offered today.

Michael sits beside him to have his drink, and Kel can smell the liquor both on him and in the glass. He listens to Michael talk crap about his work and what a week it's been. Did he see that thing on the news about an attempted bombing somewhere? World's going to hell in a handcart, right? Terrible.

Kel nods. It is.

After a while, Michael finishes his bourbon, and he leans over Kel to put the glass on the end table. His hand is on Kel's thigh, his face pressed up against his neck. Kel thinks he'll complain about the lingering traces of jasmine oil from the bath, but it seems he worked up enough of a sweat running from the bus stop to cover that. Michael licks the side of his neck.

"God, you smell... uh! Are you sweaty?"

"Uh-huh."

"Come upstairs and show me."

Kel gets off the couch and follows him. They start, as they always do, with him stripping down to the athletic shorts, socks, and T-shirt. Michael tells him he's a dirty boy, panting as he gets naked and climbs on the bed. He lies on his back, stroking his stubby, thick little dick— so hard and red the tip looks like an angry boil—while Kel kneels over him, crawls all over him and rubs his feet, still encased in those filthy socks, against his face. Michael opens his mouth, sucks on the dirt-grayed fabric, grunts out only partly comprehensible words, and begs him to take off the shirt and shorts. Kel refuses, plays shy, and Michael tells him to fucking do it. He does.

"Yes, Mr. Petersen."

There's a lot of talk about how disgusting he is, how sweaty, how dirty.

He's filth, Michael says. Filthy and revolting.

The T-shirt and the shorts are dropped to the bed, and Kel crawls over him, grinding against him. Michael's hands are on his thighs, his chest, his ass... always moving, always grabbing. He likes to watch the up-and-down of Kel's package in the stained underwear, rubbing all over his body. He tells Kel to say that he loves it, and Kel does. He's not sure how convincing he sounds, but Michael doesn't seem to mind. The briefs are in an even worse state now than when he started; he thinks maybe he'll burn them when he gets home. He hopes he can take them off soon, anyway. They itch like crazy.

Kel gets lucky. Michael's begging for them, so he peels the underpants off real slow, kneeling up to do it. He extricates one leg, then the other, and drops the dirty cotton over Michael's face. He doesn't look while Michael does whatever it is he does to them... sniffing, sucking, chewing, or who knows what. Kel doesn't really want to think about it. In any case, this is the point at which he has to start concentrating. He kneels over Michael's head and jerks off, thinking hard about something—anything—that will fill up this room and blot out the red, puffy face of this sweaty guy with dirty briefs dangling over his chin.

It ends up mostly being a hot scene from this Mexican movie Kel saw a month or so ago, where these two guys fucked in a swimming pool, colored over a little bit with Toni and the tub in their apartment. Either way, eventually Kel gets there, and he's almost able to block out the sound of Michael yelling:

"Holy shit, yeah! Piss on me, dirty boy! Piss your come!"

It's not a bad gig. Not really.

WHEN KEL gets home, it's heading on toward midnight. He had to eat the sherbet after all, but they sat at the kitchen table for it, and Michael cried while he talked about his wife. He pays well, but the guy is seriously fucked up, and Kel doesn't know where to look half the time.

He lets himself into the apartment, and the first place he goes is the bedroom, just to see that Toni's there. He is, and he's sleeping. He looks so peaceful, head resting on one crooked arm. The other arm, tribal band tattoo encircling its curved bicep, is over the covers. His face, relaxed and free, is almost like it used to be. A smile hides at the corner of his full lips, and Kel wonders what's going on in those dreams.

He can't sleep here, next to that.

He took a shower at Michael's place—God knows he needed it— but Kel still feels crusty and grimy and, yes, dirty. He had to put the T-shirt back on, because he didn't take a change of clothes with him, but Michael gave him a plastic bag to bring the balled-up shorts and gross socks home in, and Kel left that by the front door. The Pervert kept the undies this time.

The last time, he said. But he always says that.

Kel creeps back into the other room and, shucking off his jeans and the crusty tee, he takes a green wool blanket that usually lives on the back of the couch—and which Toni often snuggles into when they're watching TV—wraps it around himself, and beds down on the saggy upholstery.

He doesn't sleep well. Not until the sky's nearly getting light. Mainly he just lies there and thinks of nothing, letting his mind wander around the empty places inside of himself, and replaying snatches of memories and regrets like old songs. Finally, the pools of quiet between thoughts get longer and, at last, Kel does get some rest. If he dreams, he doesn't remember anything about it.

When he wakes up, the first thing he sees through bleary morning eyes are two black gym bags, packed and standing by the door. He groans.

Not again.

Toni is in the bathroom. He can hear water running, and see steam curling from under the door. Kel sighs, rolls off the couch, and doesn't bother to pull his jeans on before he heads for the coffee.

"So what the hell is that?" he calls when he finally hears the bathroom door open.

He jerks a thumb over his shoulder at the bags and makes like he really doesn't know. It's the only way he can think of to tell Toni he's being an idiot.

"If you don't wanna be here, you can damn well go!" Toni snarls, towel clutched around that soon-to-be changeling body, dripping in the bathroom doorway, wet hair plastered to his neck. "That's what *that* is. I packed your things for you, you lazy shit. If you don't want to be with me—"

Kel sighs. "Sometimes you're crazy, you know that?"

"I know you wouldn't even share my fucking *bed* last night!"

Kel is aware that technically it's their bed, since they bought it with pooled money, but he isn't going to argue. Toni gets moods that are wild and uncontrollable—he always has, even before he started pushing horse piss down his throat—and trying to fight that is like trying to argue with torrential rain. It's possible, but futile, and you run the risk of being struck by lightning.

"I told you I wouldn't wake you. It was late. You were sleeping."

"Liar!" Toni snaps, and Kel really doesn't know how to counter that, so he just shakes his head and says nothing.

Some days, this is the safest retreat. Today, it seems to enrage Toni even more. The towel is flung to the floor with a shriek, and after a moment, the bedroom door slams. Kel takes a deep breath, rubs his hand over his mouth and bites back on all the shouting and swearing he wants to do. It would be so tempting to kick in the damn door, grab

Toni and just shake him, slap the stupid whimpering, whining sneer off his face and make him *see*…. And what does that make Kel?

He lets the spoon in his hand clatter to the counter, half-dropped and half-thrown, his fingers still curled on the impulse to hit something. He knows what it makes him, what he could do. It's not something he wants to think about. Anyway, they've had enough fights like that, and Kel doesn't ever want to put bruises on his honey again.

So, he backs off, he leaves Toni to his mood, and he doesn't stop to dwell on things.

Kel abandons the unmade coffee and pads to the bathroom for another shower and a shave. He's put the money Michael gave him last night into the cookie jar on the top of the refrigerator, where they keep all of their cash. He's a little uneasy with that arrangement, but he doesn't want to say so to Toni, because that didn't work out well last time. Toni took it like Kel thought he was going to snatch the whole jar and run off, and there was a lot of yelling about him being called a fucking thief, and Kel didn't mean it that way at all, but Toni still got incredibly pissed. It wasn't even about the money, probably. Kel doesn't think so. He thinks it was about the fact that it's *him* who earns most of it, and how much Toni hates that, but he isn't sure.

To tell the truth, sometimes Kel thinks it would be better if *he* was the one who stole the cookie jar and ran away. At times like these—when Toni's mad, and he's packed Kel's bags for him already, and there isn't much that's going to calm him down—Kel thinks maybe he'd be better off out of it all. He thinks about taking the money and going away. He's not sure where. There are buses that go from the local bus station. Ones that go all over the place, not just the immediate services Kel uses for getting to places like Michael's house. He's never looked into it, but it would work, wouldn't it?

Just going down there with cash in hand, buying a ticket, and just fucking going.

Where probably wouldn't even matter.

The bedroom door is still shut when Kel comes out of the bathroom and, just for a moment, he catches himself wondering how many aspirin they have in the apartment, but then he hears Toni crying. Kel knocks softly on the door, because his heart is ripping itself to pieces and, of all things, he can't bear Toni's tears. He never could.

"C'mon. Lemme in."

He also needs clean clothes, and the warmth of the shower is rapidly dissipating from his bare skin. He shivers, and tries the door; it isn't locked.

Toni sits naked on the edge of the bed, bowed over and shaking, practically convulsing with all the crap he carries around inside him. Kel can't begin to imagine what it's like to live inside that shattered, coruscating mind. He thinks Toni's a lot like broken glass, or maybe a crystal vase just at the point of breaking, right before it loses its form and the echoed shape of itself.

He goes to the bed, sits down by Toni and pulls him, snot-smeared and red-faced, into his arms. He resists at first, angry and abusive, turning his head away and slapping at Kel with those long, slim hands that end in a set of short, white-tipped gel nails. Those damn things can leave scratches that really sting, so Kel tries to keep his face and neck away from them, but a few scratches don't matter next to holding Toni against him, and that's all he wants to do.

Kel gets his arms around him and, just as Toni's opening up a little red cat-scratch on his chest, that moment of safety and connection breaks through the angry bitterness, and he stops swearing and fighting. The vase falls apart, little shards exploding into dust, and Toni grips the arm around his chest hard, his face red and screwed up as he blubbers, apologizes, runs himself down again and again until Kel tells him to stop. He's beautiful, Kel loves him, it doesn't matter… he's sorry.

Eventually, Toni calms a little and lets Kel tell him it's all right without arguing back. He sniffs. Clumsily, he reaches for Kel, turning like a child in his arms and pulling him close, as if he thinks he can blot everything out with his mouth. Toni kisses him, and Kel tastes salt and strawberry lip balm. Toni's cheek is sticky, breath clogged with tears still, and Kel is aware that his lover doesn't really want him, just the validation he can give. Toni's already got one hand on Kel's chest, just below where he scratched him, and the heel of his palm grinds on Kel's nipple as his touch alternates between coercion and demand. The other hand is already delving between Kel's thighs, and he knows that if he says no, Toni's likely to throw another fit, so he has to be careful how he plays this.

"Babe…." Kel gathers up those roving hands and peels them off his flesh, holding them tight. "You have to go to work."

"I don't care! I won't go. I'll be late."

Toni leans in again, still trying. Another wet, snot-streaked kiss smears Kel's cheek. Even in the state Toni's in, Kel does kind of want it too; the hot shadow that blocks out the things that scare him. And he did miss having someone sleeping beside him last night. All the same, he squeezes those talented hands and looks apologetically into his honey's red-rimmed, puffy brown eyes. The first thing Kel noticed about Toni, that day at the outreach center—aside from the fact he was blocking the fire escape—was his eyes. It's like they lead into a strange world where Kel's never sure he can follow, but he keeps trying and trying, because they promise so very much.

"Go on. You have to go to work. Go wash your face. Get dressed. Hm?"

Toni pouts, but gets up wordlessly and stalks to the bathroom. He sniffs as he gets through the door, and Kel knows he's not done crying.

He hears it break out as Toni disappears from view—these convulsive bursts of tears that sound like someone snapping into pieces—and Kel thinks perhaps he ought to go in there, but what can he really do?

He stifles a sigh, lets the air run cold between his teeth, and hangs his head. He's really not sure how much more of this shit he can take.

CHAPTER
TWO

THE WAY he's looking at Toni makes her feel useless. Pathetic, like she's the drunk chick trying to screw everybody in the club, and he doesn't even want her kisses. Hot tears tremble on her eyelids, and the weight of more behind them pushes them out so they trail stinging paths down her cheeks. Her nose is running, her forehead's throbbing, and she wishes she hadn't started this.

It's his fault. He was late home, wasn't he? He doesn't know what she has to go through, how bad it is waiting while he's out. Knowing what... well, knowing what she knows. Toni's been all the places he has, but not going there anymore doesn't mean not knowing, or not remembering.

He's still looking at her with that horrible mix of pity and apology—like he's sorry she's fucked up. So handsome, with his crooked nose an arrowhead that's somehow landed astray on his face, his soft lips tucked into a curl of concern, his dark eyes burning into her... burning like the blush of anger and embarrassment that's rippling across her skin.

Kel squeezes her hands and, not wanting to give him the satisfaction, Toni really has to fight not to let out a sob.

"Go on. You have to go to work. Go wash your face. Get dressed. Hm?"

Toni pulls her hands away and stands up, determined not to make any more of a fool of herself than she already has. It hurts enough.

Does he not know how much he hurts her? Bastard. He's right, obviously. That's the worst thing. It always is.

Toni utterly hates having to admit that Kel's right, and she can't get back into the bathroom fast enough. Away from him, and into the arms of the pretense that he doesn't hear when she clutches the sides of the sink and cries a little more.

It's better when it's all out, like throwing up, and she can focus on fixing her hair and face. She feels even more stupid now, anyway. It was the waiting that did it. If Toni hadn't had to wait up last night, it would have been okay. It's being alone that does it.

Waiting, all alone.

Toni hates waiting. Hates it because it's lonely, and the loneliness is even worse, even more hateful than the waiting. She wasted the whole evening trying to fill the silence. Watching crappy television while she rubbed moisturizer into her legs, dry after all the goddamn waxing and shaving. It's stupid how ladies' razors are these delicate little pink-handled things, when dealing with Toni's leg hair is more like hacking through miles of Amazonian jungle. The estrogen should start doing something about that soon... maybe. Of course, pretty girls have nice legs to start with, not these knobble-kneed, scrawny, sinewy things that hang off the end of her flat, boy's ass, and that heads Toni into thoughts she should turn away from, because they're ugly and painful.

She doesn't feel right.

Toni washes the face, and pats at the eye bags and the blotchy, dry skin. Blow-dries the hair. The bathroom is still wreathed with the steam from Kel's shower, and traces of the smell of his deodorant linger on the warm air. He's left the lid off the can of shaving cream.

Toni mugs at the reflection in the mirror.

Puffy, fat, scaly, disgusting face.

That's not totally true. Some days it feels like it—a lot of days it feels like it—but not always. Some days, Toni feels awesome. Strong, sexy, beautiful, glamorous... all that and fries on the side. It doesn't matter what he's wearing, or how the pronouns fit together in his head—and fuck, are words not the most stupid, ridiculous things? It's not like people look down at themselves and say, "Yeah, I have a he-penis" and, even if they did, it blows to have to choose one set of definitions to go with it—but, some days, nothing comes together at all.

This is one of those days. This is one of those horrible, awkward, nasty, I-am-not-me-and-this-is-not-where-I-am days, and Toni hates— *hates hates hates*—these.

Kel says she's beautiful. He tells her often that she's a beautiful person, inside and out, and Toni supposes that must prove it. She must have some redeeming features, otherwise why would someone like him stick around?

This, in turn, starts her down another track that shouldn't be taken: that maybe the day's coming when Kel will realize how much better he could do. Someone not as screwed up as her, someone more stable, better controlled, better looking, better.... How does that song go?

Someone who isn't going cheap in the sales.

Toni grabs a hairbrush and pulls it through her hair, like she could yank the thoughts she doesn't want out of her head. It hurts. Last night, when she did her nails in front of CNN, she told herself she was stupid. She'll lose him anyway. He doesn't want this. He doesn't want... *her*.

Later, after all the primping and the polishing was finished, she started to feel weepy, the way she feels now, though not so bad. Toni called her friend Danielle, who's great because any time, day or night, if Toni calls she'll gossip and chat and talk to her without asking why. Danielle understands the ups and downs. Talking to her always makes Toni feel better... and maybe a tiny bit inferior.

It made her feel better last night. Just for half an hour, she could talk to Danielle and not have Kel rolling his eyes and making sarcastic comments under his breath—because he doesn't understand, not really, whatever he says—and it was okay. It was okay to admit she felt like things were out of control. It was okay to be afraid. It made her feel better and, once Danielle hung up, Toni didn't mind going back to flipping through magazines and pretending not to be watching the clock.

Now, she flings the brush down next to the sink and sniffs heavily, determined not to give in to more tears. That's over and done with for this morning. They're not her anyway. They're the fucking pills. It's probably time for another adjustment. Toni supposes she should talk to Danielle... but Danielle doesn't really approve of the self-administering thing. Which is fine for *her*, but Toni's not Danielle.

Danielle is natural, confident, and self-assured, and she has fabulous cheekbones.

Toni wishes she hadn't made such an exhibition of herself. Yelling at Kel like that. It was the waiting. If Toni hadn't had to wait up, if Kel hadn't come home so late... and he *was* late. All that time waiting, smoking in front of *Sex and the City* reruns, flipping over to catch the last half of the game—and when he did come back, Kel didn't even come to bed. Toni had woken up at the sound of his key in the lock. Waited. Rearranged her hair on the pillow. Laid there pretending to sleep.

He never even turned on the light.

Toni had turned over, tried to go back to sleep. The bed felt cold, and she couldn't stop thinking.

Most nights, she doesn't worry. Not really. Sure, there are crazies out there, but Kel's careful. They've both always been careful... Kel even more so than her. He knows what he's doing, and it's okay. It really is. Anyway, it's not like The Sherbet Pervert is one of the worst out there. So, he's got a thing about boys in dirty gym clothes. He was probably touched up by his phys ed teacher or his scoutmaster or something. So what? For Toni, it was some guy in the park; a rustle in the bushes, just a face that she'd seen there from time to time, the first person who called her pretty. Liked her like that. Mom's nail polish and a tight pair of jeans.

The first man to make Antonio Frescelli feel wanted.

Toni shakes her head, clearing the memories and the person they belong to away. For Kel, it was violent. His uncle. So, yeah, everyone has regrets.

She shivers, missing the warmth of Kel's arms around her. She feels stupid for the way she reacted—all right, *over*reacted—and later she'll unpack those bags and put his things away again. She doesn't know why he still puts up with her. Maybe he won't for much longer. He wouldn't take what she wanted to offer in the bedroom.

For a moment, Toni wonders if Kel brushed her off because he didn't want to do it, or just because he did mean it when he said she had to go to work. He's right, of course. She needs to get going. They need the money. So, she fixes her face and doesn't think about anything except how to patch up the puffiness, the reddened nose and watery eyes. Tears sting the bridge of Toni's nose, but they get pushed back. Quashed. Put away for another time.

When she finally gets out of the bathroom, Kel's in the kitchen.

He's dressed and making coffee, lighting two cigarettes in his mouth, Paul Henreid style, while he waits for the kettle to boil. He looks good. A light-purple T-shirt, spotlessly clean, clings to the outline of his shoulders, and his jeans hug the solid breadth of his hips and ass. Part of her still wants to skip today and just stay home with him. He's handsome—very handsome—with his crooked nose and his kinky hair, his broad back and thick thighs. His skin is the color of the cinnamon lattes Toni drinks on her lunch breaks, while she's thinking about him and how, one day soon, they're gonna go away together, go somewhere beautiful. Toni likes the idea of a beach with white sand and drinks that come in coconut shells. Like on Maui or Fiji, or somewhere like that with too many vowels, though she'd settle for Seattle. She's never been there, either. In fact, for Toni, the whole West Coast holds a glamour of otherness that might as well make it a different country. New York, too, and New Orleans, Miami…. They're places that happen on television, not in the real world.

Not Toni's world, anyway.

She slips back into the bedroom, dresses, fastens up her ankle boots, and comes back out feeling good. Feeling confident, almost. There's a spring in Toni's step as she goes to take the coffee and the cigarette Kel holds out to her.

"Do I look all right?"

Kel nods. "Fine. Uh… good," he corrects himself. "You look good."

Toni smiles, exhales a tight little breath of smoke, and isn't sure she believes he means it. She'd like to apologize for last night, for this morning, but the words are hard to find, and Toni's too fragile to search for them. Besides, if Kel doesn't stop looking at her like that, she might cry again. She drinks the coffee, smokes two-thirds of the cigarette, and neither of them really say anything.

She'd like to talk. Trouble is, Toni doesn't know what to say, how to put into words the things she wants him to know, the questions she might ask, or the promises she'd like to make. She watches Kel drink his coffee, his gaze fixed at a point in the mid-distance as he stares at nothing in particular, and she wonders what he's thinking about.

Toni glances at her watch. Running late. She swallows the last mouthful of coffee, passes Kel the cup, and leans across to kiss his cheek.

"I gotta go."

Kel turns his face, catches Toni's mouth against his, lips snaring hers, chaste but insistent. She supposes she's forgiven. It means a lot. She hugs him, holds on tight, and breathes in his scent. Cigarette smoke, the sharpness of soap, and a slight hint of citrus. It's a wrench to leave him, but she does, another kiss and the end of her cigarette parting gifts before she jogs down the stairs and out into the street.

THE BOOKSTORE where Toni works is a popular local landmark, less than four blocks away from the apartment. It's one of the faceless, dark brick buildings, with a strange jungle of pipes and ironwork cladding the outside, running across the worn red-brown surface like track marks. Every few months it skates very near to closing down, but somehow always rallies, like a true underdog should.

The sign over the door reads *Pink Pages*, and the paint is perpetually peeling.

Toni's working three full days and one half-day shift now, though she still has trouble with all the inventory and cash register crap. She's trying hard to nail it, because she knows how lucky she was to get the job—or how lucky she was that Danielle got her the job, she supposes—but it's difficult.

She's barely on time when she gets there, bursting through the door and into that familiar, somehow comforting smell of paper and mild damp. Karen, Toni's boss, looks up from behind the counter, where she sits on a high wooden stool a little like an old-fashioned bar chair, and smiles.

"Nice of you to join us."

She's holding a stock-checking form on a clipboard, with a copy of *Publisher's Weekly* partially over the top of it. A pencil wags between two short, stubby fingers, and her plastic-framed glasses are halfway down her nose, the multicolored string they dangle from when she's not wearing them looped against her fluffy, pale-blue sweater.

Toni shrugs and lets the door close behind her. The little bell above it gives a halfhearted *ding*. "Sorry."

"You feeling all right?"

"Mm-hm."

"Good." Karen lowers the paperwork she holds and looks Toni over. "Did you have a nice weekend?"

Toni doesn't work Mondays or Fridays, so they have this little ritual every Tuesday morning. She guesses it's Karen's way of prompting her to say she could do more... or maybe just checking she didn't go off the rails too much over her long weekend. It's like Karen's her personal counselor or something, which kind of pisses Toni off, because she's never liked talking to shrinks. Not since the ones in juvie, who just wouldn't leave anybody alone, and then Toni stops thinking about that—metal doors and long hallways—because they're not good memories.

"Mm-hm," she says again, not really in the mood to gossip too much with Karen, but not able to hide the smile that tugs at the corner of her mouth. "We went to the park."

That's true. They did, and it was nice. Early—well, earlyish—Saturday morning, after the drunks had cleared out but before it got too busy, they walked down by the fountain and back past the empty bandstand. One brief little flash of relaxation and fun between all the stuff they've had to do. Kel's blood work, her electrolysis... the pills. The constant grind of trying to keep afloat. Trying to make ends meet, when there isn't enough between the ends to stretch them all that far to start with.

Kel bought hot dogs for breakfast and held Toni's hand while they watched the algae and duckweed shift on the surface of the water. He can be really romantic sometimes. Shame she had to wreck it that afternoon, and start picking a fight about... what was it? Him leaving his pants on the floor or something. Or the right way to set the timer on the heater in the bathroom. It doesn't matter now but, at the time, it made her crazy. She wishes she didn't do that, and that they didn't fight so often, even though the bad feelings never last long.

"Kel all right?" Karen asks, one penciled-in eyebrow raised.

"Uh-huh," Toni says, aware that she doesn't sound one hundred percent convinced. "Nah, he is. He's good."

The test results are gonna be fine. He's not even worried about it, so why should Toni be? Last one was fine, and the STI sweep was clean. He got back from The Pervert's house in one piece, and he didn't even get mad when Toni acted so fucking stupid. He's good. *They're* good, right now... aside from the shouting, and most of that is Toni's anyway.

She sniffs, clears her throat, and smiles at Karen.

It's cool.

Toni spends the morning stocktaking and keeps making mistakes on the forms. It's hard to concentrate and, by half past eleven, she feels hot and shivery, like she's coming down with the flu. Eventually Karen takes the clipboard out of Toni's hands and sends her to go and deal with a couple of lesbians who have come to collect some rare archeology book they ordered. One of them—the thin one who looks like a chain-smoker and wears narrow, wire-framed glasses—says she's a lecturer at the university. The other one has frizzy blonde hair and laughs a lot. They're sweet, like they don't know they're a stereotype, and they make small talk with Toni. For a while, she feels she fits in and she likes that, because these women don't know her, and they're not treating her any different. They're just... nice. They even flirt a little bit, in a playful, meaningless kind of way, though Toni finds that slightly off-putting.

By the time she takes her lunch break, Toni's feeling much more in control, and she calls Kel from the restroom. Just to say hi. His voice will calm her, but he isn't picking up. His phone goes straight to voice mail, and she realizes it's switched off. She feels sick at first, then angry, both at him and at the fear swelling up inside her.

She gets like this, and she hates it. She hates the anxiety, the visions of things going disastrously wrong that ping into life behind her eyes. Hates the conclusions she jumps to and the things she thinks. She needs to back off, to not worry so much. Kel's probably fine. He usually keeps his phone either off or on silent when he's busy, and he is often busy. So it shouldn't be a problem… but it is.

Toni can't help that, or the building thrum of panic that starts to press in.

CHAPTER
THREE

KEL'S STANDING on the corner by the bus station, teeth working on his lower lip. He's out of cigarettes. There's a guy about eight or ten yards away selling cheap rocks, but Kel doesn't do that anymore.

He likes to come down here sometimes, not just because it's easy pickings, but because he likes looking to see where all the buses go. The big ones, with the onboard bathrooms and the shiny silver dogs along the sides. This is where he'll come, he reckons, when Toni finally pisses him off to the point that he can't take it anymore, and he'll bring the money from the top of the refrigerator and he will just fucking go. Anywhere. The buses, these great, grimy, alloyed monsters that roar and wheeze their fumes out into the air like angry animals, could get him far enough away that he could go wherever he chose.

To be perfectly honest, he's a little surprised that he hasn't run yet. He thought he would, after Toni told him. After that big fight... the fight that changed everything. Kel remembers it like it was yesterday—unusual for him, 'cause he's got real good at pushing things away and shutting them up in the boxes he keeps at the back of his mind.

Maybe he figures he needs this memory.

There was a party: a weekender at a disused warehouse somewhere not far from the river. Toni got wasted—seriously wasted—and it wasn't pretty. Kel held his head, rubbed his back, and kept the door of the old staff lavatory they were in wedged shut with his foot. The whole place was busted out; there weren't any locks. There wasn't even much plumbing, but Toni had needed to be somewhere small to puke and panic, because he kept screaming about falling through space.

It hurt to see him in that state, but it was worse to hear him. He cried, coming down, messy and uncontrolled, and the words kept pouring out just like the secondhand vodka shots. How much he hated himself, hated everything, how fucking wrong it was. Half the things he said didn't make sense, which wasn't unusual for him, but Kel recalls it being a different kind of not making sense: a disjointed rant at the world, at how everything was misplaced, or broken, or something like that.

Kel tried to help, but Toni wasn't listening. He couldn't, Kel supposed. Just kept cussing and raving, barely getting two words out between retches. Dry heaving and bawling, Toni clung to him, and Kel held on, keeping an eye on his temperature, wondering where the nearest ER was. They didn't need it in the end. He took Toni home, back to the horrible little apartment they still share now—though, at that point, it still had the gleam of novelty on it—put him to bed, sat in a chair, and waited while he slept it off.

It took three days, all told. Toni woke up after a bit, got up and dressed himself, but he barely spoke or ate the whole time. When he did speak, it was to tell Kel he was going to see a doctor.

Good. You ought to.

Yeah. I wanna get some pills.

What pills?

Toni just shut the door on him, left with no explanation. Kel didn't like letting him get away with it, but they'd already fought about that—he didn't own Toni. It wasn't his fucking business what he did or where he went.

Kel still wonders why he pushed it, though he guesses he's glad he did.

Toni didn't get back until real late. He was pissed about something, and Kel was furious because he hadn't known where to find him, and then it started.

What pills? What the fuck is the matter with you, huh?

Fuck you!

There were tears, more shouting, and finally the words came out. He'd heard Toni say them before, but always with a smile or a laugh, always in the same way he would drip with "fabulous!" jokes and exaggerate his swishiness, because even Kel has to admit that the guy is girly as fuck sometimes. But it was always flamboyancy before. It was the kind of femininity that is defiant in its queerness, an expression of genderfuckery that fitted with the whole of Toni's sharp, hard-edged identity, his multitude declarations of "fuck you" to the world. It was makeup and skintight pants and nail polish and eyeliner so thick it ran down his face when he got drunk and tearful… but it wasn't being a woman.

Sometimes, he'd say he should've been born a girl. He'd throw teasing looks at Kel through the bathroom door when he was getting ready to go out; flutter his mascara-caked lashes and say it, and he'd giggle and blow kisses. And Kel would shake his head wearily, because he didn't think it was real. He hadn't once thought it was real.

Only, right in the pit of that fist-baring, gut-clenching fight, Toni wasn't smiling, he wasn't laughing, and he said it was what he wanted.

He meant it.

Kel got mad, first off. Like Toni was saying he was ashamed, or even as if he was rejecting *them*. He told Toni so, told him he wasn't trans, just stupid. He didn't mean to, but he'd been so fucking angry.

You're not! How the hell could you even think that you—

And how the fuck do you know? You don't know me!

Words hurled all around the place like knives, screaming and ranting, sharpened and intended to cut. He'd thought he could pull Toni up short, make him see it wasn't a real solution. And it couldn't be, could it? Because if Toni was really like that, then he should've known before now. If it was real, if it was genuine, he'd have known his whole life, not just decided on it like this, apparently out of nowhere. There should have been some sign, some demonstrable glimmer of it that made him believe changing everything about who he was would be the answer… only, of course, as Kel reminds himself, it wouldn't *be* changing everything, because Toni is Toni, and if this is who he is, then it's who he's always been.

But Kel can't accept that. It pounds and pounds at the inside of his head, and he can't force his brain open to squeeze the knowledge in, because every part of him just refutes it. He's not a hater. He's not. He just… he doesn't look at Toni and see a woman.

He can't see her the way he sees other t-girls—and Kel's met plenty, between here and the outreach center, and the queer clubs and the parties they used to go to—because they're women, and Toni... Toni is *Toni*.

He knows he should have found a better way to say it. He knows he was crude and hurtful, and about as far from supportive as it's possible to get, and he never blamed Toni for storming out the way he did. He blew up, slammed out of the apartment; said he was never coming back. They were through, it was over, Kel was a bigot and an asshole and a dozen other less complimentary things.

He did come back, though. Slouched in at about three, wordless and sulking. Kel didn't say anything. He was too scared Toni would leave again. So, they maintained quiet but open hostilities. It went on for almost a week, and it could have lasted longer, even with Toni going back to it over and over—picking at it like a scab that's not yet dried—but then they had a stupid argument over trade.

Toni went out and picked up a date while he was high. Dean, a guy they both knew from the outreach center, spotted him and called Kel; he'd noted the car's model and license plate, but he thought Kel should know. Toni was a silly little bitch, he said, and he wasn't sure there hadn't been more than one guy in that car.

Kel turned frantic with worry. No one saw, heard, or knew anything. When Toni resurfaced, more than eight hours later, he looked white and pinched, and all Kel could do was explode at him, just more screaming and yelling. He didn't mean to, but he couldn't stop. Toni left in a hailstorm of broken crockery, and that night he didn't come home at all. He said he was going to stay with an old friend, and it took Kel days to find out which one.

He went there, waited for Toni to come back. Refused to give in to the temptation to smack the punk-ass roommate with the speed bumps and the really annoying voice.

Meth heads seriously fuck Kel off.

Toni was pissed to find him there. It went on for hours. Toni fought back, every wound calculated to inflict maximum damage. He wasn't rational—hardheaded to the point of absurdity—and wound so tight he looked close to breaking. Even so, Kel couldn't pull back, couldn't just stop and put an end to the way they gouged at each other, blind and furious. He remembers punching the wall, and busting the door to the meth head's apartment, and the guy yelling and threatening to call the cops, which was just the funniest thing... or would have been, if Kel had felt like laughing.

He went home, shaking with the adrenaline and the anger. They were *so* broken up. He would never see that crazy, fucked up.... But he couldn't kid himself, even then.

Not quite four days after that, Kel had found himself standing at the piece of woodchip board that had replaced the meth head's door. Toni was wasted again. He just shook his head when Kel spoke, like he couldn't hear or didn't understand. Kel grabbed his wrist, desperate to get him out of there. Away from everything. They went to the park. It was dark, except for the shiny sliver of a crescent moon, and the gates weren't locked in any serious manner. Kel was working up something to say, trying to imagine how the speech would come out if it was some grand piece of movie dialogue. It surprised him when Toni just gave a small, quiet sigh and slipped his hand into Kel's like nothing had ever happened.

They kissed in the moonlight, and it was a little bit like a movie.

Now, things are calmer. They've both had to accept a lot of things, and that has really been hard. But, at last, Toni's as clean as he's ever likely to get, and Kel doesn't get so fucking angry all the time. Obviously, sticking with going to the meetings helps with that, and he's got so many reasons to stay clean now... he feels good about it for the first time in years. As for him and his honey, well, they still break up every so often, but Kel's learned not to take it too seriously. They can get through most things by just not talking about them. Anyway, life is mostly good. And, when things with Toni are good, they're great.

He loves Toni. Loves him to death. Kel's not sure when that happened, or quite how he first realized it, but it's true. He wishes he had a cigarette, though.

Kel sniffs and turns his head, the air here gritty and rough. Exhaust fumes seep through the polluted summer breeze, mixing like wine and water until it's impossible to tell what's the bus station and what's just the general stink of the city.

A car is idling nearby—a dark-red Honda Accord—with the window down, and Kel recognizes the face of the guy inside. Been here before. A lot. He's maybe forty, maybe thirty-five, with thinning sandy hair and a sharp chin. Kel takes a glance around, but no one's fighting him for the chance. Dean, the guy he knows from the outreach center, nods at him. He's propping up another piece of wall a little farther away, and he's good for watching Kel's back on days like this. Kel saunters over, and he can see what the guy wants before he gets within six feet of the car. He waits a beat anyway, and the deal's virtually done before he even has to speak. He rests his palms on the rim of the open window, metal and plastic hot beneath his skin, and the inside of the car smells like pine air freshener and coffee.

"Julio's not here today?" the guy says, sounding disappointed.

Kel looks away up the road, takes a breath. "I don't know no Julio."

"Whatever. You're Latino, right?"

He shrugs. "Yeah, okay."

Whatever you pay me to be, you fucking cracker.

They talk money, in that brief and practiced shorthand. His figure is higher than the guy wants to go, so Kel tells him to beat it and, of course, he backtracks. Kel suppresses a smile, because some people are just too fucking easy. He glances back to check that Dean can see him, taking his time as if he has to consider whether to agree, and then he nods.

"A'ight."

"Get in."

He does, and they drive to a quiet little spot on the way to the railway. There's a disused embankment. Kel comes here pretty often. Broken glass and bits of brick litter the ground, but the sky is blue and open and, through the chain-link fence, he can see the tall wisps of golden grass wave in the breeze.

This guy must be wearing about eight layers of underwear. It's ridiculous. Kel fumbles his way in—what the hell are these, French panties or something?—and they're both getting impatient. The guy's toting attitude as well, which doesn't help. He grabs the back of Kel's head tight enough to hurt and pushes, smashing his face into the stale thatch of a crotch as if Kel doesn't know what he's doing down there and needs to be taught. He seems to like name-calling too. Nasty, sour words snarl through the hot, muggy air of the car. Ugly, mean things.

They are only words, and he's heard them before, but they still piss Kel off. Even so, it doesn't take him long to get the fucker finished. Somewhere, a train passes by, a faint rattle beneath the blanket of general noise. Kel wonders who this Julio kid is, and makes a mental note to ask Dean if he knows.

The guy grunts, gasps, gets off, and then doesn't even give Kel a lift back to the bus station. He tells him to get the fuck out of the car, and Kel doesn't mind doing that at all, because this guy is an asshole, but he still gives him the finger as he drives away. It's not really life or death, though. Kel knows where he is from here, and anyway, it's close enough to walk.

He checks his phone and picks up three angry, tearful messages from Toni. Why does he do that? He *knows* Kel doesn't pick up when he's busy. He keeps the phone off for convenience, and he has done ever since the time Toni called while he was going down on some jerk behind the movie theater. It was embarrassing. The guy's standing there with his pants around his knees, hips going like a horny Chihuahua and moaning, "Do me, Steve" (Kel never had any idea who the fuck Steve was), and then there's just this sudden burst of some stupid tinny version of an Eminem track Toni thought it would be funny to download for him.

Kel would really prefer for that not to happen again. It's a peace of mind thing.

He sighs, but, just as he's about to dial Toni's number, the phone rings. It's her friend, Danielle. He swears under his breath.

"Yeah?"

"Where the fuck are you?"

Kel squints at the blazing yellow-white flare of the sun, trailing horizontal slashes of light through the blue sky and catching on the top of the chain-link fence, spiking off it like shattered glass.

"On my way," he says.

"Huh. Yeah, but from where? Toni's going nuts. She thinks you've run off."

In Kel's opinion, if Danielle has one fault—and he's being generous, because he'd personally put the number higher—it's that she's way too quick to take seriously every single one of Toni's inevitable tantrums and panics.

"I haven't. He's being stupid."

Kel hears Danielle's quick, pointed intake of breath, and knows he's in for an ass-ripping for saying that. Not calling Toni stupid, but calling him a guy. Danielle's full of all that shit. She calls it supportive. She volunteers two afternoons a week on a phone line for trans counseling, and she makes like she's got all the answers, but she doesn't. She never has. She doesn't even like questions, because the world inside Danielle's head is totally fucking rigid. Everything is sharp and clear for her, and she regards other people's uncertainty—Kel's uncertainty, definitely—as weakness, on account of the fact she really doesn't understand it.

Kel supposes that maybe he ought to feel sorry for her, or at least a little sympathetic, but he doesn't, because he's got too much to blame on her. Besides, he knows she's not infallible. He's seen her down by the theater from time to time, just like everybody else.

He sighs wearily. "Just tell him I'm all right, okay? He still at work?"

"Yes, just finishing up. She's been trying to call you all afternoon!"

"All right. Tell him I'll come meet him there."

Another short huff of disapproval. Danielle's pissed off, big-time, but Kel guesses Toni's actually there, because she's not laying into him.

"He there now? Lemme speak to him."

"I'll tell her, Kel," she says, then breaks the connection.

Kel looks at the phone and swears. Suddenly, he really wants to see Toni, to have him in his arms, just hear his voice, bitching on about something unimportant. He sniffs, looks up at the molten sun once more. It's got to be almost five, hasn't it, if Toni's shift is nearly done? Kel checks the time on his phone.

Yeah, 4:42.

He feels vulnerable out here, and so he starts walking.

It's not far to get back where there's bitumen and concrete underfoot; the places where the shadows pool and the traffic rumbles. There's an Asian grocery store on the corner, and a street sign no longer legible beneath generations of different-colored tags. Kel pops into the grocery and buys some things for dinner—Toni has always loved crispy duck with pancakes—and he thinks maybe it'd be nice to cook, just for a change. A surprise. Kel needs to get some more cigarettes too, though he knows he ought to quit. He keeps thinking about it, but it's always next week, next month, some time when he knows he won't need them to help him concentrate, keep him calm. He buys a pack anyway and smokes one on the walk down to the bookstore. It takes the taste of his afternoon away.

Danielle's still there, which is absolutely no surprise. Kel spots her standing out on the sidewalk with Toni, who should have just finished his shift. Cigarette smoke haloes both of them, and to Kel's eyes they're an odd couple. Danielle's very pretty. She has long red hair—the color obviously comes from a bottle, but it suits her—and a knee-length black skirt, and she looks like she's always been as confident as she is now. Without the heels on her boots, she'd be about five ten, but she never stoops, and she has a knockout figure, if you like that kind of thing. Toni could pass for her gawky seventeen-year-old cousin at this distance, skinny and nervous, hair greasy and laugh too loud. Yet Kel's chest still swells at the sight of him and the way, when Toni spots him, he starts bouncing up and down, waving.

It's all Kel can do not to break into a run. He walks up nonchalantly, swinging the bag of crap he's bought, and Toni's already talking even before he gets there, telling him about his day, complaining that his phone was off, relating whatever it was that Danielle just said that was probably the funniest thing ever.... Kel doesn't care. It's just so fucking good to press his mouth against Toni's, hug him tight, and know that he's okay.

Kel holds him just a little harder and a little longer than is strictly necessary, and he plants a firm, thorough kiss right on the middle of Toni's lips. He wants Danielle to see that. Toni might be a fucked-up little freak, but this is *his* freak, whoever he ends up being.

Toni gives a small, surprised moan, lips parting and whole body softening, just ready to yield. Kel wants to deepen the kiss, to make Toni melt right here on the sidewalk, but—despite the cigarette—he still has the taste of that jerk from the embankment at the back of his throat. He wasn't the only job today either, though it's generally been pretty quiet. All the same, Kel levers Toni away, smiles, and hopes his eyes convey the promise of later tonight. Toni grins, takes a last drag on his slim, and crunches it out beneath the ball of his foot.

Danielle tucks her long, shiny hair behind her ear, a businesslike little mannerism that really ticks Kel off. The fact that she doesn't like him, in itself, does not have him flinging himself on the ground in despair, but he's aware her dislike is because she thinks he's bad for Toni. And that, in Kel's opinion, is the problem. From the minute Danielle met Toni, she has assumed his version of events is always the gospel truth... like he's been this way forever, like he's brave to suddenly make these decisions and choose to act on the needs of the hidden self he's been choking down for years.

If she really knew Toni, Kel doubts she'd be so quick to take everything he says at face value. He tried to talk to her about it once, tried to reach out to her when it was still so new, and Toni had scared him so fucking much with the things he said.... It didn't end well. Danielle made sure he was totally clear about whose side she came down on, and she left Kel hanging, friendless and frustrated. He couldn't hope to understand, she said. He was part of the problem. At the very first hint of him standing in Toni's way, she'd have no hesitation in doing everything she could to see him pushed cleanly aside.

He believed her.

All the same, plastic bag looped around his wrist, Kel sticks his hands in his pockets and smiles at Danielle. She gives him a coldly polite look, just the thawed side of icy, like slowly defrosting chicken.

If Toni notices Danielle's attitude, he doesn't say anything. He's hanging off Kel's arm, trying to peek into the shopping bag, just as curious and excited as a little kid.

"What's this? What'd you get? Oooh! Pancakes? I love pancakes!"

Toni bounces excitedly and kisses Kel's cheek, chattering happily about food, about his day, about how they all ought to go and get a drink or something. To listen to him now, it seems impossible he could ever have been upset. Danielle's looking like something crawled under her nose and died, and Kel really hopes she's going to say she's busy, but then her attention flicks to Toni and she smiles.

"Yeah, that would actually be really nice. Where d'you feel like going?"

Kel's mood sinks. All he wants to do is go home and take a hot shower, clean his teeth, and put the dinner on. Instead, he follows obediently as Toni and Danielle discuss where to go—he may as well not exist at this point—and then head off in search of wherever it is they've decided on. Kel zones out.

Rio's? Riojo's? It's something like that.

It turns out to be Prijo's, and it's a place he doesn't know, not that far away in terms of distance, but a couple of miles outside Kel's comfort zone. It's not like he only goes to gay joints but at least if a place is queer, it feels safer... and Kel doesn't like the way that people look at Toni here.

Danielle doesn't seem to get it so much, but then she looks like a girl. Well, Kel supposes she *is* a girl, not counting the plumbing—not that he'd say that outside of his own head. As Toni is prone to quoting from the Internet, gender and sex are two totally different things. He says that sometimes, preaches it like he's proud of learning how to repeat it, but Kel doesn't think his honey really understands the crap that's coming out of his mouth. It's not that he's dumb. He's not. But all those websites Toni goes on... he doesn't really read them. He knows the buzzwords, but all the conclusions he's reached, he's jumped to like a drowning man finding a raft. And he's so fucking desperate for Danielle's approval, and Kel's pretty sure that's not how this stuff is meant to go, but what can he say?

Hell, maybe he is a bigot. But he sees the way people look at Toni, and sometimes he sees what they see—sees the mask, and the pretense—and he hates it. Sure, the people here are staring at Danielle too, but they stare because she's a tall, attractive woman. If anyone clocks her at all, it's because of her proximity to him and Toni. Next to her, Kel is painfully aware that his honey looks like a camp boy with bad hair in kitten heels and skinny jeans. The baggy, genderless shirts are a better choice for him than the close-fitting tops Danielle wears to show off her boobs, but they're not very femme. Kel's thankful for that, yet catches himself wishing, in a perverse kind of way, that Toni would either look like one thing or the other.

The whole idea of him cross-living fully frightens Kel. He tries not to think about it, still clinging foolishly to the hope that Toni will somehow change his mind before then. That he'll leave the pills alone, cut his hair, and stop with the gel nails and the electrolysis, all of that shit, and just go back to the way he was.

Kel knows it's a stupid thing to wish for, but he can't help it.

They get to the bar, and he sees a lot of girls teetering about in groups, obviously fresh out of work. They come in different flavors—checkout drab to office glam—but they don't interest him. High heels and high-pitched laughs, cocktails and gossip. There's a lot of red neon and tacky fairy lights dressing up the very eighties exposed brickwork. He wonders how often Toni and Danielle have been here before, without him.

Kel follows Toni numbly through the knots of people. They look. They stare. Some giggle, and Kel doesn't even know if Toni realizes it or not. He hates it, though; hates it so bad he wants to hit something.

Danielle orders two white wines and a Bud without asking Kel what he wants, and they get a table near a window. Kel slouches in the corner with his bag of prepackaged duck and pancake components (some romantic evening in this is going to be!), and Toni slides in beside him, one hand on his thigh beneath the table. A black curl, snaking free of the everyday casual updo, dances against his neck as he talks, and Kel drifts in and out of the conversation, just watching that one bouncing tendril.

"...was, like, fuck, no! Y'know? Though the money's good, apparently."

Danielle wrinkles her nose and looks disapproving. "No, I don't think it's worth it. I mean, once you do that, honey, it's out there forever. What if it showed up on the Internet, somebody you worked with found out?"

"Like fuck!" Toni laughs his brassy, jagged laugh, and it shows his imperfect teeth. "Who, Karen? She wouldn't care."

"If you changed jobs, though," Danielle says mildly. "Got a career."

Toni snorts, his eyes creasing as his grin widens. "Oh, what? I'm, like, gonna be an accountant or something?"

"You can be anything you wanna be, sweetie," Danielle says, and Kel wants to barf until he makes the connection to what they're talking about.

T-girl porn.

He says nothing. Toni's brought the subject up before, and Kel understood the argument behind it, though he didn't like it. Toni finally stopped picking up tricks a couple of months ago, when he started seriously with the idea of this whole transition thing. It was partly at Kel's insistence, and he refuses to feel guilty for that. He knows it's worth more for Toni to trade on that sense of other—the earnings are higher the closer he gets to the point where male and female meet, at least in body—but it's more dangerous too. Horrible, appalling things happen to some of those girls. Besides, arguing the increased likelihood of some nut getting violent was easier than admitting he can't stand the thought of anyone else touching Toni.

He used to be able to deal with it—after all, it's business, and it doesn't mean anything, right?—but it's become harder and harder to handle since they've been together.

Toni's already had an offer from a guy who does shoots: some sleaze who used to DJ at one of the clubs they don't go to anymore. Kel also knows that Toni's done a couple of them before. Nothing really heavy. Hell, Kel's done 'em too, in the past. Jerk off for the camera, maybe suck a little dick. It's quick, easy money, and it's in the warm, where it's dry and—in theory—safer. If you flutter a little bit and pretend you're nervous straight meat, maybe you even earn more.

But this other stuff… this stuff Toni talked about, Kel doesn't like the sound of it at all. She's going through the same speech now: it'd be a closed set, none of the uncertainty of a date with a stranger, just working within a bunch of predefined rules. Kel doesn't know whether he hates it more for the thought of Toni fucking someone else on camera, or the fact that, if he's thinking about it at all, he's planning on it being at a time when he's got boobs and curves to show off. And maybe that time's not all that far away.

Kel tries to visualize the stuff he's read about the hormones, how long they take to make "significant physical changes." The words sound weird in his head. He stares at his beer, watches the pattern of condensation shift on the shoulders of the bottle. It's a strange little vignette, like he could be looking at it down a long tunnel.

"It'd pay for a whole lot of zap units, is all I'm saying," Toni protests before sipping his wine.

Danielle's mouth quirks at the corner. She doesn't agree, and Kel warms to her very slightly for that. He wonders if Toni's forgotten that his date with The Sherbet Pervert last night is covering the electrolysis appointment next week. That's plenty of zap, in Kel's opinion. He's too damn tired of all this to really get angry, but he feels his mouth open of its own accord, and hears words he didn't mean to say slip out.

"I don't think it's a good idea. You got more to offer than that, Toni. More'n just a body."

He's still looking at the beer bottle as he speaks and, embarrassed, he grabs it and takes a swig, but not before he feels Toni's gaze slide to him. There's warmth there, and he squeezes Kel's thigh, leaning in with a giggle and a proud grin.

Kel swallows his mouthful of beer. Danielle looks at him coolly for a moment, and then switches her attention back to Toni.

"Kel's got a point, you know."

Holy shit—that's high praise, coming from the ice queen herself. Kel wonders if maybe she's not such a bitch after all.

He considers this as the conversation segues into TV shows and the type of he-said-she-said gossip that rarely involves anyone he knows. Even so, Kel can't think of anyone other than Toni who would sit here, pressed in among the after-work spritzer crowd, and cheerfully discuss whether or not he ought to do a skin shoot when the estrogen really kicks in—not thinking for a second it might attract attention.

After the girls have drunk their wine, and Kel's been made to feel just a little bit more out of touch with Toni's world, Danielle says she needs to get going. It's one of her phone line evenings.

They say goodbye on the sidewalk outside and, just as she turns to go, she smiles at Kel and says, "Take care of her."

Kel would love to say something sarcastic and cutting at this point, but instead he puts his arm around Toni's shoulders, pulls him in real tight, and says, "Plan to." He suspects it comes off as a touch possessive, but Toni seems to like it.

He tries to trip Kel as they start the walk home, his mood playful and impish. Kel stumbles, rights himself, then swats Toni on the ass, and they laugh. It glances off the concrete and glass, sparkling with the last of the light.

"You won't, will you?" Kel asks, once the laughter dies away and a breeze, sharp with grit and the smell of exhaust, bowls down the center of the road.

He doesn't say it because he wants to ruin things, but because he really can't bear not knowing for sure. Not here and now, in the smut-stained twilight, with Toni smiling and everything feeling so restful and free.

"Huh?"

"What you were talking about. Shoots. For... y'know. Would you?"

Toni shrugs, mouth pursed. His best, most infuriating way of avoiding questions.

"I said, would you?" Kel repeats, hearing his voice harden in just the way he doesn't want it to.

His honey dances between the sidewalk and the gutter, one foot in each, hands thrust into the pockets of his jeans. It's getting dark, and the dusk is grainy and blurred.

Kel tries not to get angry.

"Why?" Toni asks, looking down at the pattern his feet make as they move, and the pit-pat of his scuffed brown ankle boots echoes through a sudden lull in the background noise. Somewhere, a car horn blares, breaking the quiet.

Kel could hate him now, if he tried. The way Toni's trying to push him to say it. Does he really need the validation, or does he just like the power this gives him? Kel isn't sure, but it's ugly either way.

"'Cause I don't think you should," he says bluntly. "An'... an' I don't want you to. Really don't. I don't wanna see you gettin' nasty with some guy just because of what you've got... or what you are. Can't stand thinkin' like that."

Toni stops. They're in familiar territory now—taking the route back behind the old library saves time. The buildings loom up on either side of them, cutout shapes against the thin strip of sky.

"Oh, I get it!" Toni looks at Kel from his uneven perch, one foot next to a storm drain, the other leg slightly bent beneath him, and grins. "Don't want no one else touchin' your woman, Big Dog?"

Kel winces. "Toni...."

Toni laughs, skips back up onto the sidewalk, and walks backward a few paces, hands still tight in the pockets of his skinny jeans.

"Come on! I'm hungry. I want you to cook me pancakes. And duck."

Kel swings the bag he still carries. They're almost home. He has the scent of it now, like salt air on the way to the seaside. He knows, once they shut the door on the world, nothing else will matter much.

If he holds on to that long enough, he'll believe it.

"Dah-ling," he says, in a dreadful fake Chinese accent. "I give you best duck ever!"

Toni squeals with laughter, and it echoes off the bricks. Kel lunges, and there's another whoop of laughter, and then Toni's running, heels clacking staccato on the sidewalk. Kel's footfalls drum after her, the plastic bag with their soon-to-be dinner in it flapping out behind him.

They run, and it's liberating. It's breathless and stupid and crazy… and wonderful. He almost catches Toni as they pelt past the parking lot beside the convenience store, but Kel's not quick enough, and he makes it to home base, running up the concrete stairs to their door.

"Safe!" Toni yells and jumps up and down, arms in the air, making roaring-crowd noises until Kel catches up to him.

"Dumb-ass," Kel says affectionately, as Toni's arms slide around his neck and the prideful grin slips off his face, replaced with a look that has a certain softness and pleading.

Kel kisses the end of his nose and sticks his key into the lock.

"C'mon. Duck time."

CHAPTER
FOUR

DINNER DOESN'T take long to do, which is good. Kel's stomach rumbles loudly as he takes the duck out of its plastic wrapping, tosses it onto a tray, and puts it in the oven. He finds clean plates, sets the two little pots of sauce on them alongside the bundles of scallions, and leaves the pancakes ready to warm through. After he tucks the money he earned today into the cookie jar on top of the refrigerator, he eases it back into place as quietly as possible. Toni hasn't asked how much he made—or how many guys it took—and Kel hasn't said anything. He clears his throat.

"G'na take a shower," he calls.

"'Kay."

Toni's voice is muffled. He's in the bedroom, probably popping something. The hormone schedule he has devised for himself is complicated—different dosages in the morning and at night, and different peaks on different days—and Kel doesn't try to follow it too closely. He sheds his clothes, strips away his day, and steps eagerly under the warm spray, reaching for the soap and the ability to obliterate things he doesn't want to remember.

Usually, the guys Kel goes with don't get to touch him. He prefers it like that, although sometimes he'll break the rules. Maybe if a guy's hot and he really gets into it, or it's someone he knows—as far as anybody ever knows anybody—then Kel doesn't mind. Sometimes, it's okay for it to be sex instead of just consciously traded favors, though he's pulled back from nearly all of that since Toni. He doesn't want to fuck anyone else, and they don't party like they used to either. That was the first thing they both chose to give up, because too much temptation lies that way. It was better to make a clean break, to leave behind the wild nights and the long kaleidoscopes of time that were made up of hedonistic sensation. No more rolling, no more favors for friends of friends, no more swapping hummers for a chance at forgetfulness. Kel's kicked all the shit he used to do, but he had to get out of that social circle to do it. That's why they got this shitty little apartment, away from the people they both knew, and the things they both did. They nested here together, like some old married couple, and it has worked... more or less.

He used to do a hell of a lot more when he was younger. Of course, he was stupid then too, and generally high. He didn't mean to start, and he didn't mean to keep going, especially once he got clean. It's not like it was easy in the first place, and it's not like it's easy now, being stone-cold sober and looking guys like Michael in the eye. Touching them. It's not always gross like it is with The Pervert, but it's not Kel's idea of the best way to spend an afternoon either. He doesn't mean it to be forever, even now. But what else is he going to do?

Kel soaps everything, cleans everywhere. Scrupulous. He washes his hair, and it'll stick out like some kind of crazy palm tree when it dries. Maybe he'll get Toni to fix it. Kel kind of likes curling up by his honey's feet and letting Toni mess with his hair. The way Toni touches him—all deft fingers and concentration, so careful not to tug or pull—makes him feel wrapped up and snug, however dumb that might be. Cherished. It's a nice feeling.

The important thing is that Kel doesn't mind doing what he does. He's nobody's victim. A lot of the time, he barely even feels it, but that kind of numbness is scary, because he finds he feels the same way when he looks ahead to the future. Kel doesn't know what's going to happen, or how anything's going to work out.

Back when he started, some of the people he partied with had plans. A couple of them made the money they wanted and moved away, went to school, got married, lost touch... but not everybody. Some of them just drifted away, faded into the night and the anonymous corners and the whole shifting, repetitive pattern of it all, and Kel doesn't even know whether they're still alive or not. He's pretty sure at least two of his exes are dead. He doesn't really care all

that much, either, and that's not a nice thing to realize about himself…
but then how many people have ever really cared about him?

He stops thinking about it, anyway, because dwelling on all this
shit is pointless. There are people he and Toni used to know who think
he's crazy—who think Toni's crazy, though they may have a point
there—and who will never forgive either of them for cutting out the old
crowd the way they did. Maybe, once, that would have mattered, but it
doesn't anymore. Not so much.

So many parts of that life are fading away for Kel. They're
growing thin and weak and sliding into nothingness, like the way the
night turns silver-gray and powdery just before dawn. It can't hold him
anymore, can't lock him up in its shadows.

He pads naked to the linen cupboard, gets a clean towel, and
smells crispy duck permeating through the apartment's base notes of
damp mustiness. The ever-present bubbles of noise that filter up from
the convenience store are blurring into the background, indistinct and
unimportant. Life is good. In this moment, in this place… at this
precise minute, it is really fucking good.

Toni's put some music on. Apparently, he's so queer that he's
actually playing Dusty Springfield. Kel shakes his head and smiles to
himself. He dries off, pulls on some comfortable old clothes, and
catches himself humming along to "Can I Get a Witness." He pulls a
very elderly sweatshirt over his head—the elbows, cuffs, hem, and
neckline are all frayed with wear, the colors muted, and the cloth soft.
Kel thinks he got this shirt from an ex-boyfriend or something, because
it's got something about Atlanta on the front of it, and he's sure as hell
never been there.

There's a lot of places he hasn't been. Someday, maybe it'd be
nice to go to some of them. Take Toni with him. Just the two of them.
It's always best when it's just them.

Kel wanders through to get the duck out of the oven, plates it up,
and carries the food over to their beat-up couch, where Toni's already
waiting for him. She's changed too. Hair loose, the curls starting to fall
out of shape, and that sweet, slender body hidden by pale-pink
sweatpants and one of Kel's old T-shirts. It looks big on Toni, though
Kel knows he's not that much broader, not really.

Toni looks up, grins, and claps his hands.

They're pretty quiet while they eat, just letting the music nibble the edges off the silence. Kel finds it relaxing and watches Toni prop the plate on his knees, roll up the paper-thin pancakes and devour them one after the other. There's something methodical and utterly determined about the way Toni shovels food into his mouth, on the occasions he actually decides to eat something. It's a tiny bit like the disconcerting level of focus he gets when he's sucking cock, and Kel files that thought away for later, grinning as he attacks his own meal. He eats with enthusiasm—he hadn't realized he was so damn hungry—and it feels really good to be holed up for the evening, alone and safe.

The outside isn't totally shut out. They still hear things. There's the noise of traffic, the intermittent sounds of things Kel's going to call cars backfiring, the thuds and clatter from downstairs, and the ever-present song of sirens threading through the city's soundscape. Over the top of all of it, Dusty's still going, and it's nice.

After they finish eating, and Toni's licking hoisin off his long, slim fingers in a very provocative manner—smirking seductively while he does it, the bastard—Kel raises an eyebrow.

"You wanna go out tonight?" he asks, looking sidelong at Toni.

Kel kind of hopes his honey's going to say no because, while he knows how much Toni loves the nightlife, and how much he enjoys playing dress-up, all that really matters right now is some quality time. He's been waiting all day, he realizes, and that's almost a surprise to him.

When they first got together, last summer, it was a tumult of desire and uncertainty. Kel couldn't remember what it was like, wanting someone so much. They edged into it carefully, each so conscious of avoiding the other's weak spots, not hurting or assuming, not taking too much or giving more than might reasonably be expected. He still doesn't know quite when it was that Toni took such deep root in his soul, or how it came to be that Kel let him do it. It's a mystery, like so much about Toni.

There isn't time to ponder it too deeply, though. The room's getting heavy with it, this need of his. Toni shifts on the couch, shakes his head.

"Uh-uh," he says. "Not really."

Kel smiles. "A'ight."

Toni holds his gaze, and he knows what Kel's thinking. He must know. A slow, lazy grin spreads across his face, and it's the nicest thing Kel's seen in days. He gets up to clear away the dinner plates, but just as he's about to pick them up off the coffee table Toni dives, grabs his wrist, and pulls him back down. He catches Kel off-balance, and he topples with a cry and a peal of laughter and lands in a tangle of limbs and giggles. Toni is clambering on top of him then, climbing into his lap and claiming his mouth, his hands pushing up Kel's shirt to rub at his flesh. He's eager, impatient, and hungry, all his girly mannerisms forgotten... or at least put away for a while. This is like he used to be, and Kel loves it.

Toni might never have been what anyone could call macho, but there's something irrepressibly male about him. He's lithe, energetic, impulsive—strong, in the way that the first green shoot in the last part of winter is, as it pushes up through the snow—and his gel nails prick at Kel's chest as he ties the two of them together with this wonderfully insistent, eager touching.

Kel reaches out for him, wants him close, and Toni leans in and kisses his neck. He grinds against Kel, and hot little moans break from his mouth, low and gravelly. Kel catches hold of the loose curls that dance between them. Smelling of jasmine, they wind around his fingers. He kisses Toni over and over, murmurs words that aren't even really words, just shapes bent around the things he feels.

Abruptly, Toni scrambles backward and hits the floor in an awkward and ungainly kind of manner, but hunched forward and fumbling with Kel's fly. He doesn't argue, just lifts his hips and lets his lover tug the faded denim down. It would have been nice to go slow, get all romantic and sappy the way Toni likes... to play the seduction ruses that make him feel good, make him feel wanted. Maybe they'll do that later. Right now, Toni only wants one thing. Kel can see that in his eyes, and feel it in the way he deftly turns aside the layers of cotton between them. Kel's already half-hard, and it doesn't take long until he's at full mast, not when Toni touches him like that. He's got a grip that feels incredible, both soft and tight all at once, like his flesh is molded directly to the shape of Kel's cock, and the only thing that's better is his mouth.

Kel doesn't have to wait long for that. He's buried halfway in the first stroke, slouched right down in the couch with Toni kneeling before him, taking it the way nobody else could ever do. The hands firmly planted on his thighs just keep going in gentle, hypnotic circles, those dark eyes fixed on his. Kel watches Toni's face intently, watches the way his cock makes first one cheek, then the other, bulge out. Those full, sweet lips encircle him, forming a tight seal around his flesh, hot tongue searing the length of his shaft on every upstroke, pausing to tease his tip before Toni swallows him again, his whole mouth buzzing with the happy little noises he makes.

He is so good at this. So fucking good... it's like the walls of Kel's brain are melting, and he doesn't even care because all that exists is the way Toni's mouth makes him feel. His heart is beating fast, his pulse thudding, but it feels like his entire body is tuned to the rhythm his honey's got going, and it is the most incredible thing.

It's hard to connect what he sees with what he feels, and Kel supposes that's one of the reasons that, every so often, fucking Toni reminds him of what it was like to get high. Really high. He doesn't do it anymore, but there are times he misses it—fucking misses it so bad it's like he'll never breathe again—and it's confusing, because he feels like that now. But not for junk. For Toni, which is stupid, because he's right here.

It's the same fear, though. Fear. It rules everything.

Toni deep-throats his cock—apparently effortlessly, but for the damp, choking noises and the way his breathing changes—and Kel groans loudly, his thighs shaking with the strain of staying still. He wants to buck his hips, fuck against the wet heat and the suction and everything that feels so damn good, but he doesn't want to use Toni like that. Not after today. He wants it to be lovemaking, but it's not going to be. It's not going to be romance and flowers.

Toni opens his mouth wide, and he's showing off now, tongue flat and broad, laving at Kel's shaft. His eyes are full of temptation and a thousand wicked promises, and that mouth has all the tricks to go with it. Before long, Kel's on the edge, quivering and sweating, and not thinking about anything other than coming. Toni takes him deep, all business now, hard and relentless. He moans around Kel's flesh, sending vibrations right through his core, shakes his head from side to side and makes more happy little growls as he sucks. He loves cock. This cock in particular. Kel loves him... and then he's there, coming and coming, his fingers buried in Toni's hair, and his teeth gritted as he crumbles from the inside out. His hips are going now, erratic twitching thrusts that Toni easily keeps pace with, and Toni meets every movement, balling the pleasure up and winding it tighter until Kel thinks it could kill him.

Toni eases off just before it gets painful, that incredible mouth restricted to cleaning him up, dotting kisses along the insides of his thighs and up to the base of his aching, oversensitive cock. His tongue traces delicate lines over Kel's balls until they want to tighten again. Kel's stomach clenches, his head light. He whimpers under his breath, shifts against the couch, and wishes they'd gone to bed for this. All the ecstatic agony fades into mild regret that he couldn't go longer, that he couldn't make it more than it was. Toni blows a raspberry on the strip of skin where his thigh meets his groin. It's wet and playful, and Kel isn't expecting it. He laughs, Toni laughs, and Kel traces the outline of his perfect crocus's ear with tired fingertips.

"Bed?"

"Mm," Toni agrees and stands up, only to collapse in uncontrollable laughter when Kel tries to do likewise and falls over the jeans he still has crumpled around his knees.

TONI WALKS backward into the bedroom, still laughing at Kel's waddling gait, pants held up in one hand. Kel pulls a face, then lets the denim drop, toes off his shoes, kicks the whole bundled mess of jeans and underwear off, and tugs off his shirt. He tosses it to the floor, and then he's naked. That wipes all the laughter from Toni's face, because Kel is so fucking stunning. He's not that tall, but he is stocky. Broad, and thick, and he makes her feel safe, and yet so nervous at the same time.

He's beautiful, amazing, and he's coming closer.

Toni just stands there, waits for him. Wants to be swept up, held… kissed.

Kel doesn't disappoint. He pounces, and he's all mouth and hands. Lips maul, fingers tickle, and breath scrapes between them. He's still flushed with the satiation of his recent climax, still a little sticky, his taste rich and heavy in Toni's mouth. Cinnamon skin under her hands, and her lover's lips on hers. His. Toni doesn't want to think about the distinctions right now, about whether wanting Kel the way she does at this moment makes her male or female, or how a woman ought to respond to what he's doing. There's too much thinking, and she wants to ditch that, because the best sex Toni has doesn't involve thoughts at all. Being like this—being with Kel—is about feeling, not thinking, and right now he feels good, feels comfortable in this awkward body that, just for a little while, loses some of its limits and confusions... because Kel doesn't judge. He doesn't look at her as if what she *isn't* matters, and he never comments on what she shaves or waxes, or the way she looks or feels. He just takes Toni as he is, and makes every little piece of him feel loved.

Toni knows that Kel is not crazy about the gel nails, but he threads his fingers through hers anyway, pulls her hand to his mouth and kisses the bony knuckles. The very first time they spent the night together—and it was the whole night, wrapped up together in a single bed in the back room of the place Kel was living at then, which smelled of weed and dry rot—Toni remembers his slow, gentle seduction. Like he was afraid of hurting her. He's gentle again now, and his hands are warm, wide, and deft. The clothes drop like petals. He kisses her neck, and her Adam's apple bobs frantically. She hears herself groan, hears her man's voice ask Kel for what she wants. What Antonio needs.

"Oh, shit... fuck me, baby."

Kel traces the hollow of her spine, two sets of fingertips diverging at the curve of her ass, one hand cupping each buttock. Toni rocks forward, rubbing her cock against his body. Arms linked around his neck, eyes closed, Toni wants to picture a different world. A different body, maybe. The two of them having perfect sex, her perfect breasts peaking under his perfect hands... but those aren't the things Toni sees. This is them. This is the way they are, the way they've always been. Kel's kinky hair—still damp from the shower, drying into crazy spirals—tickles, his muscles solid and firm, and Toni's body meets him plane for plane, the same hard lines and the same angles. The same hard, hungry cock. It pulses in Kel's palm, and Toni kisses him, swaying against him, hipbones poking out to sharp points. Kel strokes slowly, still kneading her ass with his other hand, one finger just beginning to caress the top of her cleft.

"I'm not ready yet," Kel mutters. "And that's *your* fault."

Toni smiles, smug at the recent memory of his explosive orgasm, the heat and the taste, and the power it granted.

I did that.

She hugs him tighter, wrists crossed behind his neck, pressing close and kissing his jawline.

"You could always... y'know."

Kel chuckles, hand tightening on her ass. "I know."

Toni smiles against his mouth. He always knows what she wants. What she needs. They work an awkward, four-legged shuffle to the bed, neither really willing to let go of the other, and she wishes Kel would lay her down on it, like guys used to do in old movies. Instead, she kind of flops, he climbs onboard after her, and she waits for him.

She'll always wait.

Kel's face hovers above Toni, his expression so soft. He drops a gentle kiss to the tip of her nose, and skims his hand down her body, his touch delicate until he reaches the hard, jutting rod. His cock. Toni bucks his hips, thrusts into Kel's warm, waiting hand. She reaches out, threads slightly trembling fingers into that thick, damp, kinky hair. Kel kisses him again and moans his approval as Toni snakes her tongue into his mouth, teasing and testing.

It's weird, but Toni always feels more like a man when they fuck. At least, he thinks he does. It's hard to know why... could be his body, could be how Kel touches him. It doesn't matter, because it feels *real*, and that's the only important thing, so he pushes those divisions away—they're only words, anyway—and concentrates on the matter at hand.

They're not all that crazy on toys, most times, but there's a special box under the bed. Blue plastic, with a detachable lid. Toni watches as Kel rolls away and leans down to rummage for the hidden treasures, and she hears the sound of the lid crack open. Kel's back ripples, his buttocks and thighs flexing as he reaches. One knee bends, foot raising up, a pinkish-tinged sole to coffee-colored skin. He calls himself *café au lait*, and Toni doesn't think that's right. It doesn't cover half of how beautiful he is.

Toni wants to touch him, and the urge is irresistible. Hands meet flesh and pinch and smack the tempting mounds. Kel gives a surprised grunt, and then he heaves himself back up, rolling over to wrestle with

Toni, a tangle of limbs and laughter once again. They have the best times when it's just them. When the rest of the world gets the fuck away and leaves them alone, and nothing else is relevant other than who they are and that they're both here.

Kel kisses long, slow, and deep. His tongue moves in and out of Toni's mouth, thrusting the way the toy he has in his hand is going to do. It's one of Toni's favorites—a slim jelly dildo in a sparkly pink finish—and the sight of it reminds him of how much he wants to get fucked.

"Want it?" Kel murmurs into the tail end of the kiss.

"Mm-hm. I want it, baby."

Kel grins as he reaches for the bottle of lube that stands on the bedside cabinet. Toni stretches out his arms, then folds them behind his head, relaxed and ready. He delicately extends one leg, raises it, and points his toes to the ceiling, then gets the other one up there too. He can get them as far up as his ears if he really tries, but it's not particularly comfortable. He pulls his knees up to his chest, drops them to the sides, opening out for Kel and those talented fingers of his.

There's cool wetness, and Kel's still looking at him with so much warmth and yearning in his eyes that Toni might want to cry. Or come. Maybe both. The dong isn't hard to take, and it's shaped just the way it needs to be, touching all the right places. A narrow breath skates between Toni's teeth.

"Mm."

"Good?" Kel asks needlessly. He knows it is.

Fucker knows just how well he does this. How great he is at it. He's slow and gentle when Toni wants it, and rough and hard when she needs it. He's got great rhythm. After a while, he's stroking Toni's cock with one hand, pumping the toy with the other, and Toni can see that he's hard again too. That makes it time to turn things around.

He reaches down, stills Kel's busy hands, and murmurs those special words, the ones that sound so different right now, all low down in his throat and wrapped up with need.

"Want you."

It's simple but effective. Kel pulls the toy out; Toni rolls them over and straddles his lap, aching for him. Kel murmurs something about condoms, but that just irritates Toni. He doesn't want that. He wants to feel Kel. He reaches down behind the slender slope of his ass—he's a lot of things, but bootylicious ain't one of them—and tries to guide Kel's hard cock to where he wants it, but the strength of his refusal surprises Toni.

"No." Kel grips his wrist, hard. "Not without—"

"But—"

"I mean it, T. They're in the drawer."

Toni pouts, huffs, but does what he says. For a moment, the possibility looms that Kel's more worried about the results of his last blood work than he's letting on, but the thought fades once Toni's got him suited and greased up.

He's big—among the biggest Toni's ever had—but it's worth it. He feels great. It's tough to keep a hard-on while taking him, but impossible to lose it once everything's settled. Kel fills him up, makes him feel powerful. The sensation blooms deep in him, right at his center, and it pools out, hot and yawning. Fearless. He wriggles, gets Kel's dick to hit that secret spot that melts him, and he can feel it echo back in his own cock. Pleasure in front and behind, swirling up in him, stoked higher with every stroke. He starts to move—cautiously, slowly—and small gasps break from his lips, like he's actually forgotten how good it is.

Toni could fuck like this for hours. They have, in the past. Endless rhythms, alternating between circles, bounces, fast or slow... Kel's fist clenched tight around his cock, touching him, taking him.

It's good.

Toni takes it slow tonight. He wants to feel everything, wants the steam to build gradually, blow off all the pressure and the frustration... the bad feelings that welled up and that he couldn't stop. With his free hand, Kel traces repetitive paths up his arms, onto his back. Toni kind of wishes he'd lit candles. Kel strokes him, an easy pace that matches the languorous motions of his hips, driving up with Toni's every slide down. They're a good match and at their best right now. It's an adagio, and Toni wishes it could last forever.

He pushes all the thoughts of how scared he was when he couldn't find Kel—the tears in the bathroom and stupidly calling Danielle and blabbing out all the things he was afraid of, when she didn't need to know and she's jealous of Kel anyway—right out of his head. They don't matter. They're not real.

He's forgiven.

He leans down, trading kisses and the soft murmurs he knows Kel loves hearing. His hair—hasn't been this long since he was a teenager—gets everywhere, and Kel's big, fat cock swells within him. The adagio doesn't last. Toni takes him deeper, humps harder. He wants to feel it, wants it rougher, so there's no doubt. His man, his ass. Both bodies, both cocks.

Yes.

His faster pace, coupled with those soft little moans and groans, gets Kel worked up like nothing else, and Toni wants him just as bad.

"Give it to me, baby," he murmurs, wriggling down on Kel's dick, reaching to touch himself.

Their hands meet around Toni's hard flesh—like an illicit brush of skin on skin in a popcorn tub—and Kel's face tightens. His lips quiver, as if he wants to say something, and he rubs Toni's hip with his free hand, then touches the top of his ass, caressing the point their bodies meet, pushing his shaft in farther. Toni rolls down on him, fucking harder, faster. Kel thrusts up, over and over, deeper and deeper.

More.

A shallow gasp breaks from his lips, and Toni feels him getting close. Fuck, he's big. So big. He tugs his own cock with redoubled strength, Kel's fingers still clasped around him. The pleasure blooms hotter, throbbing through him with every movement of Kel's body, every touch of his hand. His climax builds, swirling up through the pit of his gut, his balls tightening and his ass clenching around Kel's cock.

They're as close as they'll ever get to being one, and Kel touches his cheek, his eyes glazed and his mouth formed around words that have no sound, yet echo loudly through Toni's chest. Kel gasps, then pushes himself up against the mattress, sitting up with his arm around Toni, holding his waist tight as he drives up into him again and again, head bent over and his whole body focused on hitting his peak. Toni's working for it too, relentlessly. He leans back a little, the part of his weight that Kel isn't taking supported on one arm, and he stares down at his cock, his head bent the way Kel's is, both of them just watching the reality of the fuck. There's this tender union of bodies and then, above the place they meet, Toni's hard shaft, plunging ever faster into Kel's grip, burnished red and damp. His cock. Possibly the most troublesome part of him, and yet the only bit he can really believe in. Right now, it's the center of everything, and Toni's only hanging on by the very edge of his self-control.

So close.

The bed squeaks frantically. Worn springs groan their frustrations, the headboard thudding against the wall, and the entire frame creaks with a desperate urgency. The air is close, hot, and the room heaves with their hard breathing, the sounds of their flesh meeting, and—finally—the succession of hungry, animal grunts Toni makes as he comes.

He watches it shooting out in a series of beautiful arcs that land on Kel's chest and stomach. Thick, white, creamy… vivid against his tawny skin. Even the air feels different, and Toni shivers, riding the edges of sensation as Kel keeps going, his eyes screwed shut and his cock invincible. He's almost there, and Toni palms his broad chest, rubbing the hard, brown nipples, coaxing him to completion. He digs his nails into Kel's flesh, leaving little dents on his pecs, and the thought of having his lover on top of him, fucking him deep and slow while Toni rakes these bad boys down his back is a sudden and exciting vision of hotness. His head swirls with different colors of pleasure and possibility, and he feels so full, so tightly packed with sensation.

Kel groans, and he's there, his cock still pumping into Toni's ass, the thrusts dying away into slower, needy movements, the breaths that pant between them hard and ecstatic. Toni feels Kel slip out, leaving him open, defenseless, but satiated. He leans forward, presses his mouth to Kel's in a half kiss that does little more than prove they're both still alive.

Kel smiles against his lips, strokes his back… murmurs something sweet that makes Toni purr contentedly. Kel's hot cock still rubs his aching hole, presses the wet cleft of his ass, and he wishes he could go again, that there could be nothing else to life but pleasure like this. Just the two of them.

After the lights stop popping and his lungs stop screaming, Toni disentangles himself from his lover and flops over to the other side of the bed, halfheartedly kicking at the rumpled covers. He doesn't want to be touched anymore. Not yet. Inside and outside… it's too much.

Toni curls up on his side of the bed. The sounds of the night are creeping back into his consciousness. Outside, sirens wail against the shadows, and they seem to echo against the darkness inside Toni's head. He feels small and stupid and scared when Kel gets out of bed, the way he used to feel after every trick in the first few months that he did that. Hell, it seems like a long time ago. Kel dumps the rubber, goes for a piss, then finally comes back to bed. Toni doesn't say anything. There's relief—and a little bit of resentment. Some other weird shit too. He balls the feelings up and pushes them away, maybe to be examined later, or perhaps just ignored indefinitely.

"Turn out the light?"

He needs to work on his voice. Danielle's always saying that. Nobody ever passes until she can pass on the phone. The voice is definitely in guy mode tonight. Everything's in guy mode. Should that feel good or not? He's not sure. It's... complicated. He feels calmer. He doesn't know if that's the estrogen or the fucking.

Kel clicks off the light, and Toni supposes it's guy mode that keeps him staring solidly at the wall, that stops him from turning over and snuggling up close to his lover; holding on and admitting that he's scared of letting go. Kel's fingertips trace his back for just a moment—touching the fleur-de-lis tattoo on his shoulder, Toni thinks—but then the contact is broken. Kel pulls away. Maybe he doesn't want to touch anymore, or maybe he thinks it's unwelcome.

More sirens ghost their way through the night, and Toni closes his eyes, hoping for pleasant dreams.

CHAPTER
FIVE

KEL'S PHONE goes off at twenty past seven. He squints through the
bleary slits of his eyes, wondering where that metallic little pulse of
music is coming from, and it's a few moments before he connects it to
the alarm on his cell. Beside him, Toni grumbles, and a foot kicks out,
heel striking a sharp blow to his shin.

"T'n 'ff!"

Toni kicks him again, and Kel grunts a response, reaches out to
the cabinet, grabs the offending noisemaker, and jabs randomly at
buttons until it goes quiet. He opens his mouth experimentally, runs his
tongue around the inside of it, and remains unconvinced that something
didn't crawl in there and die during the night.

"Wanna coffee?" he says at last, glancing over to Toni's side of
the bed.

There's little visible of him except a couple of black curls sticking
out from the mound of covers. That mound shifts a little, and a sleepy
voice mumbles from its depths.

"Y'h."

Kel sniffs and supposes he ought to get up. Reluctantly, he slides
out from his pit of warmth and luxury, his skin prickling with the
relative coolness of the air. It's not cold. Winter is cold. Last January
they spent most of the month in bed, and not for the normal reasons.

He likes the summer better, Kel decides, as his feet touch the
floor. Toni gives a small, happy groan and wraps himself up in the
extra half of the covers until he's completely cocooned.

"Get my cigarettes?" he asks, voice croaky, husky, and muffled.

Kel stretches, enjoying the way his joints click and his muscles lengthen as he hauls his arms up above his head.

"You smoke too much," he says, looking up at a patch of greenish-gray mold on the corner of the ceiling.

Toni snorts but doesn't bother with a snappy comeback.

Kel goes to take a piss—first of the day, always the best—and fetches Toni's slims on the way back to bed, along with two mugs of hot, black coffee. He stands everything down on the nightstand next to the half-empty bottle of lube, grabs an ashtray, and lights a cigarette for himself. Toni emerges from his nest, looking rumpled and gorgeous, despite the panda eyes and sallow, papery skin. He coughs, and Kel listens to the sound of it carefully, as if he could really judge whether anything was wrong, just from that. It's stupid, of course, but he still feels a little like every single antibody of Toni's is somehow his personal responsibility.

"Ugh... what time is it?"

Toni rubs a hand across his face, smearing the last residues of eyeliner even worse, and Kel can't stop himself from smiling.

"Seven thirtyish. You got time."

He sits down on the edge of the bed, coaxes a flame from his lighter for Toni, and leans close as he puts the slim to his lips and drags. The cigarette flares into life, Toni stifles another cough, and Kel tries not to think about it. He puts his feet up, stretches out, and leans back against the pillows. They really ought to buy new sheets, what with all the cinder marks and tiny holes in these, but hey, there are a lot of things they ought to buy. Money never goes far enough, and doesn't Kel know it?

Toni leaves half his cigarette smoldering in the ashtray that he's propped on the bed and—unexpectedly—curls up close, slipping his arm around Kel's ribs and hugging tight, cheek pressed to his chest.

"Mmm."

Kel says nothing, just swaps his cigarette to the other hand and uses one finger to gently push aside the tendrils of hair that tickle his skin. Slowly, almost reluctantly, he lets his arm drop to Toni's shoulder and holds him. He's warm, pliant, smooth... dangerous. Kel's never really thought that about anyone he's loved, but he thinks Toni is. It'd be too easy to love him too much, do terrible things for him, and not even care.

He glances over at the brass alarm clock on Toni's nightstand. The bell doesn't work, and the thing doesn't tell the right time, because he insists on keeping it running a half hour fast, like that's really going to help him organize himself. The hated pill bottles stand next to it. Kel won't look at them if he can avoid it. They make the drug names, which he found so hard to learn, march through his head like an invading army… a war-torn future he can't avoid. It feels as if it's been a hell of a lot longer than it really has since Toni started taking them.

He never sat down and spoke to Kel about it. Oh, he drops the brand names and the compounds into conversation every so often, the way he might mention exciting new friends.

I gotta get this Aldactone. Can you lend me something, baby?

Kel pays, of course. Every time, and without question. It's supposed to make Toni happy. He goes with him to the Internet café where he sits, drinking lattes and buying pills, and sometimes it chokes Kel and he just feels hollow, like there's never going to be any way out.

As far as he understands, from the limited reading he's done, and the complicated and often contradictory accounts of people he's asked—not counting Danielle, who won't talk to him about this shit and just looks at him like he's a bigot—there's three parts to the pharmaceutical side of it. There's the estrogen itself, which causes permanent infertility in as little as nine months… not that they were planning to have kids, obviously. Besides, love him as he does, even Kel has to admit that the thought of a pile of little Tonis running around the place is frankly horrific.

It also puts on fat, changes the way that fat is stored in the body—and as soon as Toni read that, he quit eating breakfast and usually lunch—promotes breast growth, and induces mood swings, penis atrophy, reduction of body hair. Oh, yeah… and it can give you blood clots.

After they came in the mail, those little white plastic bottles with their bright labels and Spanish leaflets, Toni found him on the couch, reading the list of possible side effects.

Toni, have you even looked *at this shit?*

Annoyed, he'd snatched the paper from Kel's fingers.

They're fine. I need them.

The progesterone is just as scary. Toni's only just started taking those, because he had to find a pill that doesn't come in a peanut oil suspension, on account of his allergy. So far, in Kel's opinion, they don't stabilize jack shit on the mood front, and he's heard the synthetic kind can actually cause depression.

He's not looking forward to that.

"I have to pee," Toni announces and clambers laboriously out of bed, heading for the bathroom with a reluctant grumble.

Kel smiles, but it doesn't make it as far as his eyes. He knocks the ash off his cigarette, takes another drag, and dumps it back in the tray while he reaches for his coffee. Briefly, he wonders if his quitting smoking would help Toni stop, but he doubts it. He ought to—honestly, they both ought to—and Toni even more than him, with all the things those fucking pills can do.

He's definitely peeing more since he started the antiandrogens. Kel's aware, having read the leaflet, that he's supposed to watch his potassium intake, or he runs the risk of heart problems. It was there, in black and white, and yet it was hard to believe. It made the whole thing seem more real, more frightening.

Kel takes a gulp of coffee and wonders how long it'll take. He tries to picture it in his mind's eye, that first day when he'll really see how much Toni's body has changed. He imagines it will be a gradual process, but he's read that estrogen can start having effects on the body from as little as two weeks. That's certainly pretty fucking obvious in Toni's mood swings, but Kel's ashamed to admit that he's more concerned about the cock stuff. Last night was great, but he worries about what's going to happen when Toni's libido—which has always been kind of on the tiring side of healthy—starts to wane. It probably will or, at least, he'll have trouble getting it up. One day, he won't be able to at all. Kel's going to miss it, he knows that.

Worse, what if *he* can't? Will that happen? Kel supposes so. If Toni changes in that way: if his flesh becomes soft and yielding, if his butt widens out and his thighs grow round, complimenting the appearance of the swelling buds of breasts… Kel doesn't know if he'll manage to handle that.

He's never been attracted to women. He can look at a woman's form and appreciate the beauty—he might even feel a fleeting thrill of lust for the purely geometric symmetry of a great ass, a soft thigh, or a good rack—but it's not the same. He likes guys. He likes the hardness, the sweat, the scent... everything about them that makes them *men*, and only a man's flesh has the solidity, the firmness he wants. It was one of the first things that attracted him to Toni. Yeah, he was a pretty boy, but for everything about him that was soft shadows and long eyelashes, there was a hard angle, a sharp corner.

He's uncompromising, and Kel supposes that's more than half the trouble.

He doesn't know if he can stand to watch it all rub away. The pills'll do that long before Toni's found the money for any surgery he decides he wants. They haven't even talked about it, but... well, who knows with Toni? Anyway, the Aldactone—those antiandrogens—the horse-piss estrogens and the progesterones, they'll all erode everything Kel thinks of when he closes his eyes. That perfect furl of a flower will be unbent and reformed into something new.

The hardest part is not knowing what Toni might be left with then. Will he feel right? Happy? Will he have to go further—and will his body take it?

Try as he might, Kel can't avoid the feeling that it's all going to go so badly fucking wrong. Ultimately, in his soul, he doesn't believe Toni is any more a woman than Kel himself is a Dutch stockbroker. The stupid little fuck is just running, trying to cut all the pain and all the bad things out, pare them away, rotten flesh from a fallen fruit. He may even have convinced himself there's another person at that hidden core... someone strong, brave, and confident.

Kel guesses that's what Toni thinks, and it makes him so fucking mad, because he sees that in everything he already is. Good with the bad, rough with the smooth—all that shit—it's corny but it's true. Trying to make himself into this new person, this crafted, perfect image he has in his mind, is never going to work.

He won't *be* perfect. Even if they can make it happen and—one day, in some rosy vision of the future—Toni walks out of a hospital somewhere with a vagina and a brand new passport, it won't magic away every hurt he's ever gotten, or stop new ones blistering inside him. It's not an answer to what he is, where he's been, and it'll bring with it so much more that Kel just doesn't believe his broken angel will ever be ready to face.

He can't see Toni using a dilator for the rest of his life, for one thing, or dealing with all the potential discrimination. He's bad enough at that now... like the time he pulled a knife on the two fundie kids who rolled up at a local bar and started making a noise about all the fags going to hell. Pretty much everybody else was just prepared to ignore them, have the door staff shoo them back out into the street and pretend they didn't exist, because dicks like that get off on the attention. Not Toni. What should have been nothing more than a distasteful incident turned into a full-scale brawl, and Kel remembers pelting through the night with someone else's blood on his shirt, dragging Toni behind him like a wet rag, still screaming obscenities. They were lucky to get out of there before the cops arrived.

No, Toni's crazy, but he's not trans. Not in Kel's opinion, though he realizes his opinions really don't matter much. If he says to anybody he thinks Toni needs help, not hormones, he's just told he's an ignorant bigot and, if he wasn't so tired of it all, he'd find that funny.

He blinks as a shadow falls across the bedroom doorway.

"Oh." Kel blinks again. "You got dressed."

Toni's wearing his skinny-fit jeans and brown ankle boots, like yesterday, but the top half's different. The white T-shirt must be new, because Kel hasn't seen it before, and it has a bold graphic print on it that incorporates a neon-pink image of Warhol's Marilyn and a darker pink lipstick kiss. It shows just how flat chested he is, though the neckline's high.

"Uh...."

Kel wants to tell Toni he's gonna get clocked for sure, looking like that, but he's smiling, face done up with fresh eyeliner and that tinted lip balm that tastes a heck of a lot more like strawberries than the lubricant Kel bought last week. He's wearing twinkly zirconium studs in both ears, the black curls swept up and twisted into the jaws of a plastic tortoiseshell clip. He does look good and, for a complicated moment, Kel tries to pull apart the way he sees his lover and work out whether it's Toni he wants to kiss, or whatever it is that Toni's being today. Kel wonders how other people see him. Maybe their first looks take in just an androgynous, mouthy girl, and his own cautiousness about how well Toni's passing is just that—his problem.

Kel's gaze falls to Toni's crotch, and he licks his lips.

"Um. Are you…?"

"Tucking? Kinda. Looks good, right? Two pairs of panties and a maxi pad."

He turns to the side, pulls the waistband of his jeans up a little, so Kel can see the comparative smoothness behind the denim. Next to the hem of the tee, shorter than the shirts he usually wears, it does look convincing. No baggy clothes hiding everything down to the middle of his thighs today. Toni's not exactly huge, so Kel guesses it can't be that uncomfortable, though the thought does make him wince a bit.

But Toni's looking at him expectantly, so he nods and dredges up a smile.

"Yeah. S'good."

Toni grins, comes around to the side of the bed, and sits down to take his morning dosages. Kel knows he ought to try to keep a closer eye on what his honey's swallowing, but he can't. He puts the coffee and the ashtray down on the nightstand and swings his legs out of bed, propelled by an impulse he doesn't fully understand.

"What time you leaving?" he asks, pausing in the doorway.

Toni glances back at him, glass of water in one hand, small white pill cupped in his palm. "Few minutes. Wanted to be a little early, stop Karen bitching. Why?"

"Thought I'd walk with you, that's all."

Toni wrinkles his nose, smiles. "Aww. You're cute."

Kel doesn't know why he said it. He has no real reason to go anywhere near the bookstore. He just doesn't want Toni walking that way alone, maybe… and that's stupid.

He gives her a loose, absent smile, and goes to take a shower.

THEY WALK down to the bookstore, and it is early. There's not that much in the way of busy office commuters from this part of town. People are heading into work, but there are few briefcases, few suits.

Stores are starting to open, and the sunlight still moves slowly across the concrete, as if the day isn't fully awake yet.

Toni slips her hand in Kel's as they go, and it's really nice to walk like that.

She feels so bright and important, like she could shake the whole world into looking at her. The memories of last night play through the back of her mind, and they leave a warm glow behind them. Everything's good. If Toni's lucky, he might even manage not to fuck it up too badly today.

She squeezes Kel's hand and, just before they cross the street, he looks at her. His gaze flickers, as if he was thinking about something else, and then he smiles. He's so handsome. He squeezes back, and Toni floats a little way off the ground. She goes to step off the curb, still looking at him, but he pulls her back—just before a truck sweeps in front of them, the decal on the side indicating that it's on its way to deliver vegetables or something.

"Fuck," Toni mutters, as the grit swirls back down to the ground and the air stills again.

Kel says nothing, but she hears the intake of his breath. Her wrist's kind of sore where he yanked it.

Damn driver didn't even sound his horn....

Toni shivers, and the world gets a little gray for a while as all the possibilities shimmer in her head, and that nervous, anxious feeling swells out into genuinely being scared. It's not so bad, because Kel's there, but it still rubs the shine off part of the walk.

When they get to the bookstore, and the bell over the door dings, Karen's all sweetness and light, because she likes Kel. Toni figures he must remind her of a really butch ex-girlfriend or something, or maybe it's some kind of skewed maternal impulse.

"And how are you today?" Karen wants to know.

"A'ight," Kel says with a shrug.

It annoys Toni, the way he always says that. It's a shield, not an admission. He's very rarely truly honest about anything he thinks or feels. But he's got that winning smile, and those beautiful eyes, and he could tell anybody anything and get away with it. She hangs close to him when she really ought to go and start putting up the sale promotion signs Karen wants in the window, and her fingers are still twined in his.

They talk for a little, just the three of them exchanging pleasantries, and then Karen smiles at Toni.

"I left the boards out back. I thought, one in each window, then the banners across the top. Can you do that?"

Cow.

"Mm-hm," Toni says instead.

"I'll see you later," Kel promises and kisses her cheek.

The contact blooms with a wider warmth, and how good they were last night flashes back once more through Toni's mind. She wants to tell Kel she loves him, but not with Karen standing right there. So she just smiles, reluctantly releases his hand, and saunters off to get the boards, not looking back until she's right at the door that leads out to the storeroom. She kind of expects to see Kel watching her, but he's not. He's leaning on the counter, talking quietly and earnestly to Karen, and Toni has no idea what that's about.

She doesn't want to make a fuss, though. Doesn't want a repeat of that paralytic fear that makes her cry like a child and feel like she's about to die, just because the stupidest fucking thing's happened.

She's not a complete fool.

It's entirely possible, Toni thinks, as she spots the two paper-covered corkboards with the words *Huge Reductions* pinned to them in retro lettering, that Danielle is right about the pills. Everything she's been saying about the dosages—about trying to do too much at once, and using the cheaper alternatives—she could have a point. She's always had qualms about Toni self-administering, anyway. Danielle says just because you read something on the Internet doesn't mean it's true, and everybody's mileage is different when it comes to hormones, so it's important to have proper guidance. Thing is, she's never clear about precisely where Toni's supposed to get that guidance from.

The first doctor Toni went to told him to piss off and stop wasting people's time. The second one said she couldn't diagnose gender dysphoria unless he could prove he wasn't using, and that everything he said he felt wasn't swayed by that. She tried to say he needed a rehab referral, and that it was something he ought to think more carefully about, something he ought to hold off on for a while. She was a stupid bitch. They all were. None of them understood, that was the problem. They didn't know what it was like.

Toni took Danielle's advice, called some of the numbers she offered. The people on the helplines were better equipped to understand, which was something, but they still didn't help much. It seems like all anybody wants to do is fix Toni up with a therapist... even Danielle says she needs one. But she's done that before, and won't do it again. The therapists are only going to say he won't pass psych evaluation for a dysphoria diagnosis and, as it is, what the fuck other choice is there but a long, drawn-out, expensive route littered with private surgery and yet more people wanting his money?

Nobody really gets it. Nobody understands.

Toni hefts the corkboards out one at a time and totes them back into the store. Kel's gone. His absence leaves a brief void in the world, but everyday stuff soon seeps in to fill it. The boards are unwieldy and heavy and, as Toni struggles to lift them up, one at a time, onto the dais platforms that host the window display, she begins to question the wisdom of wearing heels to work. She also wants to ask Karen what Kel was talking to her about—*Was it about me?*

Toni has no idea what Kel would want to ask her boss, but it's a worrying thought. Is he checking up on her? Checking she's not going crazy?

Crazier?

Toni tries to ignore the thoughts. Moment she starts thinking like that, she proves right any suspicion Kel may or may not have about the state of her mental health... and she doesn't want to do that. There's a point of principle involved somewhere. No one's ever made her feel as special, or as loved, as Kel does. Trouble is, among the shards of worry, she has this little voice that lives at the back of her mind, and it just won't let up. It always asks awkward questions. It wants to know why he's with her at all when she so clearly doesn't deserve him, and why—when she knows how stupidly lucky she is—she wants to go and fuck it up, wreck everything just like she always does.

It's an ugly, squat troll of a voice, and it reminds Toni that everything she touches turns to shit sooner or later. This is going to be no exception.

She doesn't wanna listen, so she focuses on work, on fixing up the new window display the way Karen wants it and, if she tries very hard, Toni can block out everything else. She lifts and hefts and pins until everything looks good, but the complicated arrangement beneath her jeans is getting very hot and sweaty and, as she climbs up into the window to rearrange the books on their transparent plastic stands, something in the nether regions starts to ruck up. The maxi pad that's providing a layer of discretion between cotton and cock curls over, escaping the place it's supposed to stay, and then there's the surprisingly painful experience of the sticky side attaching itself to an errant pubic hair, and *pulling*.

Hard.

Toni whimpers and drops a hardback volume of gay mystery stories on her toe, which shoots a different and contrasting pain all the way up her leg.

Being a girl is not easy today.

CHAPTER
SIX

IT'S A nice summer, as summers go. The days stay warm and dry, and what little air there is in the city doesn't seem malign. It bowls gently along streets rimed with dust and the debris of living, but it doesn't come equipped with the kind of scalding heat that wants to burn, to choke.

The week moves on, dying and rising from its own ashes.

Toni doesn't work Mondays, but she does have an electrolysis appointment. She's nervous about it, because the treatment's painful, and going to the clinic is intimidating. It was hard finding somewhere in the first place. Initially, she made the mistake of trying to book her first consultation and trial appointment over the phone, without explaining her situation. All she said was that she was interested in facial electrolysis and wanted to talk to someone about what was involved. In a way, she supposes it was good they thought she was a biological girl, but... it didn't feel like it when she got there.

She rolled up, and the place she'd picked looked great, but as soon as she walked in there, people started staring. All those women, looking at her as if she'd just been scraped off the bottom of someone's dainty high-heeled shoe. Toni had showed up in guy mode, too, scared of being clocked or—for some stupid reason—making anyone else feel uncomfortable. It was, like, the first time *ever* he'd made a choice based on that, and he didn't know why it had seemed important.

They asked her to leave, though, and she did. She didn't want a scene.

Toni didn't just go with the first number in the phone book after that. She's done what Danielle suggested—what everything she's read online said is right—and gone with the place that seems to offer the best treatment. It's a long bus ride away, and their prices are high. Over a hundred and fifty bucks an hour, and Toni knows, in the long run, there are going to be a hell of a lot of hours.

The prospect is disheartening, but at least it's permanent. Once it's over, she will never, ever have to worry about beard growth again. And that's good, because she wants this.

She does.

Before the appointment—kind of like Dutch courage, only without the booze—she has time to meet Danielle for a coffee. Kel would probably have come with her if she'd asked, but she didn't ask. He hates needles. He even seemed to get dizzy just listening to her talk about what they were gonna do before she went for the first appointment. He gave her the money, though. Toni knows how he got it, and she's grateful. He shouldn't have to sit through needles after that.

The café is pleasant. Genuinely Italian-run, which Toni likes to see.

The family she remembers having—before the car accident and her mother's wheelchair, then the fights, the divorce, the years of foster care and the screw-ups she made along the way to juvie—had an ice cream parlor. They used to play Little Tony and Dean Martin records, and Toni's older brother would mop the floors after closing. Cream-colored vinyl, and the smell of a sickly, floral disinfectant. There were long-handled spoons and really thick glasses. That, and the velvety, fresh taste of vanilla ice cream, is all Toni really remembers about it.

She shakes her head, tries to pull everything together, to focus on the here and now. Danielle's there to greet her, waiting on the corner.

"Hey, sweetie!"

They hug, which is nice, though it makes Toni a bit self-conscious. Danielle smells of some light, sweet perfume, and she looks incredibly pretty today. She heads inside, Toni follows, and the café is cool and air-conditioned. Fake plastic ivy runs up one wall, and she listens for the strains of Little Tony playing in the background, but they're not there. Some fuzzy, generic pop tune plays instead, and that's right. It's a different place, a different time.

Toni orders a cinnamon latte, Danielle a cappuccino, and they take their coffee to a table outside, where they sit, the shafts of lazy sunlight sluicing over everything. Toni wishes she had the courage to wear a skirt like Danielle, to feel the warmth of the sun on her bare legs. Danielle looks so good, but then she always does. The scoop neck of her gray marl tee cups her breasts, and they're so rounded and big, at least a full C cup. Toni has mixed feelings about boobs. They look so incredible, and the *thought* of them is awesome—firm, round flesh, tight nipples, and all that smooth, elastic weight—but she feels weird every time she tries to wear a padded bra.

With tape and the right kind of lingerie, Toni can squeeze up slightly more than an A cup of cleavage, and that's fun to do sometimes. It's worth it for going out some nights, or when she really wants to play with the way it looks and feels… but it's awkward. It gets sweaty and itchy, and her skin doesn't like the tape so she usually ends up with a rash. Kel hates it. He tries really hard not to say so, but the look on his face when Toni takes off his shirt and reveals a black lace bra and two little squidged-up creases of flesh is just… awful.

Anyway, there are plenty of flat-chested runway models. Beautiful, stunning, amazing-looking women who don't have huge tits. Toni tells himself that. Being pretty doesn't have to mean conforming… but those amazing models don't look natural. They don't look like Danielle.

She looks so great, and it's totally, utterly unfair. She wears a sheer blouse open over her top, and it skims over everything, down to the slimly curved hips she's poured into her denim skirt. Her hair's glossy and sleek, but for a little bit of fuzz at the roots, and she has a pair of really cute blue sandals on, with a wedge heel.

"So," Danielle says, swiping a finger through the froth that tops her cappuccino and popping it into her mouth, "how d'you feel?"

Toni shrugs and watches the way Danielle sucks her fingertip clean between caramel-colored lips. Side-on, the movement quick and graceful, but still sensual…. Toni has to fight the urge to try it herself, just to see if she can do it like that.

"Okay."

She's getting sick of people asking, to be honest. Danielle raises her eyebrows.

"No more shiver-shakes and panics?"

"No… well, not really. I was stupid," Toni admits.

She'd prefer not to talk about it. Losing it the way she did last week was embarrassing. They've spoken on the phone since, and she's promised she's all right, that it was just a stupid, fleeting terror over nothing, but Danielle keeps coming back to it. Now, she's nodding and looking very sage.

"It's not stupid, honey. Being scared. You were scared 'cause you couldn't get a hold of him and—given what he does—that's not stupid."

Toni pauses with her coffee halfway to her mouth. It's cruel of Danielle to say that. Of course she *knows* that anything could happen to Kel. She puts a lot of effort into not thinking about it.

A woman passes on the sidewalk with two small children, their high-pitched voices cutting through the general chatter and noise for a moment. At another table, a man's cell phone rings. Toni blinks.

"I didn't think—"

She thought Kel had left her. They both know it. She recalls the way it felt, the burning, black pitch bubbling up inside her… terror, anger, loss. She lives with it all the time, because she can't believe she can possibly keep him. He scares her to death, just by being around, but she wouldn't change it even if it she could.

Danielle doesn't understand. She doesn't get it, and she never will.

"I mean, Kel's smart, I know," Toni continues with a petulant shrug. "I just… I'm getting kinda nervous. Sometimes."

Danielle says nothing. She drops a few crystals of sugar into her coffee, slips the spoon under the layer of foam, and stirs it in a slow figure of eight.

Toni doesn't want to say anything else, but the silence draws things out. She hates that, and she'd much prefer hiding beneath the layers of sound that cloak the street. The warm air smells of exhaust fumes, but Danielle's perfume dances over the top of it, and Toni finds herself talking without meaning to say a thing.

"We're still good. He looks after me real well. He—" She stops, pulls back on the words. There's no way she's going to tell Danielle about the money Kel gives her, or how he paid for today with a visit to The Sherbet Pervert. Thinking about that dirty old man makes Toni feel uneasy, and she can't stand the thought of seeing pitying disapproval on Danielle's face. "He thinks I'm nuts for starting this. Needles. He's so scared of 'em."

Danielle smiles politely. "Are you nervous now?"

Toni nods. "Mm. S'gonna hurt. I couldn't sleep last night."

The pain's only a part of it. Having anyone spend an hour sticking needles into your face and burning out the follicles obviously isn't going to be a cakewalk, but she can manage it. Knowing it's such a small step—that there's going to have to be a lot more sessions, just for the face—is hard, and because the effectiveness of the process depends on the stage of growth the hair is at, it's not even as easy as just doing one area per session.

"Mm!" Danielle smirks over the rim of her cup. "Honey, just wait until you get further on. Your face is *not* the worst place for zapping."

It takes a beat before Toni gets that one, but she does, and she claps a hand to her mouth.

"Ohhh… God! Have you started?"

Danielle shakes her head. "Nn-uh. Groinal electrolysis scares the crap out of me. Anyway, do I even need it? No. But you know Jada? She started last month. Hours and *hours* of it to go. She said it hurt so much she cried. She couldn't walk properly for a while after, and she got awful scabbing."

Toni tries not to picture it, but she can't help herself. It's bad enough lying on the table and feeling each tiny needle prick its way into her face, then the anticipation of the beeping, and the burst of light and heat as the hair is burned out, the follicle desiccated beyond repair. Toni can only too easily imagine the kind of pain that engenders when the skin in question is lower down, and there's no escape from that. Every single inch of penile and scrotal skin needs tackling, if genital surgery's going to be on the cards.

Is it, though? That's something Toni hasn't thought about properly. Not really. It's frightening, and a little disorienting, and it raises all these questions and complicated things that it somehow feels like she should have answers for—that she's less of a woman if she doesn't—but they're hard to separate out in her head.

When she stands naked in the bathroom at home, while their crappy shower is belching out tepid water and she's looking at herself in the small, smudge-pocked mirror, Toni doesn't feel repulsed. This body… it's awkward, yes, and Toni hates the skinny bits and the scarred bits—the pale stretch marks on his back, the bony knees and ugly feet, the brown pocks of cigarette burns on his ribs, and the little pod of a stomach that never gets flat and toned, no matter how little he eats—but it's not as simple as saying it isn't him.

The waist, the thighs, the tight little ass… the cock. They're parts of Toni, and it feels like they should be, like they belong to him when he touches them. When he touches himself, it doesn't create pain or confusion—at least, not most of the time—and, if it does, it's not because he's hurt by the ways in which he's put together wrong. Not completely, anyway.

When he was a kid, Toni hated his body violently. Puberty was horrible. He hated the way he felt, the way he started to look… for years now, he's either removed or trimmed to virtual baldness every single trace of body hair from the eyebrows down, with a kind of rigorousness that borders on the obsessive. He likes his smoothness, his delicacy, the soft, pink curl of his cock, and the slimness of his waist. He needs it, if he's going to feel pretty, and feeling pretty is on par with feeling good.

As a child, Toni picked that up early, and she didn't even realize it.

She likes the idea of a full transition. A totally new person. A woman's center to her… it could be good. She's thought before about how it would feel, though it is hard to imagine life without her dick. Toni knows Kel wouldn't be impressed, but it isn't about him, is it? This is about her. All the same, it is kind of hot, thinking about him like that. Kel having her, taking her as a complete woman… not that she can say as much to Danielle because, as Danielle would be the first to point out, who the fuck says a woman has to have a pussy?

It's complicated, and it makes Toni's head hurt. Why does anybody have to pick a gender, anyway? And why is it so hard for him? Other girls don't have this problem. They *know*, and they speak up, and they transition, and they're happy. When he was a kid—rejecting sports and cars in favor of watching game shows with his mom while she painted her nails—Toni used to think he should've been born a girl. It would have been easier, and it would have meant he wasn't supposed to like the things he didn't. It would have meant freedom, and affection, and all the ways it was okay to be who he is.

Maybe they'd have loved me more.

It's hard to know. In fact, it's probably impossible to tell, and that makes him feel so small and stupid. Being a girl—being feminine, being that cute little strip of twink who just skirts the line between male and female, at least until the pants come down—has always been a comfort. People have treated Toni right because she demands it, because she's pretty and sexy and gives fucking awesome head, and that feels amazing. Being able to do that—to *be* that—is fantastic, and she wants it all the time. She wants it to feel natural. She wants to *be* natural, to stop putting on this mask that rests against the world, and that she has to rely on to keep her safe. She wants it to be real, so she can stop being afraid of people seeing beneath it, seeing all the uncertainty, the panic and the anxiety, and the void of sheer, cold terror that fills her up so much of the time.

Nobody sees that. Nobody's there when the walls come down and the whole world is shaking, and it's all Toni can do to curl up and give in to the fear, feeling like she's going to die and every second is an inevitable fall into the fire.

Nobody sees that except Kel.

Danielle doesn't understand why Toni's so scared of losing him. She thinks—if he leaves because he can't deal with the transition, or if something as trivial as physical appearance chokes his love for her into dust—then he wasn't good enough for Toni in the first place. Only that's not fair, and it isn't really true.

Kel *does* love her. She knows that. But he never asked for this. It's new to him, and it's both unfamiliar and frightening. He's seen some of Toni's darkest places—the panic, the anger, the stupid things she does and thinks—and he's still here, and she wants to be a better person for him. They've both changed so much in the last year, and part of getting cleaner, getting out of the bad spirals they were both in, has meant grabbing hold of this, because *this* is how it ends. What Toni's doing now is the way to make everything okay, to make herself into the person she wants to be—*needs* to be—and even though it will probably mean that Kel does leave, it's still the right thing to do.

It's going to be hell, of course, because he'll always be her man. Toni's sure of that. Even if, *when*, he leaves, she'll never find anyone else she could love like him. Never anyone to hold a candle to him, and when she's maudlin she wonders how that'll feel... knowing that the one great love of her life is over.

It probably makes her a drama queen. But the thoughts are complex and troubling all the same. She flinches away from a lot of them and drinks her coffee. There's a very big difference between where she is now and where she's going to end up being, that much is clear, so who knows what's going to happen? This whole deal is supposed to be a journey, though, so it's okay to feel a little lost, isn't it? It's okay to not know quite how things are going to work out.

She pulls herself back to the present, clears her throat, her hand running absently over her face—and meeting the distinct prickle of beard growth. She didn't shave this morning, on account of the appointment, and the look on Danielle's face shows she knows and appreciates the fear that immediately springs up behind Toni's eyes.

"You look fine," Danielle says, reaching across the table and squeezing her wrist. "It doesn't show."

Toni smiles gratefully.

"How are you settling with the new pills?" Danielle asks, which feels a little like it comes out of the blue. "You had to pay the extra for the compounding charge in the end, huh? Or did you find some without the peanut?"

"Mm-hm." Toni shrugs. "Stupid allergy. Found some, but they cost more. Worth it, though. They're good, I guess. I-I think I'm feeling kinda more mellow, y'know? Balanced. Well... like it's easier, anyway."

Danielle nods, dips her spoon into the foam that rimes her cup. "What did you go for? Not more generics?"

"Uh-huh." The last third of the coffee has a stronger flavor, clovey and slightly bitter on her tongue. "They were cheaper than the others."

Danielle gives a disapproving little huff. "Toni... you can't go on cost alone. I thought—"

"They're fine," Toni says quickly, because she's getting really ticked off with Danielle telling her what she should and shouldn't be doing, and how much she ought to be paying for it.

It's okay for Danielle. She had a therapist, she had a proper consultant, and she doesn't see anything wrong with paying for the things she wants.

Danielle wrinkles her nose.

"Well, did you at least think about the dots?"

"Vivelle?" Toni takes a sneaky glance at her watch. Her smile is getting a little fixed. "Uh-huh. I don't know. I...."

"They're good. Better than most of the estrogen caps I tried. A lot of research seems to suggest it's really much better for your body to spread it out, make the hormone release a gentle intake, not a sharp spike."

Toni just nods. Again, it's all very well for Danielle, or anyone else who gets this stuff on prescription and a small copayment. Having to buy without prescriptions or insurance makes things more complicated, and Toni suspects her friend too easily forgets this. Toni's seen generic equivalents of the same transdermal patches on the Mexican website she usually buys from—they're discreet, waterproof, and probably very good—but they cost almost twice as much as the capsules she chose.

Toni doesn't have the money to throw at high-end products. She supposes she could make it, but she'd rather not. It's been hard enough so far, since she didn't exactly promise Kel that she wouldn't do anything—and it wasn't precisely a promise, not really—because there are still so many people Toni knows who try to fix her up with work. They don't see a lot of the old crowd; Toni's pulled back from so many people in the past few months. It's not a loss. Most of them were jerks. It can be lonely… it's even been a little disorienting, but it's not a loss.

It's one of the reasons she's been thinking about camera work. There's good money in that, and a lot less risk. Hell, if Kel didn't go off the deep end whenever she raised the issue, she could have suggested they get their own equipment set up, did cams or something from home. It might even be fun—and people would pay to see Kel fucking her, she's sure. They'd probably pay just to watch him clean his teeth, or sit around watching TV in his underwear. She would, if she didn't get it for free.

Toni fades back in again, aware that she's being nagged at.

"And you're still smoking!" Danielle chides. "I can't believe you're still smoking. You *have* to quit. Do you have any idea how bad those things are for you? Especially with the pills. It's not good for your heart."

Toni wonders why the fuck everybody nags so much. Why doesn't anyone want her to just get on with it and do things her way? Of course she knows there are risks. Why do they all think she hasn't thought about any of this? Do they think she's fucking stupid?

"I know," she says. "I'm gonna quit."

She takes a more overt glance at her watch and flashes Danielle a quick smile.

Danielle bites her lip. "Time to go?"

"Uh-huh."

"You'll be fine."

Toni smiles again, wider this time. Despite everything, Danielle really helps. Just the fact that she understands is such a relief. Such a comfort. They stand and, awkwardly, Danielle gives her another hug. She kisses Toni's cheek, and it sparks off a flush of warmth that Toni's not expecting.

It passes quickly, and she's able to leave Danielle behind and head off down to the bus station. The sun beats down, the air stale and coarse.

Toni doesn't look at the figures that fringe the block. She may not know them individually, but they fit into a set of familiar types that she easily recognizes. On the corner, a thickset guy with kinky hair and cinnamon skin is smoking a cigarette. Toni blinks; Kel didn't say he would be down here today. The guy looks like him, though, until Toni squints harder and thinks maybe he's more Latin than black. She remembers Kel telling her once that his grandma was from Puerto Rico or something, but she can't remember. It was kind of an aberration, 'cause he doesn't talk about his family, mostly, but as far as she recalls they were both pretty drunk.

Genetics are weird. Like everything else that makes people who they are.

Anyway, when Toni looks again, the guy barely resembles Kel at all. She gets on the bus and pretty much flings herself against the scratchy upholstery of the seat. Folded in on herself, Toni waits for the great, grimy monster to lurch into life, watching the people with whom she's sharing the journey.

There's a middle-aged woman with a dark cotton jacket far too heavy for the temperature, her face florid, and a sheen of sweat collecting in the furrows that run across her forehead. Toni wonders where she's going, with her thin mouth set tight against the world in an expression that might either be fear or determination. Perhaps both.

Farther back, there's a young couple—younger than Toni remembers ever being. No, that's not really true. Toni does remember. She takes a few sneaky looks at them, watching the way the boy's fingers are splaying through the girl's. Intertwined starfish. The way they cling, when the rest of their bodies are so loose. They slouch in their seats as if they're nothing more than two rag dolls dropped there, leaning against each other and forgotten by the rest of the world. His face rests on her shoulder, mouth pressed into the cascade of her chestnut hair, and she's laughing at something. A large, clear plastic folder rests against her leg, and there are drawings in it. Toni makes out the broken shapes of sunflowers, houses... something that very much resembles the old embankment not far from the train station. All outlined in soft pencil, figured as art instead of life. Toni twitches her upper lip as she turns away and slouches against the window.

Tourists.

TONI GETS to her appointment a little early, and she takes a seat in the waiting room. Thankfully, it's not crowded. She's self-conscious, but she knows the most important thing she can do is be relaxed—as if that's actually easy to do in these circumstances. Toni selects a magazine from the glass-topped table that stands in front of the low, black leather couch she sits on, and flips through the glossy pages. She's never sure about reading women's magazines in public places. Feels weird, as if she might be failing some kind of secret test if she's spotted spending more time than she ought looking at the advertisements for mascara or foundation, instead of reading the problem pages, or examining the articles about pleasing a man in bed.

The corner of Toni's mouth curls as she thinks about that. There probably isn't much this rag can teach her on that score—she's certainly never had any complaints.

Still, it's odd. Sitting here, looking at the pictures of the beautiful women, airbrushed far past perfection and staring out at her from their glossy backgrounds, Toni's not sure what to feel. She's nervous about the shadow she's sure is on her jaw. With the electrolysis, they use an intense magnifying plate—almost like a microscope—to get the needle right into the follicle, so there's no need to walk around with several days' beard growth. That's good, but Toni still thinks she looks horribly obvious. It's not all that noticeable, not really. Kel assured her of that before she left home—and didn't Danielle say she looked fine?

Her leg starts ticking slightly, knee bouncing in time to an inner rhythm, the heel of her ankle boot tapping on the linoleum. The pages of the magazine crackle as Toni flicks through them. There are so many things to learn, so many little rituals and rites of passage that she doesn't know, doesn't understand. Like there's a shorthand she hasn't learned, and there's no one here to tell her where to start.

Well, she has Danielle, and a couple of other people she knows through her… and there are some girls Toni talks to online, but it's not the same.

She's learned some stuff that way. Like, Danielle says, once a girl goes full-time, it's a good idea for her to start carrying a maxi pad in her purse. She says one of the first moments she really, truly felt like she'd been accepted as a woman was when someone asked her if she had a pad in the ladies' room, and she wishes she'd thought of carrying one earlier. Toni supposes that would be a better use for the damn things than her experiment with tucking.

The magazine tells her she should be applying her makeup with her fingertips this season, instead of sponge applicators. Apparently, it gives a sexy, smudgy look that's very popular on the runway, and complements the summer's hottest colors in blush and eye shadow.

The receptionist coughs gently and, when Toni looks up, she realizes it's her time to go in. She stands, drops the magazine back to the table, and smoothes her hands across the seat of her jeans, wiping the sweat from her palms. She takes a deep breath and tries to convince herself that no one's staring.

The woman who greets her in the treatment room is a different technician from the last time. Toni's a little unnerved by that to start with, but the anxiety doesn't last. The tech is called Sandy, which suits her far more than any given name ought to—she's blonde and freckly and really does look like she could be a walking beach sculpture, or as if she may be wearing a bikini under her white coat—so Toni wonders if it's a nickname. She could ask, but it gives her something to think about while Sandy's getting ready. She lies down on the treatment table, and Sandy adjusts it so she's as comfortable as she's going to get. The room is so white and clean it makes Toni anxious, and she's sure she's dirtying the place up just by breathing.

Sandy makes small talk, which is kind of her. She's read all the notes, she knows Toni's situation, and she's okay with it. She doesn't even seem to think it's unusual. Toni isn't the only t-girl who comes here, Sandy says, but that isn't much of a consolation. Toni can feel herself tensing up, and she can't stop it. Sandy wipes down the side of her face with an alcohol-free solution, smiles, and tells her to relax.

"Are you ready?"

"Mm-hm," Toni manages. Sweat prickles the small of her back.

"Okay. Here we go."

Toni screws up her eyes as she feels the probe slide into place. It doesn't hurt, but it's the anticipation that's the worst thing. Toni really hates it. The beeps come next—*one, two*—and then there's a flash of hot, sharp pain. Not so bad to start with, but it's only the beginning.

Sandy takes a couple of short breaks during the hour. Toni kind of wishes she'd just get on with it and push through, because this costs serious money, but she's also grateful for the respite. The whole left side of her face feels like it's burning, and tears gather at the corners of her eyes, the tip of her nose stinging with weltering sniffs.

"You know, you could try a topical anesthetic to take the edge off," Sandy suggests. "Apply about an hour before your appointment… you can get something suitable at most drugstores, and I've got some aftercare products you could try if you want."

Toni shakes her head, hair rustling against the paper hygiene protector that covers the table. "Naw. Well, maybe… I dunno. Stupid

Italian hair," she adds, widening her eyes and trying to blink the tears away.

Sandy smiles and looks irritatingly more like one of those wispy, willowy, Californian blondes. Toni's not jealous, and she definitely doesn't feel inferior. She needs to pee again, too, but that's going to have to wait until this is done.

She pats her palm against the edge of the table.

"Okay. Let's go."

"Sure?"

"Mm-hm."

The hour is both unendingly long and not long enough. When it's finally over, Toni isn't even sure how much they've done, though Sandy goes over everything with her in the mirror.

"It's good," she assures Toni, "especially for only your second session. Like we talked about at the consultation, we're probably going to be looking at a total of two hundred hours, give or take, but we could possibly do it in a little less. It's very much going to depend on how the, um, hormones go."

She turns a little coy at talking about that. Toni isn't sure if it's because the woman knows she's self-administering or not. She was pretty up-front about it, but Sandy made her fill in a form before they started that listed everything she's taking, and Toni didn't have a consultant's name to put in the right box. Sandy seems smart enough that she would have worked it out. Of course, the coyness could equally be because of how many thousands of dollars she's talking about draining Toni of over the next year or so.

It's worth it, though. Toni's sure of that.

She touches a finger delicately to the place they've done. It's sore and red, and she thinks it might swell. It doesn't seem like very much, either, for all that pain, but there's a limit to how much beard they can do at once. Besides, as Sandy says, hair grows at different rates, and the zap sessions only get it at certain points in its growth cycle. Her estrogen schedule will eventually stop new growth, but it's still going to take a while. Toni knows. She's heard all the talks, read all the pamphlets, but she's still faintly surprised when Sandy wishes her luck before saying goodbye.

Toni smiles awkwardly. It makes her face hurt more.

Out front, she pays the money that Kel gave her and makes her next appointment for two weeks' time. They can fit her in on a Friday then, and that's good, because it'll give her time over the weekend for the redness to go down. Toni determines she's going to think about that in the future, once she's used to this routine, and then she won't have to go into work on Tuesdays looking like she fell asleep on a tanning table or something.

She hands over the bills and watches the receptionist's face as she does so, as if the woman might somehow know where the money came from. It's a stupid, ridiculous, insulting thought, and it goes away quickly when Toni focuses on it.

Kel's told her all about The Sherbet Pervert. About the filthy socks and the dirty gym shorts, and his off-white leather couch. They laugh about him, and perhaps that's mean. Toni doesn't care. It's a hell of a lot less than he deserves, the filthy bastard. She doesn't know what he looks like but, just for a moment, she wants to wipe her hand after touching his money.

TONI FEELS people stare as she walks up from the bus stop. It's getting later, and the city's waking up; people are coming home, flowing back into the parts of town that have been fallow all day. Her face is red and blotchy, and she knows she's walking with her head down because of it. She tries not to, but she doesn't feel as confident as she'd like. She thinks about calling Kel, but settles on just sending him a text. That way he can pick it up whenever he's ready—whenever he's done with whatever he's doing—and she's not pressuring him. She's not demanding anything.

She misses him, though. Bad.

Has he been to the clinic yet, picked up his results? They might have been ready. Toni doesn't know. Should have asked if he was planning to call, should have asked if he knew yet. She's so self-obsessed.

Tears sting the bridge of her nose, and Toni fumbles a pair of sunglasses from her purse. They're big—too big, really—and she knows they're probably the worst thing she could possibly put on, but she just wants something to hide behind.

Kel should be having one of his meetings today, whether or not he's been to the clinic. About now, actually.

Toni's been to a couple, but she's not a group person. She stopped going after the session where they were supposed to talk about why they'd used. She doesn't want to talk about things like that, because talking about memories gives them power. If she's spent the past however many years pushing stuff to the back of her mind, she doesn't want to pull it all out into the open for other people to see.

If she does that, she'll never get rid of it.

Kel probably doesn't need to keep going. Toni knows he hasn't started using again. He stopped not long after they got together, though she figures he was probably already giving it up. She can't be responsible for something like that, whatever he says... and he did say it, once.

A smile tugs at Toni's lips as she recalls that day. They were making out on the grass in the park—stupid, like horny teenagers—and the sun was warm on her skin. Kel said he didn't need to forget about anything anymore. All that was gone. He was happy, and Toni was his world. She remembers tipping her head back as he kissed her neck, and watching the first leaves fall from the trees.

By the time she shuts the apartment door on the world, Toni's face is sorer than ever, and she's sick of being buffeted by people staring, the cruel glances and the sidelong looks. She may be imagining them, or she may not. Either way, she's convinced herself the whole side of her face is going to scab, or the skin's going to turn coarse and bumpy. Every horror story she's ever read is going to come true, and regrets flit through her head like moths.

Toni pours herself a ginger ale with ice and drinks it through a straw, taking occasional breaks to rest the cool glass against her tender skin. When she dares to take a look at herself in the bathroom mirror, the area does appear to still be red and slightly swollen, but she knows that's not uncommon. It was like this last time, though not as bad. Of course, last time, the tech didn't do so much at once, and she wasn't dealing with the coarser hair at the base of Toni's jawline.

A passing recollection of her father flickers through Toni's mind. He had really thick beard growth. Thick, black, curly hair and a permanent tidemark of stubble halfway up his cheeks. Hair on the backs of his hands and knuckles too. Toni catches herself tensing up in an absurd flesh-print of a memory, like she's gonna feel one of those big, meaty hands, balled up and clubbing the side of her head or something.

Stupid.

She just wishes Kel was home.

CHAPTER
SEVEN

THE CLINIC seems busier than it was last week, though Kel knows from experience that the place doesn't really get jumping until after five o'clock. That's when all the worried, white faces drop by after work, twisting tissues in their hands in the waiting room, or just sitting around looking like they want to puke. Kel could be quite tempted to come up here purely to watch them, because the entertainment value is pretty sweet, but he's seen firsthand where it can end up. If he genuinely thought he was facing a future of non-nukes and PIs, Kel's pretty sure he'd toss his cookies in fear too.

He does kind of have a little bit of that now, this knot of unease in his gut that tightens each time he breathes. It slides its tendrils all around the inside of his body, cold and vicious, like it's searching out a weakness, a spot it can exploit and break open. He's not going to give in to it, though. He's done nothing different in the months since he was last tested, and that came out fine. It's always been fine. It's not like he's been fretting about it either, because he hasn't. He only called on the off chance, because he didn't want to spend all day moping around thinking about how cranky Toni's going to be when he gets back from his electrolysis appointment.

Kel feels bad for not going with him, but it's hard enough just thinking about it.

It's brave of Toni, Kel reckons. He sure as hell can't imagine letting anyone doing that to *him*. Lying there, with no anesthetic, while somebody sticks needles in your face and blasts you with a laser or whatever…. It's one of those things that makes him uncomfortable, not just because of the thought of the thing itself, but because it sounds so awful that it kind of proves how much Toni wants to go through with this.

Kel's proud of him for that. Strange—and he wouldn't have expected it of himself—but it's true. It doesn't mean he has to like it, of course.

"Room two," the receptionist with the nice voice tells him, and he hurriedly blinks the thoughts of Toni away.

Kel walks along the hallway with his head held high, and it almost stops his pulse thrumming in his ears.

The room is light, bright... beige. A green curtain, pushed back on a metal rail over by the window, lends a murky, shadowed color to the sunshine that filters through, dappling the scuffed linoleum. The clinician is an Indian guy, maybe in his midthirties, with heavy glasses and a bored expression. Kel wonders if he expected something more from his medical career than day after day of swabbing herpes sores and explaining the importance of good hygiene and clean needles to crank-pocked kids.

"You didn't request the HIV test under anonymity?" the clinician says, glancing at Kel over the notes.

His accent is pleasantly lilting. Kel doesn't know if India has regional accents, like North and South or whatever. He supposes it must, but he has no idea how you'd start telling the difference.

"Uh-uh. You guys got all my details anyway, and I come here for everything, so...." He shrugs. It's none of the guy's fucking business. "It okay?"

The clinician squints down at the notes again, and his hesitation panics Kel. It's a yes or no response, surely? He edges forward a little on the uncomfortable, low chair, trying to pretend he isn't holding his breath.

"There were... no antibodies found present in the blood."

Kel breathes again. He listens to what the guy says, all the stuff about how things can change, how the window period is like a sliding scale, and simply means there is no definable presence at this time. To Kel, it's barely a breath away from preaching and, when the clinician slips a couple of leaflets across the desk, he guesses he hasn't been working here long. He takes them anyway, nods like he really gives a shit, and leaves as soon as he can.

Coming out into the sunlight feels like surfacing from the deep weight of cloudy water, like always, but this time Kel can shake that weight off easily. He's doing good: clean STI sweep, no nasties in his blood, not even a head cold. He supposes he could go and catch up with some people, celebrate a little, but he doesn't want to jinx it. Besides, it wouldn't be good to show up at his meeting stinking of drink, like he's just replaced one habit with another.

Kel checks the time on his phone. Speaking of meetings, he ought to get going. He can't be late, even if he doesn't want to go. He can grab something to eat before he has to head down there, though, so he swings by a sandwich bar and orders something involving chicken, bacon, and peppers.

As far as Kel's stomach is concerned, most really satisfying food comes prepackaged between two layers of something starchy. He doesn't know why, but he isn't going to question it. He sits on one of the place's high metal stools and eats slowly, sucking on a caffeine-free Coke and watching the people go past outside the window.

BY THE time he has to go, Kel's mild antipathy has had space to work itself up into a fit of really not wanting to do it, and he's seriously considering ditching everything and just heading home. He knows he can't. His meetings are one of those things he can't let slide, however tempting it is. He knows how he gets if he skips one: tense and pissed off at everybody. He slapped Toni around once. It was a while ago, before he started the pills and everything, and his honey just gave as good as he got, but Kel's still so fucking ashamed of himself. He can't begin to imagine what would happen if he did it now. It doesn't bear thinking about. Anyway, just like always, Toni still hurts himself too much to need a hand in that department from anyone.

It's true, Kel supposes: things have changed between them. He just isn't sure if those changes are for the better or not.

He starts to walk, and that sloping, ground-eating trudge of his soon pushes the feel of asphalt and concrete out from under his feet, until it seems like the world isn't much to do with him. He's just walking. There's a serenity to it, an awareness of his body and his heartbeat, and he can just let his mind run on autopilot, thoughts buzzing away below the surface, but not bothering anybody.

On the way down there, Kel tries to pretend to himself that it's not a selfish, running-away thing, this not wanting to go to the meeting. He tries to pretend it's about Toni, that he's thinking about her electrolysis appointment and the long bus ride home. She'll be sore and grouchy, and Kel would like to convince himself that he needs to be there when she gets in, to provide the TLC and listen to the complaints.

Toni does need him, after all. And, on its own, that's not a bad feeling.

The locations shift around, although more often than not the group meets at the church not far from the old train station. It's squat, ugly, faced with weather-stained brick and rusted pipes. A peeling yellow poster, trapped forever in a cracked Perspex case on the wall by the door, reads, "All We Need Is Love." Kel considers that to be complete crap, though he wishes he did truly believe it.

In some ways, he kind of does.

Obviously, love doesn't pay the rent or put food in the fridge—not love like the poster means it, anyway—but loving Toni has already saved his life. Kel believes that's true. Sure, it's made it so much more complicated, brought with it a whole world of new problems, and sometimes he wishes he'd never met the fucking guy, but Toni does keep him going.

Maybe that's all that really matters.

Kel shrugs off the philosophical wrangling and goes inside, hands shoved deep in his pockets, and his shoulders hunched against the world. It's dark inside, intrinsically dark, from the heavy wood panels and the steel mesh over the stained-glass windows, banking what should be bright, luminous colors with murky, shadowed light. The church has been stripped back to its very barest essentials, which feels more right to Kel than altar cloths and the loud, sharp sounds of choirs. Those remind him of the religion of his childhood, which he was only too pleased to leave behind him. Sunday mornings with no cartoons, and Aunt Gina's enormous bosom imprisoned in pale-green cotton, her voice plowing through hymns with total disregard for pitch or stave.

Uncle Matt used to stand on his other side… right where God could see him.

Kel shakes his head and glances around the place.

There's a trestle table in here now, with a blue paper tablecloth, a coffee urn, and several stacks of Solo cups upon it. Someone's brought a couple of packs of Oreos, and some juice boxes stand, looking faintly forlorn, beside the cookies.

People are already milling about, but nothing's really going on yet. There's usually this loose, awkward period of waiting. Wooden chairs scrape on the scuffed floor as the guy who runs the group starts to drag them into a misshapen circle. Technically, he's Father Morgan, but he tells everybody to call him Ian. The usual faces fringe the edges of the room—Kel knows them, and they know him, as far as anybody knows anybody—but there's no movement toward any kind of cheerful, chatty conversation. They all just stand there, waiting.

There are a couple of new people too, guys he hasn't seen here before, but he has noticed them around. One's short, wiry, mousy-haired, and looks like he's stumbled in here under the impression there was a free buffet, and now he appears lost, almost confused. The other one is taller, skinnier, but quite good-looking, in an unpolished, careless kind of way. He seems arrogant, the way Kel knows *he* was at first. Refusing to believe talking about anything would actually help. Refusing to share his weaknesses, as if keeping them close to his skin could stop them thrashing around and getting bigger, splitting and multiplying, and making every promise he made a lie.

He remembers those days. There used to be a lot of them and then, in the dying embers of last summer, something changed. All the things he'd been trying to shake away for so long just didn't seem to have so much of a hold on him. Toni made them go away, just by needing him… though Kel thinks of it as more than that. He thinks there was something secret to it, something hidden.

He doesn't dwell on it right now.

Dean's here. He's standing over by the coffee urn, though it's an unwritten rule at these things that no one gets coffee until at least one person's broken down in tears. At least, that's the way it usually works out. They have to earn it, Kel supposes. Dean glances at the new arrivals, then catches Kel's eye, and they share a smirk of amusement.

Kel's never known how old Dean is. They're probably about the same age, though he doesn't look as hard, he thinks. Dean always seems like he needs a really good ironing: his acne-scarred skin is crinkled and uneven, and the troughs that cross his forehead and run at each corner of his mouth seem to have been gouged out, leaving dark places behind them. He has a shaved head and a narrow, thin face, and though he smiles a lot it's never a truly pleasant expression.

Ian stops dragging the chairs around and, with his sleeves pushed back to his elbows, he smiles at the gathered group. He claps his hands together, rubs his palms like it's cold, or he's about to start a barn raising or something, and he suggests they get started. His voice has a bright, enthusiastic tone to it that makes Kel's gut sink.

He hates this. Hates these things so much. Hates being here, hates talking.

Hates that it helps.

AFTER THE meeting's over—the sitting on the hard, uncomfortable chairs, making eye contact that isn't quite eye contact with people, and letting the snakes of fear and failing free to coil across the floor—Kel heads fast for that free coffee. The room still seems to echo with everything that's been said, and it's darker than ever, and stuffy.

Dean joins him, raises his plastic cup, and nods.

"Hey."

"Hey," Kel says, pulling a face at the taste of the dishwater beverage.

They have a well-practiced shorthand for catching up on things. By the time he's got two-thirds of the way down the cup and eaten a couple of cookies, Kel's learned a few things about people he hasn't seen in a while, places he hasn't been.

For his part, Dean doesn't ask many questions but, when he does, he's cautious with them, almost like he's expecting bad news.

"And how's, uh, how's Tony?"

Kel hears the inflection in his voice, the little flick that makes it a *y* instead of an *i*. It's silly, he knows, because there's no damn difference. There's no difference between vowels in the way *he* says it, either, but somehow it just sounds wrong. Dean does it all the time. He thinks Toni's bad news because he stopped coming to group… first at the outreach, and then here. And not just that. Dean's not exactly sympathetic. Most people who know about the stuff Toni wants to do are okay with it. Kel supposes it's one perk of living in the part of town they do, and knowing the people they know. They may not understand, they may not know everything that's involved—fuck, some of 'em just don't give a shit either way—but very few of them give out the hard-eyed sarcastic crap that Dean does.

As if he's proving a point, Dean says, "He wearin' dresses yet?"

For a brief moment, a flare of anger crackles through Kel. It's hot, protective, and irrational. He blinks it away.

"He's okay."

"Still fucking with pills, though?"

"Uh-huh."

"Hm." Dean takes a swig of the coffee and doesn't appear to flinch. "He gonna do it, y'think?"

Kel shrugs. He honestly doesn't know. In a way, he doesn't care, and that strikes him as odd. Whether Toni goes through with the transition or not—and how he ends up afterward—is going to determine the rest of Kel's life too. Seems like either just one of them's gonna be happy, or neither, and he supposes he ought to be more concerned about that. But, right now, all he wants to tell Dean is that it doesn't really matter; that it's their business, and they'll deal with it.

"I don't know," he says instead. "Maybe."

Dean gives him a long, hard look. His brows draw low for a moment, then his whole face changes, as if someone turned on a light somewhere, and he says, "Hey, you know that kid, Julio?"

Kel frowns. The name rings a bell, but he can't remember from where. "Who?"

"Latino. Been workin' the bus station."

"Oh." He shakes his head. "Nah. Why?"

"He ain't been around a few days," Dean says before draining the last of his coffee. "I figure the little prince just got scared, 'cause I ain't heard nothin'. But some friend of his was down there this morning, kicking up a stink. I said, he's not here, and he hasn't been. Guy looked like he was gonna sit down in the gutter and bawl. Started spoutin' off in Spanish."

Kel doesn't say anything. He's trying not to think the kind of thing that it's logical to think, because that's haunted too many bad dreams in the past. His mind drifts back to last year, when all he had on Toni's whereabouts was a partial license plate and a bad feeling. They've never talked about what may or may not have happened in that car, and Kel doesn't ever want to.

"Just saying," Dean says as he refills his cup. "I figure he'll show up. Hell, he could be back down there now. Didn't need all that fuckin' fuss."

Kel wonders how he can drink so much of the stuff. Has he had the inside of his mouth steel plated or something?

"Uh-huh."

"Yeah." Dean takes another mouthful of the appalling coffee and swallows slowly. "Fuckin' spics."

Kel keeps his mouth shut. It isn't worth it.

He leaves not long after, still feeling a little raw, like he always does after these things. They're good for him, he knows that. They stop him going back to places he doesn't want to go to, and he knows if he's left to himself that willpower won't be enough.

Toni isn't enough either. He's a lot of things—and being with him stops Kel doing so much he knows he otherwise would—but he's not a panacea. Not that Toni's still using. He isn't, but he's not as firm about it as Kel. Up until the point he started the hormones, he was still far too likely to score some X for the weekend and—while fucking Toni on X is intense, incredible, amazing, and probably one of the best memories Kel has—he doesn't want to fall back into partying that way. He knows that if he keeps doing it, then it leads onto other things, things he can't control, and those are the horrible tendrils that spiral out of him, hurting people and destroying everything. He's done it before, and he won't do it again.

It's dark outside, almost, the summer evening soft and grainy. He scowls at the sidewalk, hands deep in his pockets, the occasional orange glow of a streetlight brushing across his thoughts.

Kel wonders how Toni's getting on with his face, whether the skin's going to have taken it better or worse this time. At nearly two hundred dollars an hour, he'd have thought they could manage not to lay him up for a day. It's going to cost thousands in the long run... though it's not going to be the most expensive thing out of all the stuff Toni could do. Kel finds himself thinking about that—about surgery—as he walks.

Toni's so beautiful already, whether he dresses up or not, that Kel can't imagine he could ever convince himself he needs facial feminization. All that scary stuff about nose jobs, shaving cheekbones and reshaping chins... he won't want to do that, will he?

He knows Danielle's had her Adam's apple shaved. Maybe Toni'll consider that because, Kel thinks bitterly, if Danielle told him to jump off a bridge dressed as the Easter Bunny, he'd probably do it. Especially if she made him believe he'd feel better for it, like it would release his true self or something.

Kel fucking hates that phrase. He's heard it too often. It's on the front of that book he got Karen to special order him at the bookstore—a so-called "guide for friends and family." He picked it up last week, keeps it tucked under his half of the mattress, and so far he's read about a quarter of the way through. The more he reads, the less it sounds like Toni. Kel was so hoping he'd be wrong, that he'd understand a little bit more with every page, but it isn't happening.

He has these dreams where Toni's telling him he's going to go to Cambodia for surgery, get boobs and a pussy done. Kel doesn't want him to go, and they fight. When he comes back, Kel's waiting at the airport. It's not Toni who comes to find him, but a girl with long black hair and almond-shaped eyes, and she hugs him and won't let go... until he wakes up, choking.

It's stupid.

Kel kicks at a pebble on the sidewalk, a loose piece of gravel that pings away into the dusk and debris. If Toni did do it—the whole sexual reassignment surgery, SRS—he wants to believe it wouldn't matter. Maybe it even wouldn't. He'd still be the same person, still be himself. All it's supposed to mean is that the outside will finally match the inside, so that wouldn't be a problem, would it? Sure, Toni's hot, but Kel loves more about him than his body. And, if this is really the right thing for him, then the person Kel's known all along has always been a chick anyway. Fuck, maybe he's been bi all this time and never known it. He smiles at that thought, because it's such fucking bullshit.

Kel sighs, too tired to keep trying to convince himself with the same worn-out arguments. He's nearly home, and his mind drifts away from the worrying mechanics of bilateral orchidectomies and neovaginas, and back to how his honey's gonna be feeling after her appointment.

He takes a right off a familiar street, adds a few more minutes to his walk and stops by a bakery that sits hunched right up next to what used to be a pizza place before it closed down about a month ago. Amazing that the bakery's still going, really, but it stays open pretty late and, Kel has heard, also does a nifty line in super-special muffins, so that's probably why. He hasn't asked.

The guy who runs the place is big, Turkish, and hairy. He smiles broadly at Kel and packages up the order like he asks for, fussing with the gold organza bow before handing it over with a knowing wink.

"You make it up with the girlfriend, huh?"

Kel just grins.

As he's leaving, heading back out into the street and the night, which is slowly awakening around him, his phone rings. Kel fumbles for it, answers it abruptly without checking the number. He assumes it's going to be Toni, wanting to know where the hell he is, but then his gut tightens at the sound of a familiar voice.

It's Michael.

"Yeah?"

The Sherbet Pervert usually leaves much longer between his appointments than this, but he wants Kel to come over on Thursday.

Huh... some "last time," buddy.

Kel expected it, despite all Michael's protestations, but just not so soon. It feels sudden and desperate, and he doesn't like that, but he's not really concentrating. He's still wrestling with other, complicated stuff in his head, and they need the cash, so he just says sure, he'll come. He makes the same arrangement he's made plenty of times before and hangs up, not really giving it a whole lot of thought.

It's not important.

He walks on, and a car sluices through the night beside him, trailing a fluid band of distorted, tinny music through the air.

CHAPTER
EIGHT

BY THE time Kel gets in, Toni's face has settled into a dull ache, and she's slumped on the couch watching TV, almost dozing off from the relief. She jumps at the sound of the door slamming, and as soon as she's connected it to where she is, who it is, and what's happening, Toni's getting prepared to give him a hard time over not being here when she wanted him.

She straightens up against the couch, waits for Kel to come in, but he doesn't.

Toni frowns. "Baby?"

There's clunking around, heavy footfalls and the sound of him shedding his jacket. She smells cigarette smoke and turns against the upholstery, one arm along the back of the couch.

Kel appears in the doorway, looking tired but smiling. He's holding a white box, about six inches square, tied with a sheer gold ribbon.

"Hey. Got you somethin'."

"Aww!"

Toni hops up, goes to him, and bounces excitedly in anticipation. She recognizes the bakery's logo embossed in gold on the glossy white card lid, and knows what he's bought her. The smell of honey, almonds, and spice is already making her stomach rumble.

"Baklava?"

Kel nods, and Toni grins, eagerly pulling the box open. One of her favorites. He leans in to kiss her cheek—not the sore one, the other one—but she still flinches, so he pulls back and, instead, kisses the very tip of her nose.

"Thought you prolly needed cheering up."

Tenderness wells up in Toni, and she bobs forward, puckers her mouth and touches it gingerly to Kel's. He's so thoughtful. So romantic. So good to her. The little voice at the back of her mind wants to know how his meeting went—whether this really is just sweetness, or whether there's something he thinks he needs to make up for—but Toni tries to smother it. She delves into the box, snaffles a sticky, crumbly morsel of nutty pastry and bites down hard on it, hoping that'll quiet the troll voice. It doesn't. Not fully. It feeds on the unease she's felt all day, and now she almost wishes she'd swallowed a couple of aspirin and gone to bed, as pathetic a response as that is to just a little bit of hair removal.

"Good?" Kel asks, indicating the pastry.

"Mm." Toni nods approval and feeds him the other half, a snatch of desire running through her when he takes it deftly from her fingers with those talented lips, sucking the pad of her thumb clean as he does so.

His tongue traces the nub of her flesh, and Toni giggles.

Kel chews, swallows, runs his tongue over his lower lip, catching an errant crumb.

"Mm," he agrees, eyebrows raised. "Good."

There's just a tiny little gloss of stickiness on his lip, in part from the glaze and in part from where he licked up the crumb. Toni stares at it and catches her own lip between her teeth, hungry to have his mouth on hers again. Kel's eyes glitter with a glancing mischief, and he grins.

"Put the kettle on, hm? I'm gonna go take a shower."

"'Kay."

Toni folds the lid of the box down—more little pleasures for later—and Kel touches her arm very briefly as he passes by. She aches to hold him, but it won't be long. If Toni could be sure he hadn't been working today—she didn't think so, but it's usually why he springs straight for the shower when he comes home—she might sneak in and join him, surprise him under the warm spray. Then again, screwing actually *in* the shower is more trouble than it's worth. Doing it once you're just out from under the water is way better, and it's not so easy to slip over. Toni likes running a bath, making sure there's candles, fluffy towels… and plenty of time to waste.

She blinks, realizing Kel's almost at the bathroom door, and she hasn't yet asked him what she wanted to know.

"Hey! How was your meeting?"

Kel hesitates before he answers, his fingers already grazing the door handle. He doesn't look at her, just shrugs.

"A'ight."

It's all he says, then he shuts the door behind him and, after a moment, Toni hears the water start to run. She frowns. Taking her box of baklava, she turns away, goes to the kitchen, and sets about making the coffee he wants. They drink more coffee than they used to since she started the hormones; it's Kel's way of trying to get her to lay off the booze.

Toni can't help wondering about his meeting. Did he even go? He doesn't go every time. He should do—and he always says he will—but sometimes he doesn't. He blows the meetings off, and takes it out on everybody afterward, and Toni can't fix it. She can't make him go, and she can't complain, because *she* didn't stick with the group sessions. She supposes it might be easier for Kel if she started going again—they could go together or something, not like it's the best date imaginable— but she doesn't want to, and so even though she feels kind of selfish about it, Toni's not going to give the idea much of a chance.

It probably is just that the meeting was tough. That's all it is. She guesses so, anyway. Therapy isn't fun at the best of times and, sometimes, going to things like that only makes you wish you'd never tried to get clean to start with. Just reminds you of what you miss.

But Kel wouldn't do that, she knows. Besides, if he did, she'd be the first to find out. Toni is all too well aware of what it looks like— what *he's* like when he does that—and she'd spot it in a second. He was still doing it when they first met, back at the outreach center. He was the only good thing about that fucking place… the only bright spot among the rules and procedures and fucking pious charity from people who didn't understand shit.

She remembers the first time she saw him, just looking up and seeing this dark silhouette against the sky. He hurt his hand on the railing, clumsy guy that he is. He was kind. Funny. He didn't give up, those first few months.

Toni never meant to play hard to get. He was just... confused. Lost, maybe. It was hard to know what was going on inside his head at that point. Like trying to listen for one chime among a thousand bells, or a whisper in a fairground.

Kel didn't give up after that, either. Toni expected him to, but he never did. Even when she told him. He just keeps going. Danielle says most relationships don't survive the whole transition deal. Twenty- and thirty-year marriages can snap in an instant, which doesn't seem to leave them much chance. Danielle says that's probably a good thing. She says sex drive gets totally screwed up for most women. She says *she* went through a whole six months, early on, where she really didn't even like the idea of doing it at all. She says she's still not that bothered now, that finding a man would probably be nice, but it's just not a priority.

Toni supposes that's a very empowered place to be, in a certain kind of way. She read a book about empowerment a couple of months back, but Kel teased her and said she didn't need any more attitude.

He doesn't get as angry since he gave the shit up, doesn't lash out the way he used to do, which is good. It's all got to go somewhere, though, hasn't it?

The kettle boils, and Toni's aware she hasn't been concentrating. She makes the coffee, puts the baklava on a plate, carries everything through into the other room, and sets it down on the table for when he's ready. She runs a hand over her hair, tugs at the hem of her shirt to straighten it. Flicks the stereo on. It's a Do or Die greatest hits album, which she bought Kel for his birthday, and Toni selects the songs she wants to hear. Smooth beats flow out, rounded and easy. Toni chose it because she knows he likes it, not just because it's their style of make-out music... though it is, and she smiles to herself.

The shower goes off, the door opens, and she can hear Kel clumping and bumping about out there, changing into his sweats. She kind of wants to go to him, be nonchalant and ask about his day, but in a way it's nicer to let it all fade away into the distance. Toni would like to think that, if he wants to tell her something, he will. She doesn't have to ask, and he doesn't have to keep secrets.

The song changes and Kel comes in, sloping over to the couch to sit beside her. He smiles, and the ugly voice in the back of her head starts over again, making her question how she ever got here, and telling her she's stupid if she thinks she can keep it. Kel doesn't seem to hear the troll. He's kissing Toni, and she slides her arms around his neck, a little surprised by his intensity. He wants her, it seems, right now. She doesn't plan on complaining. She doesn't even really care if the coffee goes cold.

He unbuttons her blouse, tickles her tummy, and exposes her chest. She lifts her arms, lets him pull off the garment. She tugs at the hem of his shirt—if she's getting naked, they're gonna be even about it—and helps him shed the time-worn tee, its front crackled with an old baseball team logo in green letters. It lands somewhere on the floor, and Toni doesn't know where, because she can't stop staring at his beautiful body. A smile bursts from the corner of her mouth as her gaze touches every part of him—the wide, square planes of muscle that make up his chest, the intricate little points of his deltoids. He's incredible.

Her stare makes him chuckle, and he flexes, pulling a face. Toni laughs, drags him closer, plants her lips on his. The sore part of her jaw protests, but if she tries to ignore it, it's no worse than bad beard burn. Kel's being as gentle with her as his desire allows, and she loves him for it. His tongue slides against hers, sweet and tempting. Toni's nipples are tight with anticipation even before Kel leans down to buss each one in turn, teeth and tongue making delicate circles around the flesh. He plants a vine of kisses down the line of her sternum and toward her navel—hard, like he means them—his fingers already working on her fly.

Kel fumbles that, forgetting that girls' jeans do up the opposite way to boys'. Toni reaches down, helps him, and wishes she knew what this was about. She lifts her hips, and he starts to pull the pants down, kisses the tops of her thighs as they become available. His stubble scratches her soft, shaven skin, and it's good. Pleasure shivers through Toni, knots at the pit of her stomach, and she puts a hand to his head. He hasn't washed his hair. He's wearing it braided, and she rests her fingers on the firm, neat ridges. It took her ages to learn how to do cornrows right, but it's worth it, and it suits him. Kel's broad, blunt-tipped fingers skim her flesh, tracing the outline of her underwear. Toni shifts, shivers again... not so comfortable this time. She's vulnerable, exposed. Under the jeans—a little treat because of how horrible part of today had to be—she's wearing a black lace thong. It's a lot more delicate and a lot smaller than the high-leg cotton panties she usually wears, and it feels really sexy... or it did until Kel had his face right next to it.

Toni thinks she sees him smile at the wisp of lace before he glances up, gaze meeting hers. In the split second before his eyes change, the look in them softening, Toni isn't sure he's not laughing.

Kel moves back up and kisses her again, his body close and his solidity reassuring. She slides her arms around his neck once more, holds on tight, and inhales his freshly washed, clean scent. He loves her. Toni feels it, knows it, believes it. She lifts her legs, wraps them around his waist, and squeezes, laughs softly when his hand runs up the outside of her thigh. Kel's mouth is on hers again, enveloping her, lifting her higher... and then the feeling becomes more literal, because he's physically lifting her up, holding her tight, and pulling her to him. Toni giggles, holds on, squeaking with laughter as they rise, lurch, and almost fall.

Kel grips her waist, one arm across her back. He won't drop her.

She trusts him.

KEL THINKS it's crazy how Toni can wash away everything. He meant to take it slow, kick back and relax for a while. Coffee, pastries, music—maybe talk a little bit. They really need to talk, and about so many things. The skin on the left side of Toni's face looks red and slightly shiny, puffy and probably sore. That's what does it, and it occurs to Kel that it's the stupidest thing in the world to get turned-on by. It just says something to him about how brave Toni is, and whether Kel agrees with what she's doing or not doesn't seem to matter. It doesn't seem relevant. He just has to go with what he feels, and what he feels right now is Toni's body under his hands, Toni's mouth on his, and all that buoyancy; the barely stifled giggles and infectious smiles are spilling out over Kel. He's warmed by them, like basking in sunlight, and it feels like just maybe a shade of Toni's courage could rub off on him.

He likes to think so, but he still wants the girl clothes off.

Kel pops the buttons on Toni's pink shirt, starting at the bottom, his fingers dipping in to caress smooth skin and hard muscle. Toni's happy noises continue to burst against his mouth, and Kel feels eager hands tugging the hem of his T-shirt, so he holds out his arms. Toni pulls the thing over his head and tosses it to the floor, gaze tracing Kel's body with approval.

Kel does a quick flex for him, though he's not as ripped as he could be. He knows Toni doesn't care, 'cause they go way deeper than flesh and bone, don't they? She wraps her legs around his waist, tangled with the unfastened jeans, and wants to be carried into the bedroom. It's no mean feat when they're both still partly clothed, and almost the same height, though she's not really heavy.

Too damn scrawny to be heavy.

Kel manages, albeit with some clumsy thrills and spills, bumped elbows, banged knees, and death-defying stumbles. They're laughing all over again by the time they hit the sheets, and Toni pulls him close for a sweet, scorching kiss. Her not-quite-breasts rub his chest—those incipient bloomings that he may or may not be imagining—and they feel like more than nipples. They seem more real now than they have before, and maybe it could just be a change in the way Toni's body feels, just a shift in what's muscle, what's the softness of flesh. Just for a second, Kel thinks it's the hottest thing he's ever felt, but, when they part and he looks down at her, he's not so sure.

He kicks off his pants, not having bothered to put underwear on after his shower, and Toni wriggles and writhes to help him get rid of the jeans he'd already started to pull down. She's lying there, flushed and wanton, hair coming out of its clips, lips parted and eyes dark and clouded. Naked except for a black lace thong, she's everything Kel wants, and yet she's ridiculous at the same time. Her thick makeup is smudged, and the silly little black lacey panties are totally inadequate for what they're holding.

Kel doesn't want to admit it, but he can see all the cracks in the finish of the master artwork that is Toni. So, he gathers her up in his arms and buries her with kisses, and she wraps those smooth, pretty legs around him again and grinds, scratching his shoulder with her fake nails as she murmurs his name. Kel edges the thong down, and Toni's cock is a blushing, awakening mouse. It was never a monster, but it's starting to get more docile. Kel's noticed that. Toni hasn't jumped him as much as he used to this past month, and even over the last week or so he seems less inclined to take the initiative, to go for things at the spur of the moment. It's not like his libido's diminished, just… like it's softer somehow, and that worries Kel. He doesn't know how much of it is the pills, or just how Toni feels in himself, and how much might be the fact they're at that deadly one year mark, when the free fall of honeymoon romance really starts bottoming out. Thing about that, though, is who's to say it hasn't done that before now? How would he know?

He's already seen Toni puke, seen him cut his toenails while sitting on the john, seen him do a dozen less savory things. Life wasn't exactly all hearts and flowers when they got together either, but it didn't change how he felt. That hasn't changed much now. Sure, perhaps the glow has rubbed off a bit, but Kel never had that many illusions to start with, so it's not a big deal, is it? In any case, it's been replaced by something way more important.

Kel tugs that dumb lace thong past Toni's knees, pulls it the rest of the way down, and drops it to the floor.

That's better.

It's not that there's nothing to be said for Toni in lingerie… just not now.

Kel leans farther down, nuzzles Toni's thighs, parts them gently and bats away the nominal protests. Toni's getting harder, though he's not there yet. Kel thinks he can fix that. He palms his lover's thighs, kisses along the soft skin of their inner length, his warm breath grazing Toni's balls.

His honey lets out a soft moan, pushing his hips toward Kel's mouth in a needy, hopeful little movement. Kel obliges, pressing his lips to Toni's sac and delicately juggling the orbs within. He sucks one at a time, pulling Toni's flesh into his mouth and swirling his tongue over the thin, sensitive skin, dragging a succession of hot, ragged gasps from his honey. Toni raises his legs, whimpers for more, and Kel dips down, mouth on the lowest part of his cleft, entranced by the spice and musk of him. He's tempted to go lower still, to hoist Toni's hips up or turn him over, then lave his hole until he screams. It's perfectly possible to make him come like that, but it's not what Kel has in mind right now. He presses his thumb into that narrow valley, feels the tiny ring of muscle flinch against his touch, and rubs slow, torturous circles around it.

"Oh," Toni murmurs, those fake nails gently skimming the back of Kel's neck. "Fuck, baby... you feel so good. Do it?"

Kel knows what she wants. She's not getting it. Not yet.

A low, playful growl rumbling at the back of his throat, he leans up and snatches at Toni's cock with his lips, then encircles its swollen, pouting head. Toni curses again as Kel's tongue twirls wetly over the glossy, firm flesh, and that only encourages him to suck harder, savoring his taste. Toni is harsh, salty, pungent... a flavor just as uncompromising as the rest of him, and just as complex. He thumps his fists on the sheet, hips twitching hungrily, wanting more.

Kel can't refuse him.

He plunges down on Toni's shaft, takes him right to the root, and then pulls up tight and slow, his free hand rubbing circles on his lover's thigh. Kel's thumb slides deeper, pressing into the hot, narrow channel of Toni's ass. She coos, reaching down to spread her cheeks, and he feels her relaxing, taking his digit into that hot, tight clasp.

Kel keeps his rhythm strict, fast, ruthless. Toni's cock thickens, hardens, twitches in the wetness of his mouth, throbbing against his tongue. With every stroke upward, Kel pulls harder on the slick, stiff flesh, and he knows how much Toni's loving it, not just from the way he's making those hot little noises—each breath riven through with cracked groans and gasps—but because his own cock aches in sympathy with every touch.

He wants to touch too, to feel them in concert with each other, to push Toni even higher. He's hard, but not yet close to the edge, and Kel knows the ultimate way to take him there. He pulls away, reaches across to the bedside cabinet, and pulls out a tube of lubricant that has a cute trick to it. One-handed, his fingers still massaging Toni's ass, he unscrews the cap. She sits halfway up, watching what he's doing, hair messily tousled and expression wonderfully naughty, lower lip caught in creamy teeth.

Kel touches the cold gel to Toni's crack, and as he moves his fingers in slow, steady circles, he knows his honey can feel the lube heating itself. It's got this special ingredient in it, makes the skin warm and tingly... fuck knows how it works, but it does. Toni wriggles down on him, and Kel crooks his index finger, seeking out the secret spot that'll make him melt. It does. Toni presses his lips together, lets out a long "hmmm," and closes his eyes. He looks so fucking good, and Kel can't wait any longer. He lets Toni's glistening flesh slide from his lips, pulls back, and sits up on his haunches.

Toni smiles broadly, opens those gorgeous legs and raises them, cheeks spread and cock hard. Kel takes hold of himself in one hand, guides his cock to her pucker, pushes... it's fast, urgent, and he's not using a condom. He hasn't told Toni about the clear test results yet, and for a fraction of a second Kel's angry with him for not asking, for not demanding that he gets a glove on before he gets in there.

He doesn't say anything, a little scared by Toni's trust in him— because he'd rather believe it's that than anything else—and anyway, he knows how much Toni wants it like this, wants to be able to feel him. Kel tries to think of it like that, as if it's all for Toni, because he's also afraid to admit how much he wants it. How much he wants to go hard and raw, to make Toni feel it... to mark him.

He's definitely feeling something. Kel suspects he skimped on the lube and preparation, because Toni's teeth are gritted, and the noise that breaks from him is just as much a protestation of pain as encouragement. It's so fucking good—so tight, so hot—but Kel forces himself to wait, trying to give Toni time to adjust. He didn't expect to want it so much tonight, to need it so bad, but he does. His cock pulses deep in Toni's ass, and a tingling trail of sweat starts to run down Kel's back. A muscle twitches in the back of his thigh, and his arms ache from taking his weight. Toni's face is flushed, so close beneath him, expression a strange mix of dreamy dislocation and total concentration, a tiny frown lodged between those overplucked brows.

Kel can't help it; he leans down, kisses her temple. The perfect flower unfurls just a little, and Toni's beautiful dark eyes flicker open. She looks up at him, and her slim, warm fingers curve around the top of his arm, nails digging into his skin.

"C'mon, baby."

"You ready?"

"Mm-hm."

Kel tucks his hips, drives his cock deeper, feels Toni's legs wrap tight around him, and hears the sharp intake of breath. He goes slow, adds more lube, and tries to bite back on the maddening pleasure swelling in the pit of his gut. He wants to go fast, deep, hard… he aches for it, burning with the effort of holding back.

Toni turns his face to Kel's, trading kisses and soft promises. Kel surges his hips again and again, and gradually the thrusts do get harder, faster. The hot little gasps Toni makes keep time with them, a low, sensual rhythm panting between their bodies.

"Fuck… do it, baby. Give it to me…."

The words are more than Kel can take. He pushes Toni's legs back, knees folded and thighs pressing down on his chest until they almost obscure the complex, troublesome buds that will swell there. Kel doesn't want to picture the image of boobs wobbling, doesn't want to waste time thinking about what is or isn't there, what Toni is or isn't going to be. He needs to get off, and he wants nothing more than to fuck—hard, fast, and long—until he gets there.

Toni's ready, and he's man enough to take it.

Kel pushes down on Toni's knees, loving the way his face, neck, and chest are flushed with heat and want. It's hard even to see where he's tender from the electrolysis. Kel thrusts deeper, and all he can think is that he's filling Toni with his cock, that this is a man's fuck, and that it's vital, indelible, and eternal.

DAMN, HE'S on form tonight…!

Toni wasn't expecting this sudden outburst of Kel's, but she's not complaining. She tilts her hips higher, closes her eyes. The burn as he fills her—chafing every nerve she's got with his ruthless, swift energy—makes her wonder if this is what it's like for girls. Maybe. Maybe this is better, though it's not something she focuses on for too long.

Kel wants to fuck hard and fast tonight, and Toni lets him. He needs to get off, and he's so beautiful when he does. His face tautens, the bends of sweat glimmering very slightly on his forehead and upper lip, and his eyes hold storms within them. Toni feels it, feels each hot, wet spurt right inside, and it's profound and terrifying. Kel leans down, spent, folds against his lover, face buried in Toni's neck.

Toni holds him, listens to his harsh breathing. She isn't sure how she feels now. Passive, incomplete, maybe even frightened. Her cock didn't really wake up for the majority of the fuck. She lost the hard-on when Kel breached her, and now it's rubbing sleepily against his belly, as if it's not sure whether to stiffen properly or not. Toni wants it to, wants to come, but so much still lingers unanswered... both in her own body and in Kel's embrace.

Kel reaches down, strokes idly, fingers clasped around Toni's cock, grip slack but tender. They shift their position, and Toni almost wants to laugh at him, because he's already on the way to falling asleep, but he's determined to get her there before he does. She's damned if she's going to tell him how difficult it is.

Toni hits it eventually, an agonizing climb to a difficult peak, but it's good. Kel coaxes her through, tells her she's beautiful while the droplets of thick, white fluid spatter her stomach. He rubs them in afterward, smooth motions of his square, broad palm... and he makes a joke about beauty regimens. Toni smiles despite herself, swats his arm, and hopes he'll hold her while she falls asleep.

She's sore, but comfortable. A pleasurable kind of ache that's mixed up with love and pride, and she can live with it. Kel sighs, and his warm breath filters through Toni's hair like a desert wind.

"Hm," he says sleepily, shifting against her. "Oh, yeah. Went t'the clinic. S'all good. All clear."

"Oh."

Toni hadn't forgotten about it. You don't just forget about things like that... but she never has believed it would touch either of them, so his news isn't unexpected. The flood of relief is still jagged and sudden, but she isn't sure what else to say—what else he *wants* her to say—so she settles on flexing her fingers against his chest, and says, "That's good."

It sounds a little weak, but Kel knows what she means, doesn't he? Anyway, perhaps there isn't any major requirement for anything but acknowledgment. All the same, Toni doesn't like the silence and tries to slide something in to fill it.

"Well, you knew it, huh?"

He doesn't respond, already three-quarters asleep. Toni thinks fondly of the coffee and baklava in the other room, and then she's not really ready to sleep anymore. Kel's breathing changes, and his head feels heavier on her shoulder, so she doesn't move.

She waits until he's properly crashed out, and then she eases herself out from underneath him and steals into the other room. The coffee is cold, but Toni drinks half of one cup anyway while she wolfs down the baklava. Midnight feast. It's naughty, but good. Feeling very slightly queasy once it's all gone, yet not entirely guilty, she leaves the plate and cups in the kitchen and goes back to bed. Kel's turned over, one arm spread across the place Toni would be occupying if she hadn't got up, and his skin is dusky against the paleness of the sheets, his outline soft in the murky light.

For a brief moment, the strength of everything she feels tightens Toni's throat, and affection stings in the bridge of her nose. If he wasn't snoring quite as loud as he is, he wouldn't even look real. She climbs back in beside him, just lifting his arm so she can slip beneath it, and she's amazed at how easily he accepts her presence. He shifts, mumbles in his sleep, and lets his hand fall across her chest. Face crushed to the pillow, before he starts calling the hogs home again, he looks so perfect.

Toni lies still and watches him for a while. Just thinking.

CHAPTER
NINE

ON THURSDAY morning, Toni sleeps in. It's a naughty luxury—pure sybaritic bliss—but she can't resist. As Kel leaves, he reminds her not to be late for work, and she just waves a hand at him from the warm, smooth, wonderful world of the covers. He mumbles something under his breath and, as the door closes, Toni hears the sound of a street sweeper a block or so away, the buzz of the truck's brushes humming through the morning.

She's vaguely aware that Kel told her where he was going, but it hasn't really permeated the aura of snugness that's enfolded her, and she finds herself just easily, quietly, slipping away again, back into pleasing clouds of slumber.

An hour later, or thereabouts, she's clacking down the sidewalk as fast as she can possibly go without spilling her takeout latte down the front of her baggy cord shirt, determining to buy an alarm clock that not only works, but has a motherfucking snooze button. The sunlight is bright, the sounds of construction filtering into the narrow, brick-clad street from somewhere—what could they possibly be building? Toni's coffee tastes scalded, so this is the absolute last time she's gonna buy anything from the stand on the corner by the old library, and she's fucking *late*. A lone cloud drifts lazily over the sharp, empty sky.

By the time she makes it to the bookstore, Karen is already dealing with some customers. Toni recognizes them as regulars, a big friendly bear and his hubs. To look at them, you wouldn't think they were into anything except red wine and foot rubs, but Big Friendly comes in every week, regular as clockwork, and picks up any number of the various leather and kink subscriptions he has on order. Hubs scoops up so many free weeklies, newsletters, and fliers that Toni wonders whether they actually keep toilet paper at home. Today they're buying in bulk: the latest novel from an author who writes hot bondage thrillers featuring a gay PI, and a compendium of erotic scene photography that's heavy on the latex and bukkake. Also—rather surprisingly to Toni—a book about planning a gay wedding, and one that professes to be about the emotional process of adoption as a same-sex couple. She supposes everyone has different parts to life, the different masks they wear. And most people have so many places they can keep the bits of themselves, little compartments that get filled up with things like work, family, politics, and car insurance. It must be nice to feel so organized.

Toni mouths an apology at Karen as the shop bell gives its anemic *ding*, and thinks maybe it would feel good to live like that. Not a so-called "normal" life, as such… Toni hasn't had one of those in a very long time, but she recalls the trappings of it being constrictive and unpleasant. They make it hard to breathe. So no, not like that, but having somewhere nice to live, enough money to buy everything they need… that could be good. And maybe, one day, Kel will put a ring on it. Whether it's legal or not—and in how many states—doesn't really matter to Toni.

She goes through to the back, nodding in greeting at Big Friendly and Hubs. They smile, and Karen seems cheered enough by the money they're spending not to glare outright at Toni across the counter. The ass-chewing will probably come later. Toni glances at the clock and wonders if she has enough time for a cigarette first.

She has some nicotine gum in the pocket of her shirt, but it tastes terrible. She pops it anyway—it's better for her, and she won't look like she's trying to run away if Karen comes back here and finds her already hanging out the door. Toni supposes she ought to get on with something useful, and she casts an eye over at the hated inventory forms, pinned to the clipboard that sits neatly on top of a stack of boxes. New stock.

Toni can still hear Karen talking to Big Friendly and Hubs, and she cautiously slips her fingers beneath the lip of the top box and pulls it open, breathing in the slightly astringent new-book smell of paper and potential. The covers wink at her, layers of glossy darknesses with embossed gold titles and jewel-like flashes of color. Toni likes books. They give her somewhere to go to, and people to be, when she can't face the world outside her own eyelids.

She takes one of the uppermost copies out and starts to read the blurb inside the jacket. It's a romantic thriller, a story about a CIA agent who falls for the reformed gang member testifying in a major case and then has to protect both himself and the guy he loves from the gangbangers, who get acquitted on a technicality. Toni flicks through a few pages, starts getting into the rhythm of the book. The description of the CIA guy sounds kind of like Kel. Strong, silent—the type of guy who keeps everything locked up inside him until he trusts a person. Once that starts to happen, it's like daylight coming in through a broken window, like colors fracturing off the glass and dancing together in unexpected places. They start out pale and fleeting, but as the sun gets warmer, they grow stronger, until they're dazzling and bright.

"Toni?"

She flinches. She hadn't noticed that Karen had finished with Big Friendly and Hubs, but apparently she has, and she's standing in the doorway, looking expectantly at Toni.

"Are you okay, honey?"

Toni smiles, closes the book. "Yeah. Hey. Sorry about—"

Karen shrugs, gives a resigned lift of her pencil-shaded brows. She still has her glasses perched halfway down her nose and, with one pink-tipped hand, she reaches for the clipboard with the stock form on it.

"Don't worry about it. You're here now, but maybe you could just *try* to be on time for the whole of a week sometime, hm? Y'know. Just for kicks."

She gives Toni a sweet, sarcastic little smile, and Toni wrinkles her nose.

"'Kay. Sorry."

Bitch-whore-dyke-fuck-slut!

Toni doesn't say the words, and the sneaky impulse to do so goes away once she takes a couple of breaths. She likes Karen really, just not the fact that the woman's her boss. Toni isn't really comfortable with anybody being her boss, and she's starting to feel hot and prickly again, which she puts down to the fact it's a warm day.

There's stuff with forms to do, and restacking of shelves, and by the time lunch comes around there hasn't been a customer in since Big Friendly and Hubs, so Karen's got Toni doing some dusting and tidying up before she scoots. Toni doesn't really mind; Karen says she doesn't have to come back after lunch.

"You look tired," she adds, by way of justification.

Toni knows it's kindness, but she doesn't really like it. Anyway, she thought she looked pretty good. This kind of concern undermines what scant self-confidence she's clinging on to, and she knows she doesn't need that. She quirks an eyebrow.

"Oh?"

"Well, I thought…." Karen presses her lips together, does a small, cutesy tilt of her head that makes Toni want to smack her. "It can't be easy, what you're going through, however hard Kel's trying to help. How's he getting on with the book?"

She slips it in as if she wants to switch Toni's attention away from what she just said. That cardinal sin—*What you're going through.* Like it's some kind of long convalescence, or a violent stomach bug or something. Toni never thought she'd be sensitive about it, but she's finding she is, which is weird. Just another part of herself she has no control over. It pales next to what Karen's let slip, though.

"What book?"

Karen smiles tightly, and it makes her upper lip crinkle. "Well, I suppose he did say he wasn't going to tell you, but… he's been reading up, you know? Ordered a bunch of stuff. That roadmap guide, and that *True Selves* book for friends and family…."

Toni couldn't feel worse if she'd been slapped with a dead fish. No, she hadn't known Kel was doing that. It makes her feel lumpy and stupid, and more of a bitch than usual. So typically him, of course. Not talking to her, not saying anything. Just letting her think—

"You're lucky to have him," Karen says, as if that's remotely helpful.

Toni just nods, unable to speak without embarrassing herself. Tears want to spill out of her tired, sore eyes, and for no good fucking reason. She sniffs, tries to salvage her dignity. Wants to go home.

Thank God it's only a half day.

The time passes really slowly. It grinds on and on the way Toni remembers it doing in school, when the minute hand used to tremble and tremble just before ticking over, and for a moment it would seem to go back instead of forward, like the whole hour was just going to repeat itself.

She wants to call Kel, but she just sends a text. He doesn't send one back, so she figures he's busy, and that's okay. It really is. Toni tries believing she isn't validated by or dependent on him and, when there's a little midmorning rush of shoppers, that becomes true for a while. Toni loses himself in being busy, in smiling and making small talk, and it feels really great, really… strong.

Strong is good. Just for a little while, strong makes the world seem easier, and the anxiety seem less, and Toni doesn't feel like the seconds are sleeting past in some kind of breathless rush. It's like there's a handle on things, and maybe people aren't just waiting to watch the train wreck she makes of everything.

Danielle's coming round later. They had some girly time planned, just manis, pedis, and gossip. Like a day spa trip, but without the expense or the people looking at her funny. Danielle says she never gets pedicures done professionally because people always stare at her feet. They are big, but then she's a tall girl. Supermodels all have big feet, Toni reckons, on account of how they're all tall. She told Danielle that once, but she just laughed.

At last, lunch comes, and brings with it Toni's release for the day. She smiles at Karen as she's packing up to go, and promises to be on time on Tuesday—hell, the whole of next week. Honest. Karen shakes her head and rolls her eyes, but it's affectionate. Toni grins, and the bright sunlight outside warms away the last lingering traces of discomfort. Makes everything better, somehow. She is lucky. She's lucky to have Kel. Lucky to have Karen, too, and Danielle.

Lucky to be me.

Toni crosses the road, takes a deep breath, and doesn't feel so jumpy anymore. A strange kind of security seems to blanket her, and she supposes it's the thought of Kel squirreling away self-help books and guides to transition, reading them in secret. Trying to understand— and he is, isn't he? So maybe he's not just gonna bundle up and go, the way she's been scared of for so long.

There's a message from him on Toni's phone. Just a few short, simple words: he'll be back tonight and he'll bring dinner, Toni and Danielle are not to go crazy—like he's really going to come home and find Toni's gone platinum blonde—and he loves her. Toni smiles to herself as she sends back a one-line reply. They won't, and she loves him too.

The sun beats down, and it sparkles a little on the mica in the sidewalk.

IT'S NICE having Danielle round. They can just let their hair down, be stupid together. She makes Toni laugh so hard that ginger ale almost comes out of her nose, and the bubbles sting like crazy. There's wet nail polish and wet towels, and it feels safe. It feels safe to talk about anything, to say all the things Toni isn't sure she can even allow herself to think most of the time.

"Am I doing the right thing?"

They're sitting on the couch, and there's an open bottle of wine on the coffee table, next to a pepperoni-and-mushroom pizza in a greasy, steam-dampened box. Danielle's got her feet—freshly pedicured and tipped with maroon polish—placed neatly together on the cushion, her glass of wine held in the hand that isn't resting across her bent knees. She peers at Toni over the rim of it, concern clouding her face.

"As in?"

Toni frowns and looks down at his lap. Sitting here in sweats and foam rollers, with the astringent odor of nail polish mixing with the smell of the pizza, Toni doesn't feel confident or secure. Toni doesn't even feel much like the person she thinks she is, let alone the person she wants to be. And, once those words have been said, everything seems that little bit less safe and secure. It's funny how fast things change.

"Um... y'know. Just generally." Toni clears her throat, tries to sound like it wasn't a big question. Like it wasn't important.

She starts to think that, no matter how safe things felt a few seconds ago, this is a bad idea and she shouldn't say this stuff to Danielle. It might upset her, or she'll get mad and they'll never speak again, because she'll see Toni's a screw-up who can't do the simplest thing right—not even understand how her own head works—and everything's going to go wrong.

Toni's forehead starts to sting as the room goes fuzzy and the panic threatens, and his stomach twists in on itself, folding in on the empty nervousness. Danielle doesn't seem to have noticed, though. She looks consideringly at Toni, and her expression is serious but threaded through with just a little tiny bit of pity.

"Honey, you told me you'd thought everything through. We talked about deep thinking, and you said you were sure. Has anyone been—?"

"No," Toni says hastily.

Why does everybody always have to assume it's someone else's fault, someone else's responsibility? It's like no one thinks Toni could possibly do anything—even fuck up—without a shove in the back and a clearly labeled diagram.

"It isn't that. It's not Kel, before you even say anything, okay? He didn't... he didn't say anything. I just... I don't know. What if I'm wrong, huh? What if all of this ends up not being right for me?"

Danielle's mouth twists, and she's about to say something, but Toni doesn't want to hear it, whatever it is.

"You can't tell me you've never spoken to someone that's happened to! With your helpline stuff... you know it happens," Toni finishes lamely.

Danielle doesn't respond right away. They both know the horror stories: women whose nerves or cold feet worsen during the time they spend in transition, instead of improving. Perhaps they push on, go all the way only to realize—once the surgery is over—that they've made an irreversible mistake. It can leave people miserable, drive them to suicide. It can ruin lives.

Danielle takes a long, slow sip of her wine and swallows. She looks carefully at Toni, as if watching for some sign of possible implosion.

"Yeah, I know it does. But why ask these questions now? You told me, and I quote, you'd never been more certain of anything, and that you wanted it, no matter what. Has something changed?"

Toni slumps back against the couch, unable to meet her gaze. It's hard to know what it is... whether it's an inside thing or an outside thing, or just nerves. Maybe it's just the pills, maybe it's good old-fashioned rational what-if thinking. Who knows?

Toni shakes his head. It's hard to feel like a woman next to Danielle. He feels awkward and ungainly, like he's wearing heels two sizes too big and trying to run in them. Maybe this isn't right. Maybe he doesn't want to be like she is—or he does, but not the way it first seemed. Kel keeps telling Toni that he's not like Danielle, that he's not trans at all, and it gets Toni so fucking mad because—as if it's not enough that Kel *dares* to try and tell him what he is or isn't—he never offers a solution to go along with it. He just shoots it all down, and he never helps build it up.

It's hard to know whether any of the answers are the right ones. They felt right when Toni started. Hell, they still feel right most of the time... at least half of the time, anyway. But it's complicated. Maybe he just never thought it through properly, like the fucking idiot he is. But, then again, if it's a journey, there's lots of directions to go in, aren't there? Lots of ways to go, lots of different paths.

Maybe not all of them are wrong.

Toni would probably cry right now, only she doesn't feel any tears. She's not even sure she feels real. She's like a whisper, a sliver of paper-thin flesh pressed to the world. There's nothing banked up, no weight pressing in. She *does* want it. She does want to be that person, that brave, confident, perfect self she can see in her future... but what if it doesn't work? It's not just the troll voice talking either. It could happen. It could go wrong, couldn't it?

Danielle sighs and leans over, resting a comforting hand on Toni's wrist.

"Is this about surgery? I know you've been thinking about it more. You don't have to start getting into that until you're ready. Hell, Toni, you don't have to get it at all! I haven't. I'm not gonna. No one says you *have* to."

Toni twists her head away from the comforting words, and she crumples her glossy lips into a sneer. Danielle's still talking, and her voice is so easy, so calm. Toni doesn't understand how anybody can be calm, but then not everybody feels like this, do they? Like the sky's going to break and the air's on fire.

"The helpline's got all kinds of support group numbers and therapists," Danielle says, as if that shit is actually helpful. "Toni... oh, come on, don't pull that face."

Toni doesn't stop grimacing. He doesn't do groups. Or shrinks.

"Anyway, it's true. A lot of women are choosing to live without SRS," Danielle says, obviously convinced she's found the source of his discomfort. "There's no golden rule that says you've got to do it, that you have to transition any one single way. You can be nonoperative if you want, for as long as you want after your RLT. You can always do it later. It's just as much about waiting until you're ready as waiting until you can afford it."

Toni scowls. She sounds so fucking patronizing when she's like this, though he knows she just wants to help. Most days, he can take it as help too. Most days, Toni would be grateful for this... but not today. It shouldn't come down to money either—*she* shouldn't think it comes down just to money. It does, of course. That is, it will, when Toni's ready for it. Surgery. Changes that can't be stopped or reversed. The estrogen is irreversible as well, or it will be. By this time next year, if Toni keeps up the dosages, she'll be about as far changed as she can get without a surgeon.

It doesn't seem very far away and—all of a sudden, all of a crashing, horrible sudden—it seems a hell of a lot more real. It seems... scarier.

The tears do start to come then, but not the way they so often do. Not desperate, uncontrollable, and heartbreaking. Just a heavy dampness that spills from eyes too hot and too full to hold it, silent and unstoppable. Twin salt tracks trace his cheeks. Danielle wraps her arms around Toni, pulls her close and holds her. Rubs her back, kisses her hair. It feels good. Toni's a little alarmed to discover how good, and he pulls away, clumsy and confused.

Danielle wipes his face with her thumb, and it's such an intimate gesture, such a sweet, kind thing to do that it very nearly feels wrong. Toni swallows heavily, clears his throat, sniffs, and smiles. Danielle smiles back, and things lighten a little.

"Thanks," Toni says, voice thick and rough at the edges.

"It's all right. You'll be okay, you know? Whatever you choose, you'll be okay. And you can talk to me. You can call the helpline if you want, if you wanna keep it confidential—all right, all right. I'll shut up."

She grins, and Toni realizes how pissed off he must have looked at that idea. The helpline doesn't offer much in the way of information or suggestions either; it's all about listening. Not that listening is bad, but it's not what Toni needs. He's done enough talking, throwing words out into the darkness and waiting for them to make sense where they land. He scrunches up his nose, and they laugh, and the tension seeps away. Danielle refills the glasses, and they finish off the pizza. Screw the diet. Toni tells her about Kel reading up, about the books on order from Pink Pages… about the one she found hidden under his half of the mattress when she got home this afternoon.

Danielle smiles indulgently at that, says it's good, says it's progress. Toni wants to ask if that means she thinks they have a chance, but doesn't dare. That would be complicated, and it would raise up once more that whole issue of how things are going to be in the long run.

Some things don't need asking right now, and they don't need answering yet.

They slide back to the loose comforts of gossip and idle chatter. Danielle makes some coffee, and Toni puts the TV on. They half watch a talk show, laugh at the people on it, and push the problems of this life away until they fade into the background of the brightly colored television one. Toni suspects Danielle didn't really listen. She believed in Toni totally from the very first time they met, the very first time they talked about things. She'll have put all these worries down to nerves and nothing more.

Maybe they are. Maybe it is only that.

Toni looks at Danielle, watches the way her fingers are folded around the white china mug, and watches how her mouth crinkles at the corners when she laughs. Her roots are beginning to show through—dark brown at the base of the red—and there are slight traces of crows' feet edging her eyes.

It's a funny thing, Toni thinks, not knowing who you are. Whether it's a passing crisis, or just nerves, or even a slowly changing point of view, it's unsettling. It doesn't feel safe. When he fights with Kel—those horrible, prickly times when, even though Toni doesn't want to argue, he can't help it and he can't stop the vile things that come out of his mouth—there's this thing that Kel does. He gets this really resigned look on his face and he sighs, and he says Toni's name, and it's pleading and long, like a low breath of wind. She used to think he did it that way to make it sound like a guy's name.

It is, of course. It's been what Toni's gone by since the age of thirteen, and he's not yet picked anything else. That probably needs to happen soon. A new name, some more things in the wardrobe... proper full-time living. Danielle says that's something that shouldn't be rushed, but Toni doesn't see why not. If this is right, then why wait? The way it feels when girl mode's working—the fact that everything seems so much better with the world then—must mean it's the way to go.

Names are hard, though. He doesn't know where to start, who he wants to be. What he sees in his head, when it'll all be over, that person who's smart and brave and clean and free... she doesn't have a name. Toni's not even sure he connects with her all the time, that she's really a part of him, and that gets him so mad. It's like Kel's fucked with his head, changed his mind—it's got to be Kel's fault, hasn't it?—and he's going back, slipping inexorably back, into those dark places he doesn't want to go.

It's got to be Kel's fault, because Kel was the one who didn't want this. Kel didn't like the idea. Kel didn't think it was something he needed to do.

You're not trans, you dumb fuck, you're just stupid!

Cruel words. He isn't usually cruel, but when he is, he's very good at it.

Toni thinks of the book tucked under his mattress, sips the coffee, and pulls a face. Danielle always oversweetens everything. The talk show's over, its bouncy theme music leading off into commercials. Danielle channel surfs a little, and Toni wonders if that's to avoid talking. There certainly is a slight awkwardness to the silence between them, which isn't normal. Not for them.

Other questions are just starting to dance through Toni's head— things that might be worth asking, even if the answers aren't popular—

when Danielle finds a local news report, and she's just about to flick past it when they both stop and, in silent, horrible unison, stare at the screen.

A reporter with a pastel-green blouse and red lipstick stands before a flapping line of crime scene tape, and the sallow light of late afternoon glints on a chain-link fence. Behind the woman, police officers and criminalists in those heavy black nylon jackets are picking over the dusty ground and, past the metal honeycomb of the fence, tall, golden grass waves against a gray sky fringed with clouds.

"Oh, God," Danielle says. "That's the old embankment, isn't it?"

Toni doesn't say anything. She knows where it is, what it's for. The report is live, and Danielle turns up the volume.

"...was discovered approximately two hours ago," the reporter continues, presumably recapping whatever it is the station already knows, "and is believed to be that of a young man, preliminary reports suggesting African American, who appeared to have been beaten severely. Police officers have yet to make an official comment...."

Toni is aware of Danielle's gaze, of the look of horror on her face before she catches herself and reels it in.

"Isn't that awful?" Danielle says, voice pale and thin. "I wonder what happened. What do you think—?"

Toni doesn't answer, trembling fingers already stabbing at the keypad of his phone. Kel's number goes straight to voice mail. It's stupid to be so panicky, to immediately have this thing open up inside that's too big and too terrible to even be real. It's not a fear that has a name, it's just a dark aura on the world, and it echoes back at Toni with all kinds of possibilities, all kinds of sick, twisted things that shouldn't be thought about in case they're conjured into being. Her stomach hurts really bad, like it's clenched up so tight it's going to burst, and her head's floating as she tries to focus.

"Toni?"

Danielle's voice comes through a shroud, distorted and fuzzy. Toni shakes her head. It's hard to breathe, to hear, to see. She's choking on something she can't identify. It's not tears, not anger, not panic, but some combination of all three, and it hurts. Her forehead burns, a panicky dizziness sweeping in and out of her. Kel is still not picking up, and she can't even get the words out to leave a message.

It's him, isn't it? Something bad. Something bad was always going to happen....

She could take most things, but not that. Not Kel.

"No."

The word slips out, small but stubborn. Danielle comes over to her, reaches out, takes hold of her wrist and tugs on it as if she's trying to get a recalcitrant child to move away from a stand of toys.

"Honey, c'mon. I'm sure it's all right. It's nothing to—"

She wants to say no again, to stop all the words and all the feelings, the images that dance behind her eyes and the fear that pools under her skin, cold and greasy, but she can't. Danielle puts her arm around Toni's shoulders, squeezes gently, and she is warm but totally devoid of any comfort.

"Toni, come on. You mustn't panic, okay? Don't panic, honey."

They're different words, but they've been said before. Kel's said them, all the times they've partied too hard, and all the times he's treated her like a stupid kid, like a crank.

Don't freak out on me now, Toni. Pull it together, 'kay?

But Danielle is not him, and Toni stiffens under her touch, resenting things that aren't even there. The reporter is still talking. One of the small, fragmented parts of Toni that is not currently sleeting through space on the wings of total terror wonders why this is making the bulletin. The local news doesn't usually cover every single dead body that shows up in the shitty parts of town... but the embankment is right at the point where you can see across into the nicer neighborhoods, and maybe they can see across to you. The reporter's fine blonde hair is blowing across her face as she uses words like "brutal" and "discovered slain," and apparently it was some little kid that found the body.

"Hey." Danielle rubs her shoulders. "Just because it sounded like—"

"No!" Toni snaps, because putting a name on it is wrong. "It's not! It isn't... it isn't anything. It...."

The words dry up, hissing away into nothingness like water spilled on a hot stove, and all she can do is stare at the TV, watching the dying light touch the long grass that waves against a dull sky. Other news stories are running across the bottom of the screen in a blue ticker-tape band, as if anything else actually matters, and then the camera breaks away, and it goes back to the studio. The anchors are suave, polished, well made-up, and they just go back to talking about the local economy. You could almost believe that nothing's happened.

Danielle kisses the top of Toni's head. "Look, sweetie, if you're worried, we could always just get in the car and drive down there... find out what's going on. I'm sure it's nothing to do with him."

Toni just nods. Yes, she wants to. Needs to. Danielle understands, hugs her one more time, and pulls her to her feet.

"All right. All right, come on."

IT DOESN'T take all that long to get to the old embankment, though, by the time they arrive, the golden glow of a summer afternoon has given way to the soft light and faint chill of early evening. It's like the texture of the world has changed a little bit, and Toni notices it, looking up from the bleak autopilot of dialing Kel's number over and over—the same tattoo of beeps on the keypad, the same fucking voice mail message—and wonders if it means something, the fact it feels colder.

Danielle says she might want to stop dialing. It takes a little while before Toni realizes she means because the cops might have found her number on Kel's phone, might be tracing who he is and where he lives, and who cares about him. They'd go to the apartment, though, wouldn't they? Fuck, maybe she shouldn't have left. If it's him—and at this point, the conditional seems stupid, because a whole well of horror is filling Toni up with foreboding—then it won't take anyone long to work it out, because he's been fingerprinted before. He's in the system—and fuck the fucking system, and all the fucking things it does—and they've got him now, haven't they?

Closed up tight. Shattered.

The whole place is still crisscrossed with scene of crime tape. Beyond the chain-link fence, the tall, golden grass has become a row of dark wisps against the shadowed sky, though it's not yet properly dusk. The sun is just... gone. Whoever was here has been taken away, but there are still people hanging around—a couple of uniformed officers, and criminalistics people taking tire impressions or something. There are a few rubberneckers too, and Toni recognizes some of them.

She pulls away from Danielle's grasp and bears down on one of the uniforms. Toni sees the look in his eyes when he registers their approach, but she's just not in the mood for that kind of bullshit.

"Can I help you… people?" the cop asks with a smirk.

Fuckwit.

Toni wants to hit him, and the rage swells up like thick nectar, but she chokes it down.

"There was a body. Right? Who is it? Who was—"

"I'm not really at liberty to comment," he says, and Toni knows the bastard is wavering between tacking "sir" or "ma'am" on the end of the sentence.

It doesn't matter. She knows what she looks like, what she sounds like right now. Her voice is shot, and she hasn't even thought about the way she's walking. He can think what he fucking well likes.

"We just want to know if the body has been identified," Danielle says, taking firm hold of Toni's arm, like she really thinks he's going to windmill the guy.

Toni wriggles away.

"Has it? Is it a black guy? Mixed. Whatever. Light-skinned, and he had… he had braids. Short cornrows. He's about five nine, maybe 175?"

She blinks hard. She can't remember what he was wearing when he left home this morning—fuck it, she didn't even look. Toni slept in, barely threw a word after him as he went. So fucking self-absorbed and now the most unthinkable thing might have happened and she'll never forgive herself….

The cop's talking. Toni hasn't heard, doesn't understand at first. Danielle squeezes her elbow.

"Are you sure you want to do that, sweetie? You don't have to."

Toni shakes her head, frowns. The cop repeats himself, looks at her like she's a retard as well as a freak. Identifying the body… it sounds clinical and strange. The cop's on his radio now, so Toni's description must have hit a note somewhere. Dizziness pulls at her knees, and the sickly, woozy feeling she gets around police officers takes a firmer hold than ever.

"You don't have to," Danielle says again, urgently this time. "Don't rush it, Toni. What if it's not him, hm? He could just be held up somewhere. He might just show up at home. Why don't I take you back to the apartment and—"

She thinks it's him. Toni can tell from the sound of her voice. She wasn't sure before, but now Danielle really thinks it's him, and that scares her all over again. Toni can't countenance it, can't believe what Danielle so clearly does, but now she's thinking about it afresh, and all she can see is the image of Kel shut up in a coroner's van or a morgue, abandoned in some black bag, all alone.

She can't stand it.

She says yes. Of course she'll do it. It's one word, but it feels huge, and it yawns out in front of her after she's said it, like something endless and heavy that she's got to fight her way through. Even the word itself seems to stretch out. Toni hears the sound that leaves her mouth as if it comes from some unidentified animal. It's a raw, ugly, creaking noise, and she wants to scream, cry, and probably puke, but she can't... because that'll mean it's him.

It's not. It can't be.

The cop asks more questions, and Toni answers them numbly. When she last saw him, his age, his relationship to her. The asshole smirks and actually asks if she's tried calling him, asks if maybe he could just be out with friends. Toni knots up tighter, her shoulder blades drawing together like wings and her fists starting to bunch, but Danielle's hanging on to her arm and helping her answer, guiding her through the whole thing and helping her explain that this is real, this is serious... and she doesn't let go of Toni's arm for the whole journey.

The cop starts to treat them with a little more respect after a while. He's not that old, Toni realizes, seeing the nervousness in his eyes and the acne scars on his chin. He reminds her of the cop that picked her up for solicitation on her eighteenth birthday. The cop car smells the same as it did that day too: pine air freshener, upholstery cleaner, and stale sweat. There's an undertone of coffee. Only, this time, Toni's not sitting here facing something that can be made to go away with a handful of notes and a blowjob.

The city—the parts of it that aren't familiar, aren't worn in to the comfortable shapes of everyday life, like an old sweater—flies past the windows. She doesn't really give it much thought, because she's clutching her phone tight as a talisman, still dumbly punching in the numbers. It'd be so stupid, wouldn't it, if she went all the way to the police morgue and then Kel picked up, said "hey" the way he does when he knows it's her and she's been trying to get hold of him, and she's going to be mad that she couldn't. He always manages to sound slightly pissed off... not the way he sounds on his voice mail message. She lets it play when it starts up now, instead of hanging up as soon as she realizes he hasn't switched the thing on.

It's Kel. You know what to do.

Only Toni doesn't know what to do. What if all there is left of him is this single recorded message? What if she never hears his voice again? Just one brief glimmer left and nothing else. He almost stops breathing, and stars of glowing blue burst in front of his eyes.

"Toni?" Danielle touches his arm lightly.

She doesn't respond at first, and Danielle pokes her again, harder.

"Hm?"

Toni looks up. Danielle's expression is strange, like she's trying to be cheerful, but all the comforts and consolations are slipping off her face, leaving just the fear in her eyes. She smiles a little bit, and it makes the corners of her mouth look tight and unnatural.

"Don't... don't let's jump to any conclusions, hm?"

Toni grunts a noncommittal reply and turns his attention back to the cell phone. The same sequence of numbers beep their repetitive rhythm, then:

It's Kel. You know what to do.

THIS IS one thing that Toni hasn't done before, but the novelty isn't something to be cherished. The building is low, concrete, square... kind of like a giant grayish-beige lump of sugar dropped onto the sidewalk among the office buildings and industrial leftovers, and gradually melting into the dirt.

They pull up at the back, where white vans with blacked-out windows come and go, and it's weird. Any time Toni's had anything to do with cops in the past, they've always gone in the front door. There's none of the commotion and the frustrated anger of the bullpen back here; it all just feels empty. Just a big, concrete void.

It's busy, certainly. All the corridors she walks down have people bustling around at the ends. Other rooms, other doors... there are lives beyond each of them, and she should be able to feel that, to recognize their existence, but she can't. They're nothing more than drones. Walk-on parts. Danielle tries to hold her hand, but Toni pulls away. She doesn't know why.

She has to fill in a form before they'll let her go in. Give all her contact details, prove she is who she says she is, and then there's checkboxes for gender, and this box that demands a full legal name. Toni doesn't know what to put—at that moment, the whole concept of saying either thing aloud, or marking the paper in any way seems just completely absurd—and the blurry print mocks her. Everyone's waiting. She doesn't think about it as she ticks the same thing it says on her birth certificate, and then she moves the pen to the long box for legal name, writes "Antonio Sebastian Frescelli" in shaky block capitals, and hands the pen and the clipboard back with as much dignity as she can manage.

The morgue smells, but mainly of bleach or something like that. Toni's seen death before, but never in such clean and tidy circumstances. It's not really what she was expecting.

There's a woman here. Toni missed whether she was police or CSU, or just some passing morgue employee they've grabbed and shoved out front and center because she's female and looks as if she could have a caring smile. She's petite, with a high ponytail and killer cheekbones. Maybe Korean. The badge she wears—when Toni blinks at it, because she can't stand looking at the charitable confusion and disjointed sympathy on the woman's face—says Christine Hong.

It's strange, Toni thinks, how so much metal draws the walls closer in, yet reflects the tainted, sallow light. It should make this room feel hard, tightly enclosed, but it doesn't. Instead, it's soft, disconcerting... and that makes it hard to know where the walls end or the floor begins; in fact, where anything really is. The whole room echoes and swoops around the edges, and it's disorienting, like being beneath a great weight of water, murky and deceitful.

"Are you ready?" the Hong woman asks.

Toni nods, but she's not sure. She told Danielle to wait outside, and now she wishes she hadn't, but if some things can't be done alone, then there's probably not much point in doing them at all.

She closes her eyes and wishes she could find words to pray with.

The sound of metal on metal is all at once silky and hard and violent, and Toni clenches his teeth in an effort not to give in to the sudden burst of nausea. In the long, dark nanoseconds before he's brave enough to look, he can see the agonizing blackness, the shape and the coldness of the void Kel will leave behind him. It's big… too big for anyone to go on into, surely? Toni shivers, the weight of it pressing in hard and inescapable, until he feels as if his feet are slipping on the first tiny stones of a collapsing scree slope. There's something unavoidable about it. Just like the fact that—at some point—he's going to have to look down at the body in front of him, and at that point Toni knows he's going to fall. He'll fall and fall, torn by rocks and betrayed by gravity, and he'll die falling, the air choked out of him and the darkness cold and terrible, until there's nothing left at all… because what else can there be without Kel?

Toni opens her eyes.

There's cinnamon skin. Black hair, braided but rebelliously fuzzy. A soft, wide mouth is different in this kind of repose to the way it should be in life. Cold and unmoving, no spark of humor or sign of warmth touches it, but that isn't the worst thing. An ugly, broad wound runs across one temple, the edges chewing away at the skin, revealing the slickness of muscle and the hardness of bone beneath. There are other cuts and bruises too, and the unevenness of a jaw that was broken before death.

Toni sags a little at the knees. The whole world's opened up inside her. No one could ever understand it. She can see the vastness of time and space, the unending hugeness of everything, and she knows exactly how insignificant she is. She can see the reality of her own death, feel the coldness of it inching closer with every breath, without choice or escape, and she's more scared than she's ever been. It's like the biggest K-hole Toni's ever looked down, but reversed so that, instead of everything being depersonalized—numb, like a fat lip after the dentist—it's focused on her, and she can't get away. She feels everything, and it's intense and inescapable. She almost wishes she could stop breathing, do anything to make the seconds stop ticking by, but she can't, and every single fucking one weighs down like a suffocating mantle. They're agonizingly slow, and yet so fast as well, and they just won't fucking stop. She's falling, and falling, and everything's black. The only sound is of pebbles cascading down along the sharp, steep ground.

"Are you all right?"

The Hong woman hastily covers the body over and steps back a little bit as she looks at Toni, which suggests that they get a lot of pukers in situations like this.

"Do you need me to…?"

Toni shakes his head over and over, reaches out and is surprised to find that the woman's white-sleeved arm is warm. It's a good thing to hang on to, to drag himself back to land. Breathing. Breathing is good too, but harder to do.

"Nn-nn."

He doesn't want Danielle. Not right now. Not in here. The Hong woman's pretty dark eyes—such a nice shape, not unflatteringly round and faintly buggy like Toni thinks his are—widen a little, and she's trying to coax a proper response out of him. He knows that, but his mouth's still numb and his tongue feels fat. She must think it's weird that he's grinning. But what can Toni do, except grin?

It's wrong, really. It must be. This poor bastard is still dead. So young, so handsome, and so very cold. Toni glances back at the smoothness of the sheet, broken only by the strange, stark valleys of shadow that the folds and drapes cast, deeper somehow than they should be beneath the electric light. He wants to reach out, touch the guy's face, and apologize for being so fucking relieved.

"It's not him."

The words are small and hollow, but very important. Oh, it's like him. It's so like him… but it isn't. And that's not denial talking. The bones are finer, the busted jaw longer and a little slimmer, the cheekbones not shaped quite the same. The skin is a subtly different color, the lips thinner and not so well-defined. There's more Latin there than African instead of the other way around, and the forehead doesn't have that crinkle in it that comes from too many small frowns—the kind Kel wears when Toni's doing something he doesn't approve of, or when a bottle has really small print on the label—and it's not his crooked arrow of a nose.

It's not him.

Toni shapes the words over and over behind her eyes, until they become real and take on a life and color of their own. It's still a terrible thing, what people are capable of doing to each other. Somewhere behind all the glee and the relief that knowledge still lingers, and it does feel wrong to be so jubilant in the face of it. But Toni's got time to worry about that later.

Right now, the world is just a little bit more okay.

CHAPTER
TEN

THURSDAY COMES around. Kel wasn't really expecting it to do anything different.

He's been having second thoughts, on and off, about agreeing to what The Sherbet Pervert asked for. It is very soon after his last date, and Michael doesn't usually want him to visit so early in the day either.

Kel knows he ought to be a little worried. It doesn't fit the guy's usual pattern, and if Kel's learned anything since he started doing what he does, it's that people have patterns. They're predictable. Only, when they stop being predictable, it means shit can get really fucked up.

Still, he knows Michael. He's safe, as much as anything is safe.

Kel has some other business lined up for the day but, once that's over, he's free. He picks up a message from Toni as he leaves the bus station. It's only short, just checking in, saying what a quiet day it is at work. The questions are silent but noticeable.

Danielle's coming around later, so that ought to cheer her up, and Kel plays on that when he texts his honey back. He tells Toni that everything's okay, and he promises to bring dinner with him, on condition they don't go crazy and he lets Danielle dye his hair blonde or something. He pops the phone off again then, planning to swing by the gym for an hour. It seems like a good idea to start working up the sweat Michael's going to want on him—especially as Kel hasn't had time to really yuck up any socks. He still has the gym shorts, and he slips those on in the locker room, a pair of sweats over the top for decency's sake. Toni never lets him keep the socks or the disgusting T-shirts in the apartment without washing them between dates.

Kel likes the gym. The one he usually goes to is small, not part of any glossy franchise, and it's opposite a vegetarian restaurant that does pretty good samosas. It's clean and quiet too, and not blatantly cruisey the way so many places are. Not that Kel doesn't enjoy extended eye contact—or eye-to-crotch-or-ass contact—with highly toned strangers. There's definitely something to be said for that type of window shopping, especially when Toni's been caught up in one of her periodic whirlwinds of fake nails, new hairdos, and mail order catalogs. Kel suspects she looks at more lingerie brochures than a horny teenage boy, but he doesn't say anything. He knows, no matter what hunk of beefcake might walk in here and start exchanging lingeringly lustful looks with him over a program of lateral raises, it wouldn't make the slightest bit of difference.

Once he's done, he skips the showers and heads across the street. Lunch is a vegetable samosa with some kind of grated carrot salad on the side, washed down with a large Coke. Kel sits by the window, watching the people go by and inventing stories for them. He's still wearing the clothes he worked out in, and the thin cotton jacket he has on over the top is too warm for the day, but he'd rather not take it off. It's nice to sit here, pretending that he fits in with everyone else.

As if, underneath, he's not filthy.

Kel gets to The Sherbet Pervert's place around fourish, and it's a little nerve-racking to walk up the drive when other people are bringing their kids home from school and shit, like he's stumbled into someone else's life. Michael answers the door almost before Kel's pushed the bell, and he looks paper-white and pasty, as if he hasn't slept in a week.

"Come in."

Kel steps into the hallway, the door closes behind him, and he notices a faint smell of bleach or something. Some kind of cleanser. He stands awkwardly, weight on his back foot, slips a hand into his pocket and fumbles for his phone. It's on, but on silent, not set to vibrate or give any other outward sign of the irritating just-checking-up messages Toni will invariably send. Still, just having the weight of it in his hand is a comfort. Like it's there if Kel needs it. A line to the outside world, an emergency window on the places that stopped existing once he stepped in here. That's one of the things that makes it easiest for Kel: pretending nothing else exists, not even what he's doing. He leaves the room completely, in his mind. Just hangs on to enough to keep an outline on everything, a basic guideline of what's okay and what isn't. Beyond that, concentrating just isn't necessary.

"You, uh, you all right?" Michael asks, half a cough lingering at the end of his question.

"Yeah, a'ight," Kel says. "How 'bout you?"

Michael chuckles dryly. "C'mon upstairs, hm?"

Kel nods, but that's not usual. The Pervert normally wants some kind of pretense of familiarity first, the whole bullshit routine that surrounds the dirty socks, the crusty T-shirt, and the gym shorts that ride up on his ass because they're so fucking small. It's not that he's desperate for all that crap—he would much rather dispense completely with it and just get on with things—but it's a break in a pattern.

He follows Michael up the oatmeal-carpeted stairs, into the bedroom he shares with his wife. Kel notices a certain strangeness up here. Things aren't the way they've been before. If it was anyone else, he'd be looking for uninvited guests, cams, or heavy, blunt objects. He casts a quick eye around the place anyway, and it seems okay, though something's still off. For a moment, Kel thinks about backpedaling, saying he can't do this now and they should make it another time, but that's a major way to lose business, for a start, and also there's no real actual *thing* he can put his finger on.

It's just that it feels so empty.

Michael's definitely not playing the way he usually does. There's no hint of the role he normally likes to take. He's pleading, desperate—pathetic. He pulls at Kel's clothes, showing little interest in the playacting that normally surrounds the barbecue sauce and sweat stains. Something's happened. Kel thinks about the wife... it's very soon for another business trip, or a visit to a relative. Has she left him? Maybe she found the dirty underwear from the last time Kel was over here—shit, what would that be like for the poor bitch?

Kel tries to picture that while Michael gets naked. Not only is your husband cheating, but it's like this. It's dirty socks and filthy boys, and sucking on crusty underpants as he lies on the marital bed, screaming abuse at the very thing he wants most in the world.

The guy's fucked up, Kel suspects. Irreparably. But he's not here to think about that, so he doesn't, and that makes it easier to zone out of the room while Michael strips. He pulls his clothes off, revealing his saggy, hairy chest, his pink, round belly, and bandy legs. Kel gets naked too, and Michael's all over him while he does it, tugging his pants down, touching him. He didn't say that was okay and, for a moment, Kel's vulnerable—almost scared.

"Fuck, you're so big," Michael murmurs. He's sitting on the edge of the bed, shoulders slumped, staring at Kel's cock. He looks like a man totally defeated, pushed to the brink just to watch his life slide away from him. When he glances up at Kel, his blue eyes are bloodshot and misty. "Leave the socks on?"

Kel shrugs. "A'ight."

They're old and dirty, but only a day or so's worth, not the kind of gross Michael really likes. Kel almost regrets that. He actually feels sorry for the poor bastard. He always has, in a way, but it's been easier to compartmentalize, to forget once he leaves here.

Tonight, Kel doesn't know what Michael will do when he's gone.

The Sherbet Pervert gives terrible head. Kel supposes it could be because he's used to Toni—nobody will ever come close to him—but he doubts it's totally that. Michael tries, but he has no idea what he's doing. His eyes bug and water, and he gnaws at Kel's dick like a beaver on a tree trunk—no finesse, no subtlety. Kel thinks it would work better if he held Michael's head and just fucked his mouth, but The Pervert starts to panic when he tries that. They end up on the bed, Michael jerking Kel's cock frantically, rubbing against his body, and moaning over and over this mantra—that he's a bad, dirty boy, going to come so hard, so filthy. Kel's still wearing the socks, and he has one leg pulled up, the foot turned slightly out to the side. He lets Michael hump it, his stubby penis scrubbing the gray, stained fabric. Kel splays his toes, gives him something to work against, and moves it all along that little bit faster.

Michael comes first, a strangled cry and a whimper, depositing his load onto Kel's sock. He sighs deeply but surprises Kel by turning his attention to his pleasure as best he can, instead of just quitting. He kisses Kel's shoulder, and it's not as off-putting as Kel thought it would be. He puts his hand over Michael's, tries to coax him into a better grip, a better rhythm. It starts to work.

Kel's been with older guys before. Some of them were sleazes, some just wanted his youth. Some liked to believe they were in charge, some knew he wasn't naïve. Generally, older men have been around the block a couple of times. Generally, in Kel's experience, they know what to do with a dick, but Michael is seriously lacking in that department.

He remains strangely resistant to learning too, and Kel flings himself into the fantasies of memory. There was a guy, a long time ago, who used to give him money for everything he needed. Drink... and other stuff. He kept Kel supplied, and high, and doing what he asked for in return didn't seem wrong, because the guy really liked him, or so Kel thought. He wasn't attractive, but that didn't matter, because he could make Kel feel so good and, anyway, thinking about people only in relation to how they are on the outside was really shallow, wasn't it? He thought he liked the guy, anyway—liked how it felt to please him, liked being treated as if he mattered—and he missed it when it was over, at least a little bit. Of course, it had got weird by then, but it hadn't all been bad. Not at the beginning.

Kel decides it's probably wrong of him to think about Michael the way he does, but he's not going to beat himself up about it. He's never been the filthy one in this room, whatever The Pervert likes to say.

Eventually, Michael's technique starts to improve very slightly— or maybe Kel's just thinking harder—and he starts getting there. He could still do without the puffing and blowing noises Michael makes while he does it, but you can't have everything. Kel doesn't come a whole lot, but he makes a performance of it for The Pervert. Michael sighs happily and kisses Kel's shoulder again. His tongue feels wet and flabby against the skin, and his breath is hot and stale. He makes a satisfied "hmm" in the back of his throat and, reaching across, peels the sticky sock off Kel's foot. Tenderly, he wipes Kel's cock and belly with it, and Kel closes his eyes. He doesn't wanna watch that happen. He can hear Michael sniffing and sucking the fabric, tasting their combined semen, but he chooses to ignore it.

For now.

He thinks he'll get away with leaving it at that, but Michael doesn't kick him out or show any sign of wanting to move just yet. He... aw, hell, he wants to cuddle. Kel's not happy with that, but he doesn't say anything.

"C'mon." Michael tugs at his arm, not content until they're lying back against the pillows together, his thick fingers splayed on Kel's chest. "There. Nice, hm? Relax."

Kel doesn't like it. The Pervert, pressed up against him, fingertips tracing circles on his pecs, rubbing his nipple lazily, feels too familiar. Michael's trying to take something that's not his to have, and Kel isn't in the mood to share it anyway. His skin wants to crawl away somewhere, and it's hard to keep his mind from drifting to Toni, which would be wrong, because he's got no place here. He's set apart, clean and... well, not pure, not Toni, but something a little like that.

Of course, it doesn't take long until Michael starts to cry.

Kel's lying there, looking at the cracks in the textured ceiling through half-closed eyes and wondering if he can get away with having a cigarette, and he hears it. It's quiet at first, just a heavy breath that quavers a little as it goes in, then rushes out, moist and harsh. The tears come in earnest then, and The Pervert balls up beside him, naked and fetal, pressed against his body... still touching. Kel's embarrassed, but there isn't much he can do except put his arm around the guy and pat one shoulder gingerly.

All his suspicions are confirmed, somewhere in between Michael's wet, gulping sobs. The wife has left. She found the dirty underwear he kept stuffed right at the back of his drawer. Wanted to know what the fuck it was, who the briefs belonged to when they sure as hell weren't his or hers... he says he wanted to tell her. He wanted to be completely honest—because he knows he has a problem—but he couldn't. And then she just wouldn't stop shouting. She demanded to know if he was gay, if there was another man.

"I told her I'm not a fag."

The words come out disjointed and mixed up in between the tears, but they fall like stones anyway. Obviously, he's not. He's just lying in bed, crying his heart out in Kel's arms, still stained with traces of his spunk, the taste of Kel's cock lingering in his mouth.

Of course he's not a fucking faggot.

Kel doesn't say anything, however tempting it is. He stills his hand on Michael's flesh. The wife didn't believe him. Accused him of all kinds of things. Threw a beef casserole on the kitchen floor—that'd be the smell of bleach, then—and left shards of white china and a twenty-five-year marriage all over the terracotta tiles. How sad.

Abruptly, Michael sniffs, rolls away, and pulls himself upright on the bed. He sits hunched over, wipes his face with his hands, and he doesn't even bother to look at Kel when he says, "You can go."

Kel runs his tongue over the backs of his teeth, like a kid banging a stick against metal railings. He doesn't take kindly to being dismissed this way. For a start, he wants his fucking money. Come to think of it, he wants more. He deserves it, putting up with this shit. Terrible head, boring stories… old man snot all over his chest. He shouldn't have let the bastard get away without paying upfront in the first place. It's not something he usually does—it'll teach him to be nice, won't it?

Kel swings his legs out of bed and catches the waistband of his jeans with the toes of the one foot that still has a disgusting, crusty sock on it. At least Toni'll laugh when he tells him. They get a lot of mileage out of The Sherbet Pervert, though sometimes he thinks Toni's only laughing to hide how appalled he is.

Sometimes, so is Kel.

He bends over to reach his jeans and start pulling them on. Michael can keep the whole fucking gym outfit this time. He doesn't want it, and he'd rather go commando than wear the shorts home on the bus.

He sees the flicker of a shadow against the oatmeal carpet, but there's not enough time even to turn his head before the blinding pain hits. It floods through the back of his skull, his neck… sends his eyes rolling in their sockets. Kel's aware of something that sounds like breaking china, and all he can think of before he falls is beef casserole, spilled over a clean-bleached floor.

Kel blinks, shakes his fat, throbbing cloud of a head. The world feels like it's melting. He seems to be made of nothing more than impulses of pain, loosely connected together and linked by trembling threads of fire. He can't feel his hands, though he can see them digging, clawlike, into the oatmeal carpet in front of his face. A few drops of blood have spattered onto the pale floor, blurry but very bright red.

He knows his mouth is open, and that he's trying to speak. No… trying to yell. That's more like it. He's naked and bleeding, and it's Michael's fault. Michael hit him. As strange—as totally fucking absurd as that sounds—it's true. Kel can't assimilate it, can't work out what happened, but then his ears kind of pop, and the sounds of the world start to flood back in. They mainly involve Michael screaming and crying.

Kel flails, grabs at the bedside table that must, until recently, have housed the wife's things. Passingly, and not very clearly, Kel wonders what she kept in there. Hairbrush, photographs... contraceptive stuff, maybe. Did they use condoms? Or did she use pills? Did Michael screw her raw after he'd gotten his dick wet with some dirty boy? Kel, or someone like him. He doesn't know if he's ever been the only one. He doesn't like the thought... and he might wanna puke, but the two things aren't connected.

He's pulling himself up, stumbling around to face Michael. Kel claps one hand to the back of his head and feels the wound there. Wet and warm. A rivulet of blood has trickled forward, where his head was hanging down, and it's damp and sticky beneath the base of his ear.

Standing nude at the foot of the bed, breathing hard, Michael should be ridiculous. His pink, hairy belly, his bandy legs, and his saggy, south-facing man boobs; his stubby little dick hanging down all worthlessly shrunken and shy. He should be pathetic, but he's not. His face is red, and a vein stands proud on his forehead, his features all scrunched up and squashed into one another, pressed in together as part of this strange, violent rage.

Michael lunges at him.

It's stupid, but Kel's not expecting that. It isn't that he can't believe it's happening—this is the thing he's been prepared for, in some secret, back part of his mind, since the first time he played this game. No, he's still woozy, still barely joined together, and his reaction times are off. It's like being drunk, or high, and everything's slowed down and speeded up all at once, just colors and shapes smeared across the blurry, sharp light.

The blow knocks Kel off-balance, making the world sound woolly and the ground pitch beneath him. He hears himself cry out, hears the curse the pain wrenches from his mouth as Michael hits him again.

Fuck, that really *hurts*.... Michael's got something in his hand.

Kel looks blindly about him, rolling his head from side to side in order to try and squint through the stars. It's flattish and heavy, like an ashtray or something. Glass. Michael brings it up again, aiming for Kel's face. He's screaming, barely coherent. Ugly, twisted words, thick with hate. Kel's disgusting, it's his fault, he's filthy... he's filth. The ashtray doesn't meet its target; Kel raises his arm, absorbs what he can't deflect of the blow, and pushes back, shoving as hard as he can. Michael roars. His face is horrific, mired with snot and tears, contorted and creased into tight folds that look ready to burst. He fights Kel every inch of the way, even when Kel manages to pry the ashtray from his grip. He could hit Michael with it, but he doesn't. He flings it away— he knows he has, because he hears it hit the floor—and tries to wrestle out of Michael's grasp. It's harder than it ought to be. Kel's not got that much spare flesh on him, but he's strong. Sure, Michael may be heavier, but what really counts is his anger. This crazed, sightless fury is frightening, and Kel can't get away from it. He tastes blood, not knowing why, because the struggle doesn't end. The punches and the fingers in the eyes, on the throat, they keep coming. He can't breathe. Michael's actually trying to strangle him.

Kel gives one last shove, brings his knee up, and connects with Michael's most intimate parts, and they're fleshy and soft on his bare skin. There's a coarse, saggy groan, and Kel lands a fist in The Pervert's gut as he starts to sink to the ground. Michael gurgles, yells in pain and anger, and Kel can't help it. He balls up his hand and clubs the bastard in the side of the head, hard. Fire shoots up his fingers, melting his knuckles together, and he guesses he's broken something. He hits the fucker again anyway, because he wants him to suffer. He ought to. He should fucking *hurt*.

Michael goes down. He slumps and falls over sideways like a sack of gravel.

Kel just stares at him for a few strange, long seconds. Michael isn't moving, and his face is marked with blood and snot. His lips have slackened, his eyes sagging shut, and Kel thinks maybe he's not breathing. He doesn't want to reach out, though, doesn't want to touch him and feel for a pulse. Doesn't ever want to touch him again.

Won't.

He doesn't see the blood at first, but then it's seeping, smearing the red, sweaty skin, matting the hair at Michael's temple... staining the pale carpet. Kel wets his lower lip with a thick, nervous tongue. Shit—what the fuck has he done? Michael isn't moving. Kel doesn't take his gaze off him, but he edges around the pallid flesh-lump cautiously, and he goes for Michael's clothes. More particularly, the wallet in the back pocket of his pants. There's cash, so Kel takes it, leaving the cards and all the other shit that can be traced. He glances around the room. His fucking DNA or whatever is all over the place... fingerprints too. Will that matter? Is Michael even dead?

Shit... fucking fingerprints. Fucking... fuck....

Breathing hard, Kel steps over him and snatches up his outer clothes. Pants, shirt, jacket... he can get himself presentable enough not to attract attention on the way to the bus stop. Wipe the face and hands, smooth down the hair. The wound on the back of his head isn't that bad. It's not bleeding much. He just needs to remember not to panic. His hand doesn't want to work—fucking agony, just to cram the lifted bills into his pocket—and it should never be so hard to get shoes put on. Kel manages it nevertheless and takes one last nervous look at Michael. Is it his imagination, or does the flabby, hairy chest seem to be moving?

Maybe he's okay. Maybe he's just gonna come around with a bad headache and a worse temper, which would make what Kel knows he's doing now theft, and not... anything else. He sniffs heavily, wipes the back of his hand across his face.

Sometimes, he and Toni watch those science cop shows on TV, where all the criminalists are preternaturally good-looking, multitalented, and usually sleeping with each other. They laugh their way through them and have running jokes about the secret story lines that the shows don't cover—how some big butch character is secretly in love with the blond guy in ballistics but can't work up the nerve to tell him, or how the pretty female fingerprints expert all the male characters lust after is actually a dyke.

He wishes he hadn't laughed so much, and had maybe actually learned something. There's enough of his bodily fluids in this room to put him in prison, isn't there? Even if The Pervert doesn't die. He prods Michael with his toe, and the weight of that ugly body resists him, rolling back against the carpet. A groan of air issues from the wide, flaccid mouth, and Kel jumps back, cussing the way he hasn't done since he was a kid, when Aunt Gina used to clobber him for it and tell him he wasn't raised to be a hoodlum.

He doesn't know. He can't think. All he wants to do is get out. He *needs* to.

It's hard, though, because Kel can't move. It's as if he's made of nothing but lead and clay, and all the breath has run out of his body like water. The spell breaks, just as suddenly as it started, and the silence roars in his ears. He lurches away from the crumpled flesh, the... body... and he shakes his head, as if he could throw off what's happened, make it not real, or somehow have it not matter. The panic fills him, washes everything out of its path, and all he can think of is getting away. Kel backs out of the room, and he runs.

He runs, and he doesn't look back.

CHAPTER
ELEVEN

TONI DIDN'T want to come home. She wanted to look for him, to do everything and anything to find him. If Kel wasn't in that fucking morgue, then he's out there somewhere, and he's not answering his phone.

He's still not answering. She's essentially given up on trying, not even really wanting to hear his voice mail message anymore, and her thumb hurts from the repetition of the same string of numbers. So, Toni's just slouched on the couch, the phone cupped loosely in her hands, hanging between her knees. Danielle's taken charge. Danielle said, unless anything really had happened to him, this was where he'd come back to, and Toni ought to be here when he does.

It sounds like she's talking about a cat or something, and it pisses Toni off, but he's not going to say anything.

What they both leave unspoken is the fact that, if Kel doesn't come back tonight, the police won't even listen to a missing person filing until more than twenty-four hours have passed. How much they'd do after that is definitely open for debate as well, but Toni purposely pushes that out of his mind. It's easy to imagine what it would feel like, going down there, walking into the precinct, feeling all those eyes, all those stares. Toni frowns at the cell phone he still holds, sees his hands as if they're totally new, totally unconnected to anything he remembers being there. His fingers look to him like men's fingers, long and thin, with knotted joints and sharp knuckles. They link together loosely, and the gel nails are incongruous and troubling. They don't give Toni the same flush of pleasure as they used to, the same sense of security and satisfaction.

"Honey?"

Danielle sets a mug of coffee on the table. It chinks on the scuffed wooden surface, and Toni glances up, both grateful for the gesture and also kind of resentful. Danielle hunkers down, her face an unsettling mix of pity and foreboding. She gives Toni a lopsided, tight smile which doesn't do much to ease the tension, and reaches out to squeeze his wrist. The pressure is neither reassuring nor soothing, but Danielle means well. Toni can't quite manage to smile back, but a wrinkle of his nose and a quirk of his lips seems to suffice. She doesn't say anything else, and Toni's grateful for that.

They just wait, mostly in silence. It seems like all there really is to do. There have been a couple of phone calls—that asshole Dean from the outreach center, and one or two other people Kel knows—and Toni doesn't know why they bother to call here. Not when they don't even have the balls to admit they've tried calling Kel and they can't get him, that they're scared and concerned. Toni thinks it takes a special kind of spinelessness to weasel out of it the way Dean did, to um and ah and say "never mind" in that tone of voice that suggests it's somehow Toni's fault Kel isn't here. And that is such fucking shit. Toni doesn't have the time for it, or the patience.

So they just wait. They just keep waiting.

He'll come home soon. Toni knows he will. He'll come home and they'll laugh about how scared Toni was, how much everyone's panicked, and how all the things that could have gone wrong just haven't... how they've been lucky one more time.

Yeah, Kel'll come home. He has to.

IT SEEMS like a longer walk to the bus stop than it's ever been before. Kel has to try real hard to keep calm on his way down there. He struggles to hold a cigarette to his lips, to light it with a shaking hand, and, once he finally manages it, even the nicotine doesn't calm him down. He can't run, must act normal. Thing is, he doesn't know exactly what "normal" means, even at the best of times. Is it something he ever does? Or does he always have the taint of wrongness on his forehead, like people can see who he is, where he's been, just in a single glance? A whiff of suspicion that follows him around like a bad smell, alerts everybody he passes to what he's done.

What I've done.

That's a strange thing too. Kel doesn't actually *know* what he's done. Among all the bad choices he's made, the things that have gone wrong today, the truth remains that he doesn't know. Michael could be dead, or could just be unconscious. Yeah, he's probably just unconscious. That makes it less dangerous, doesn't it?

Kel's breathing hard as he gets to the bus stop. He doesn't have to wait long, and he's grateful for that. He pulls himself up onto the great, wheezing beast, and he just wants to hide in the greasy, gritty smell of it, to fade into the scratchy, grubby upholstery and melt away into nothing. It feels like people are looking at him, though he knows that's stupid. Before he left Michael's house, Kel made sure he looked okay. There was a baseball cap in the closet. He took that to cover the blood on the back of his head and, with his jacket zipped up, there's no mess, no stains, no evidence of what's happened. Not on the outside. He knows it isn't obvious, but it still feels like it is, like everybody can see, everybody knows.

Thing is, if Michael's not dead, he could call the cops when he comes around. Sure, so he probably wouldn't. People don't do that… they don't like to incriminate themselves. And he *did* land the first blow. But, Kel did take a substantial amount of money and, when The Pervert does come to, he's really gonna be hurtin'. If anger wins out and he reports Kel for taking the cash, or files a complaint of assault, it won't look good. Kel has no idea how he'd get out of that. He wouldn't, obviously. Oh, he's been picked up before, more than once, but it's never stuck as far as conviction.

Maybe there's a first time for everything.

Of course, it'll be just as bad—and probably a whole lot worse— if Michael never gets up again. Someone will find him, and it won't just be the matter of a wad of bills snatched and folded into Kel's pocket. Not just theft, but the kind of fuckup that changes everything.

Kel leans his forehead against the grimy window and tries to let the movement of the bus shake the thoughts away. He didn't mean to. He'd turned his phone off before he left Michael's place, leaving messages unchecked and missed calls ignored. There'll be something from Toni on there, no doubt, and Kel just doesn't know what to say to him. How is he supposed to explain this? Toni panics over the least little thing, invents dramas and crises even where there aren't any. How the hell is he going to deal with something like this?

It's one of those moments when Kel wishes he could change things. Change people, maybe. It would be so much easier if Toni was harder inside; if he didn't come so close to breaking, shaking apart with every breath, and if Kel could rely on him.

They say a friend will help you move, but a true friend'll help you move a body.

He pushes the thought away, wonders if Toni being tougher would mean Kel loved him less. That'd be ironic, wouldn't it? If all Kel really wants is someone who makes him feel needed, a lover who can't cope without him and bolsters his own sense of manhood by flaking out every time things get difficult.

It's bullshit, though, and Kel knows it. For all the drama, all the histrionics and the flailing about in a sea of self-created chaos, Toni is one of the strongest people he's ever met. In so many ways, he truly is and—in this single moment—Kel really wants him. Just to hold, to breathe his scent and feel his lips. Sometimes, when he wakes up really early in the morning, fresh from the cobwebs of slumber, or maybe pulling away from the vestiges of some horrible dream, Kel turns over and just looks at Toni. He's incredible when he's sleeping, when he's not trying to be anything else and he's just natural, relaxed... the way he ought to be.

Kel shivers as his stop comes up. He's almost missed it, and he swings off the bus fast, lurching into movement from the lumpy, unconscious stupor of thought so quickly that his stomach flips. He's still sure he stinks of violence, blood, and failure. Everyone can see it, and it's not going to go away. Not until he gets home, and maybe not even then. There are things Kel knows he can't lose in Toni's arms, and whatever he's done to Michael is probably one of them.

All the same, he wants to try. He hunches his shoulders, lets his feet think for him, and just points himself toward home. The evening—not quite night, though it's growing later—is warm, the air stale, heated through and overcooked with hour upon hour of exhaust fumes and heavy sunlight. The darkness is coming and it will bring with it the cooling of all this heat, satin fingers to stroke through the summer's zenith and smooth away the tensions of the day. Experimentally, Kel clenches his sore hand, and jolts of searing agony shoot through the joints before they've barely moved. Kel winces, relishing neither the pain nor the way he guesses Toni's going to react when she sees what he's done.

Kel skirts past the convenience store and its smells of cheap food, of warmed-over donuts and corndogs, and makes for the concrete stairs at the back of the building. There's a light on in the apartment. Kel gravitates to it like a moth. He'll take the shrieking and the swearing, the fussing and the panic, because it'll be over eventually and, when it is, he'll be able to curl up with his honey and forget any of it ever happened.

But, from the moment he puts his key in the lock, Kel knows something's wrong. He feels it, like a pin left in the folds of a new shirt, or the shift in the air just before a fight breaks out. The first voice he hears is Danielle's, and Kel is getting ready to be seriously pissed off by that—he doesn't want her here tonight, doesn't want her so close to Toni all the damn time, even though he knows it's a stupid, useless thing to be jealous of—but then he hears how she sounds. He hears the heightened pitch of her words, the tone of what she's saying, and then the door's open and she's staring at him, her eyes wide and her lips parted. Something's more wrong than anything ought to be, but he doesn't have time to figure it out. There's a wail—the drawn-out, intense bellow of a wordless cry—and Toni charges him, cannons into him like a scrawny freight train and locks on tight.

He's crying. Kel doesn't know why, but he holds Toni hard all the same, feels the depth and breadth of those sobs, and they're threaded through with a strange relief, a catharsis Kel can't comprehend. His hand hurts, his head is still throbbing, and all he really wants is a couple of painkillers and a warm bed. He starts to move inside, which is kind of hard to do when his honey won't let go of him, and Danielle's shepherding them both, closing the door behind Kel as if it's important to shut out the world somehow.

He doesn't know what the hell's going on, and he starts to turn his head to ask her, but that makes sharp little glitters of pain dance in his vision, and Kel just winces and shuts up, concentrating on the quivering body in his arms. Toni pulls back suddenly, roughly. His face is red, contorted, and blotchy, and his nose is running. He starts hitting Kel's chest with the sides of his fists, and the screwed-up ends of words grind their way between his teeth.

"Ever! You don't fucking *ever*…. I'll fucking kill you myself, I *swear*…."

He stops, hiccups, and flings himself on Kel once more. A glance at Danielle confirms that, whatever insanity this is, it's not confined to Toni. The ice queen is crying too, though it's not so dramatic.

"We were so worried," she says, her voice cracking a little. "I really thought that you…. Well. I'll go and— You know."

She puts a hand to her mouth and dives for the kitchen. The clinking of cups follows, and Kel can't remember a time when Danielle's ever made him coffee. He doesn't dwell on it, because Toni's busy making the front of his shirt wet and—tears or no—Kel wants a proper answer to what the fuck's going on.

"I knew you'd come back here when it wasn't you," Toni's saying… or something like it. It's garbled and doesn't make sense.

"Wasn't…? What?"

Kel frowns, more confused than ever. It doesn't really need explanation, though, because Toni's wrapped so tight around him. He strokes the back of Kel's neck, presses his cheeks and his forehead, as if Toni needs to learn him by touch, to prove he's truly real. It's okay, though. His arms are warm and strong. He's here, taking care of Kel, and the fear and all the pain runs out of him, cold and sharp like a needle bite in reverse, to be replaced with warmth. Comfort. There's a kiss, a twisted oath of truth and possession, and Kel winces into it when he forgets and tries to cup the back of Toni's neck with his sore hand. It hurts, and he stifles a cuss. Immediately, Toni breaks away, looking worried. He takes hold of the hand as Kel lowers it, and brings it between them. Mottled blotches of deep purple and blue are starting to color the knuckles, spreading out below the skin. Toni's fingers delicately skim the puffy flesh and he winces, as if he can feel the pain himself.

"Baby…."

"It's okay," Kel lies, because he wants something to be.

The corners of Toni's mouth pull back, tense little wrinkles appear around his eyes, and his brow furrows.

"Jesus," he whispers.

What *he's* going to do about it, Kel doesn't know. The thought makes him smile a little, and that's when the tears want to start coming, but he won't let them. He holds them in until the bridge of his nose stings and his eyes hurt. Toni doesn't ask any probing questions. A couple of curls have escaped his updo, and one drapes softly against his neck. He lifts his gaze to Kel's, dark eyes so serious, so… bruised, as if he's been looking at ugliness all day. Kel's moved by a sudden pang of protective regret. Toni should never have to suffer things that make him look like that. Kel ought to be able to prevent it, somehow.

"It's busted," Toni observes, still holding his hand.

Kel doesn't say anything. Sometimes, silence makes Toni talk. Only, right now, it doesn't. Toni looks up at him soulfully, tears still trembling in his eyes, and all he says is, "Fuck."

Kel sniffs, pulling his lips in tight, like he could really hold things back. Another breath drags over Toni's teeth, and he screws up his eyes, not resisting when Kel wraps his arms around her again. They don't move for a while, him just holding Toni, and Toni just hanging on. Holding him. They're pressed so close together, but there's this distance between them that Kel doesn't understand.

"I thought it'd be you," Toni whispers after a while, the words clotted with so much pain. "I really thought…."

Kel hasn't got a clue what he's talking about, but he almost doesn't want to ask. He spent so long on the way home working out how he'd explain what happened with Michael, and this still doesn't seem real. He's hungry, he realizes. How weird is that? Starving hungry, right there in the middle of all the hurting and the soreness and the cold. The residue of Toni's tears wets his neck. Another sniff follows, then, "He looked like you, a little bit. The guy."

Kel's not following, his mind bouncing fuzzily over the things Toni's saying like the words are just cotton-candy clouds. He feels dizzy, and he wonders if that's because he hasn't eaten.

"What guy?"

Toni pulls back, looks at him in utter amazement, tip of her nose red and eyes bloodshot and puffy. "What…? The fucking *dead* guy, you f— Jesus, Kel! What did you think was— Haven't you heard? It's been all over the news. At the embankment. This guy, he... oh, God. Baby, I didn't know what— I couldn't get hold of you. I thought...."

Kel strokes his cheek, presses the pad of his thumb to Toni's lips, and they quiver just a tiny bit under his touch. "You thought—?"

Toni nods. More tears spill, and Kel's heart breaks.

Danielle comes in with a tray of coffee, stopping at the doorway and clearing her throat loudly, then taking an uncertain step backward. He looks over at her, more grateful than he's ever been for her presence.

"Wh-why don't we all sit down, hm?" Danielle raises her beautifully plucked eyebrows and glances at the couch, like it's the magic answer for all things.

Kel nods, and then regrets it because it feels as if his head may fall off. Still, sitting down doesn't sound like such a bad idea. They've been standing here like idiots in the middle of the room, all this fear and pain pouring out, and maybe for a minute he even forgot how tired he feels. He stumbles over to the couch and flops gratefully onto it, and his limbs still seem loose, barely connected to his body. Toni slides close under his arm, nestles against him, hand on his chest, as if he doesn't want to let go. Kel squeezes him tight, reassuring and, he hopes, comforting.

"It's okay," he murmurs and presses his lips to the side of Toni's head in a tired, lazy half kiss as his honey's lighting two cigarettes.

It's not okay. Not okay at all. He's going to have to admit to that, but it's so incredibly hard to do. He feels like he's walked through the wrong door somehow, lurched into a narrative that isn't his own, like a sitcom actor emerging onto the wrong set, bumbling around with the wrong lines in the wrong place. Plus, his head really hurts, and so does his hand.

They sit and smoke, and drink the coffee Danielle made. She's found half a box of cookies at the back of a cupboard or something too, and laid those out on a little plate. They look sad and ridiculous somehow to Kel, but he eats a couple all the same, and they remind him how hungry he is. That goes away, though, when Toni's faltering, damp words relate what's happened today.

It's insane, some comedy of errors that is so far from being fucking funny Kel would like not to believe it, but he doesn't have that

luxury. There was a body, a death... a murder. And that they thought—
no, that *Toni* thought the absolutely impossible. It's beyond believing.
It's a sick, horrible coincidence.

Kel had no idea. Not about any of it. He listens, and he doesn't
interrupt, because cutting across Toni now would be the worst move he
could ever possibly make. Kel hears how he found out, how the whole
thing went down, spreading over the afternoon like a long, dark
shadow, poisonous and evil.

"You went to identify th—?"

Toni nods and hushes him with words that are so simple that
hearing them aches.

"I had to. I kept thinking, if it was you... alone in a bag
somewhere. I couldn't leave you like that."

Kel can't look at her face then, all torn up with pain and the
leftover, relived fear of this awful day. Every time in the past he's said
how brave Toni is, Kel knows he hasn't even cleared the half of it.
Sitting there, with his hair starting to look lank and greasy, his eyes
rimed with the traces of smudged liner ineffectually wiped away, Toni
is the best, bravest person he knows, and more of a man than Kel thinks
he'll ever be. He wants to say so, but he doubts it would go down too
well. So, instead, he glances at Danielle's pretty arrangement of coffee
cups and the plate of cheerless, incongruous cookies. It's weird, like
life is breaking in across tea with somebody's grandmother. The
crushed, bent ends of cigarettes sit like worms on the china.

Once this got to be about them, not about passing on news,
Danielle excused herself from the couch and went to get something for
Kel's hand. Now, she calls from the bathroom, asking if they have any
bandages. Toni doesn't look away from Kel's face and calls back that
the bandages are in the cabinet, behind the Tylenol.

Danielle brings in a tube of antiseptic cream and some bandages,
sets them down on the coffee table, next to the mugs and the half-eaten
plate of cookies. The whole thing feels so fucking bizarre. She stops
dead—funny how words gather meanings like moss—and Kel realizes
she's caught sight of the wound on the back of his head. He'd already
taken the cap off and let it fall to the floor, because he doesn't want a
single piece of Michael's house still on him. He thought he'd cleaned
his head up pretty well too, but Danielle still gasps.

"Your *head*! Oh, Kel…. Do you need to go to the hospital?"

"Nuh-uh." He turns quickly to hold her gaze, not wanting the fuss, and lights pop in front of his eyes. "It's okay. It doesn't hurt, and I don't have any double vision."

It's mainly true, except about the hurting, but Kel's had enough concussions to know this will pass soon. He holds on to the eye contact he has with Danielle, because she's always been so stable, so normal. She's what Toni has always held them up against—yes, himself, but Kel too, in that strange way of his, where he wants everything to fit into this idea he has of what things ought to be.

Danielle nods, seems to accepts his judgment, and helps him dress the hand. Toni sucks his teeth and shakes his head. He tuts sympathetically and holds on to Kel's other hand while Danielle binds the fingers.

"Two broken knuckles, and I think these fingers are fractured," she says, tying off one strip of gauze. "You ought to get this looked at properly. What on earth did you do?"

Kel says nothing. It's strange; he's both grateful for her presence and resentful, like maybe it's time she pissed off and left them alone. Truly alone, for the first time in months. Not with her shadow dancing on the wall. He'd like that, although he finds that, oddly enough, he doesn't really want her to go. He needs her.

Toni'll need her, before tonight is out.

"Kel?"

Toni's voice, gently prompting. It can't be ignored. He has to tell. He wants to, and Toni is impossible to deny when he just sniffs and says, "So? What did you do? Where were you? How come you didn't…?"

Kel's not sure what he wants to say. "Call me?", "see the news?", or maybe "show up until now?" Could be any of those things, could be something a great deal angrier. It's occurred to Kel that Toni's taking everything—as far as is possible—extremely well, and that has to be good, doesn't it? He would, under usual circumstances, have expected a lot more screaming, hurling of abuse, and general fury, anxiety, and panic. Kel can't imagine what it must have felt like for her. The wave of guilt, of regret, comes hard and high and crashes over him until he thinks he'll drown in it. He feels like he's choking on it when he tries to talk. It's agony.

"I was…." He stops, clears his throat, tries again. "I was at Michael's today. I told—"

I told you where I was going. No, that's the wrong thing to say. He is mad, to a degree, that Toni didn't remember, didn't know where he was, when Kel distinctly remembers telling him. He always tells, always makes sure his honey knows, and he can't do a damn thing about the fact Toni never fucking listens.

He tells the story. Goes from the first to the last and doesn't spare details. Kel hears the sound of his voice change when he talks about The Pervert turning nasty, about the bits that went really badly wrong. He doesn't recognize a lot of the words, or the pictures they conjure. It was over so fast, such a strange, random jumble of events, that it doesn't deserve the way the girls react. Danielle turns pale, blinks rapidly and keeps glancing between him and Toni, but it's his honey's face that gets Kel the worst. Toni's lower lip trembles, his eyes well, and then he's touching Kel, touching his cheek, his arm, his neck, like there's something he could imprint there, something he could prove. Kel catches Toni's hands in his, squeezes with the one set of fingers that are working properly.

"It's okay, I promise. I—"

"How is it okay?" Toni demands, the words getting choked up with that note of hysteria Kel has been expecting to hear. "How is it anything fucking *like* oka—"

"I promise," Kel says, over and over, trying to make both of them believe it. He reaches into his pocket, pulls out the folded wad of bills, and presses it into Toni's hand. "See? Look, it's…."

Toni stares dumbly at the money. His mouth opens, but it's Danielle's voice that cuts through the moment.

"Oh, Kel…!"

He blinks. This isn't going the way he wanted it to. Toni's fingers close around the cash, and he shakes his head slowly as he flicks through the notes. When he raises his gaze once more, there's a whole new kind of fear in those dark eyes.

"Baby… I don't think this was smart."

Kel swallows, wets his lips. No, they have to understand. This was the only thing he could do, wasn't it? His due, his recompense for… for everything. He hangs his head. It's still throbbing, in a dull, low-level kind of way.

"Nuh-uh. I know."

He sits, mute and stupid, and lets the arguments break out around him. Danielle starts getting arch about it, declaiming it was wrong, not to mention frankly idiotic, and adding in what she must think are hushed tones that he could have done *who knows what* to that guy.

Yeah, like I didn't think of that!

He doesn't say it. Doesn't say any of it, no matter how tempting it is. Toni's defending him, and Kel loves him for it. He and Danielle start arguing with each other in that strangulated way of pretending to be civil, pretending to be quiet. The words are clipped off at the ends, taut and strained. Kel lets them fade into the background, absents himself from what they're saying the way he does when the conversation's about estrogen dots or hair removal.

None of it feels real yet. What he may or may not have done, the things that may or may not have happened, they don't matter. He's just sitting here, wavering in and out of some kind of conditional space, and it's really, really strange.

Danielle stands abruptly, glares at Toni, and says something like at least she can find out what's going on, but she's not getting involved in it. Kel doesn't know what she means, but then she's fishing in her purse and muttering under her breath. She tosses one last glance at Kel before she stalks out, and Toni goes running after her. They pass behind the couch, and Kel just sits there, the uselessness and weakness burning against the inside of his forehead, like his whole skull's bursting. He hears voices whisper, knows Toni sounds scared and frustrated, and then the apartment door slams.

Toni heaves a long sigh, and cusses.

Kel doesn't say anything. Words seem kind of inadequate. He just waits, gaze poking at the edge of the room until Toni slouches around to fill it, his shoulders hunched and his hands in his pockets. He's frowning, and the frown only deepens when he looks at Kel.

"She's going to find out what's going on. Just get out there, go take a look. I told her where it was. Just see if there's any sign of... y'know."

Kel nods, just once. Yeah, he knows. Cop cars, yellow tape. Evidence. Has he really been that fucking stupid? The fuzzy, loose-linked memories play over and over in his mind. How Michael was in bed, aching to please and desperate to receive, and how Kel thought of laughing. It changed fast, and that part's blurry. He remembers the ugly, violent scream of a face, screwed up and horrible, and he remembers crawling around on the oatmeal carpet, naked and with that thudding, crushing pain running through his head. Michael's hands around his throat. Now, Kel's fingers climb to his neck almost without him noticing. He touches the skin, wonders if it'll bruise. It isn't as sore as he expected. A little bit, but not really bad. His head is worse. It feels sore now, the whole of him aching and ready to flake out, the way he gets after a really long night or a party he should have left hours ago. He's tired, and it's hard to concentrate on the things Toni's saying. Kel knows it was probably something important, and he looks up apologetically.

Toni lets out a breath, and the air jets, harsh yet resigned, over whatever he just said, obscuring the traces of the words and leaving them forgotten, abandoned. He stands there, hands on those slim hips, body still framed by the uniform of skinny jeans and baggy T-shirt. He looks chalky and washed-out, and Kel thinks he flinches when a siren ghosts its way through the soundscape outside the window.

Toni shakes his head. "C'mon. Let's get you into bed. Sleep for a little bit, huh?"

"It's early," Kel protests, but Toni's already making his way over and, when he holds out his hand, Kel can't help but take it.

His honey shuffles him into the bathroom, strips him, and leans past his naked shoulder to turn on the shower.

Kel stares numbly at the water as it starts to beat against the bottom of the tub, pressure picking up and making the pipes thump and rattle. Toni cranks the thing up to the highest setting it can manage and they wait, watching the spray lurch and spatter. After testing the temperature, Toni shakes the droplets from his hand and—still so close, still leaning across him—kisses the point of Kel's shoulder.

"Don't scare me like that again," he murmurs and pushes Kel gently in the middle of the back.

He lifts one leg, then the other, and climbs obediently into the tub. Stepping under the spray is nice, like entering a quiet room off the street, where the noise is muffled and the door can close on everything that's happened. He looks around for Toni, but he's edged off to the door, leaving Kel to it, the flimsy shower curtain pulled half-closed. Faded palm trees dot the crinkled plastic fabric. Kel sees Toni's hand on the doorjamb, the flicker of his body in the doorway, and then he's gone.

Kel frowns, then reaches for the soap and starts to wash his day away. He doesn't think about it at first, but he realizes that it'll wreck the bandage Danielle put on his hand. Not that it seems to matter too much—it'll dry, and he can't use the hand to do too much anyway. For a moment, Kel wants to call Toni back and get him to help with the bits that are hard to reach, but he doesn't. It doesn't seem right. Briefly, Kel wonders why not, but the thoughts don't linger.

Nothing lingers under the hot thrum of the water.

When, finally, he gets out, Kel finds that Toni's left him clean towels. He dries off as best he can, and wraps one around his waist before wiping his good hand across the bathroom mirror and squinting at his head. He cranes his neck, tries to get a good look at the damage. From what he can see and what he can feel, it doesn't seem to be too bad, but he wishes Toni had stayed in here to help. Kel feels a little insecure about it, if he's honest with himself. It's not the kind of thing that usually gets to him, but... did Toni not want to stay? Can he not look at him anymore? Sometimes, he has moments like that, like when he packs Kel's bags for him in the middle of the night and tells him he's moving out. He hears whole conversations in his head, Kel suspects, plays out scenes that will never happen, just to prove some twisted point of logic he's got into his mind.

Is he thinking something like that now? Ascribing guilt, imagining the scenes Kel described and inventing new flourishes, awful additions? He could be. Kel doesn't think he'll ever fully understand how Toni works. He's crazy. But Kel wouldn't change him for the world.

He leaves the bathroom, comforted by the hot shower but still stiff, aching, and generally feeling kind of sorry for himself. The guilt isn't fun either. With time and distance, the whole day is starting to fall into place, and Kel's convinced it's all his fault. He shouldn't have done things the way he did. He should have listened to his instincts, got out of there before things got screwed up and—most of all—he should have been here for Toni. It still doesn't seem as if it can have happened. A body at the embankment. Someone who... who could have been him, but for the slimmest of chances. Those chances seem that much slimmer today, and that's what Kel can't get rid of, that cold thing gnawing away at his gut.

He lets out a low breath and rubs a hand over his forehead. He never knows whether he's doing the right thing—hell, he's pretty sure he doesn't even know what the right choices look like anymore—but he wants to see Toni. Needs to. Needs to be with him right now. Kel knows he's been stupid, and he deserves everything he gets, be it a slap in the face or a mouthful of abuse. It doesn't matter. He tracks his way through the apartment, worried by how quiet it is but resigned to how he feels. Nothing's going to be right until he's made this up, because nothing's going to be right until he's got Toni in his arms again. In one way Kel really does hate that but—next to everything else that happens in the world, all the pain and the suffering and the shit that goes on— why should he be ungrateful? Why it is, how it happened... neither of those things matter. Just the simple truth of the fact that they are who they are, they have what they have, and it's real. He wants to call Toni's name, but the word doesn't want to leave his mouth, like he's actually protective of it.

Kel hears a noise from the bedroom, and he heads in there. The carpet by the door is threadbare and stained—not their mess, and he doesn't want to know about the history of that little patch of floor—and the door's paintwork is scuffed and has the greasy scratches of nicotine stains on it. He curls his fingers and knocks gently.

"It's me."

He can hear rattling, the sound of pill bottles being moved about. Packed? Maybe this time Toni's filling those black gym bags for himself, and a cold fear squeezes Kel's throat. He pushes the door open.

Toni stands on the far side of the bed, stuffing things into a backpack. Pills, leaflets, a bottle of that strange, crusty, grainy glue that is supposed to hold false eyelashes in place, and a white cotton wash bag with pink daisies on it, that holds who knows what. He glances up as Kel shuffles awkwardly into the room, and he looks terrible. There's a pile of folded clothes on the bed. They look like Toni's, and Kel's chest tightens.

"Packing?" he asks anyway. He wants to go in, fish out some clothes for himself, something comfortable and loose-fitting, but their bedroom doesn't feel like his territory now. That's kind of frightening.

Toni shrugs, lifting the corner of the backpack he's holding to show Kel that it's already pretty full. Things inside it rattle.

"We're gonna need stuff. Clothes, a few essentials. Cash."

Kel stares, nonplussed. "Wh—"

"Danielle called. She says there's no cops, and she saw a light on. She said she wasn't about to go sneaking up to the house and peek in the window, but it looks like there's someone in there."

Relief. It's a weird feeling, on top of everything else, but it sleets through Kel like hot rain nonetheless. If someone's in there, then Michael isn't dead. He didn't kill him... or, just maybe, the wife has come back and is sitting in there deciding whether or not to call the police. He groans. He can't take this anymore—the not knowing, the nerves, the possibilities, and the great motherfucking shadow of it, lingering over everything. He exhales sharply, and Toni sniffs.

"So, I don't know," he says, carefully avoiding Kel's gaze. "Danielle says we should get away for a few days, just make sure there's nothing going to come from all of this. No... fallout or whatever."

He reaches for the pile of clothes, tucks them carefully into the backpack. Kel grapples with a strange and sudden flush of irritation. All the days and weeks and interminable fucking months of sentences that start with "Danielle says." He can't take it anymore.

"Toni, just because—"

"Don't!" Toni snaps, glaring at him. "Okay? Don't start that."

"Oh, c'mon. 'Danielle says'...."

"What Danielle *said*," Toni retorts, "is that *you* ought to get away for a few days. Yeah? That's what she said. You should go. And I said no, I wouldn't let you do that. I said we'd go together or not at all. I said everything would be okay, and we'd just take a couple of days away. It's a vacay, yeah? That's all. Just until...." His voice wavers a little, and the tip of his nose reddens. "Fuck it, Kel! You have no idea what it was— You don't know what it was *like*!"

Kel moves his mouth around the empty husks of words. Toni's right. He had no idea, not about any of it... except for Danielle. She said that, huh? Well, he wishes he could feel surprised.

Toni shakes his head and goes back to the packing. He hasn't said what the plan is, where he wants to go. Kel aches to cross the last few feet between them, to touch Toni and promise it's all going to be all right—whether it's true or not doesn't matter—but he can't. There's too much stiffness in the air, too many things lingering on it.

Kel wets his lips. Toni glances up at him, an old sweatshirt in his hands.

"Th-thanks," Kel says quietly.

It's a small, simple word. Slowly, the silence changes. It doesn't exactly soften, but it feels less jagged, less insurmountable. Toni nods at the chest of drawers by the door.

"You can start passing me undies. Can't have enough clean ones."

CHAPTER
TWELVE

THEY'RE WAITING at the bus station, sitting on those lightweight black metal benches with the curved legs and perforated seats, angled just the right way so it's utterly impossible to get comfortable on them. It's getting late, and it's dark at last. Toni slips a look at Kel. He's slouched up on himself, feet turned inward on the shoe-squeaking, grimy floor, hands scrunched deep into the pockets of his sweatshirt and his gaze half-focused, fixed on some invisible, distant point.

He hasn't said much, but Toni doesn't mind that. Somehow, it makes things seem clearer, more defined, the edges unblurred by neither of them trying to work their way around words they can't handle, or saying things they haven't thought through.

Not that thinking really came into it. Toni didn't even have to think about it for a minute. That's funny, isn't it? After all the drama and calamity, it just seemed the natural thing to do. Maybe it shouldn't have, because what happened—this whole business with The Sherbet Pervert—that's supposed to be the kind of thing that changes how you see a person, isn't it? Toni suspects it should be. It's supposed to make you think, change what you believed they were capable of doing. The doubts are meant to creep in, to gnaw at the dark places—the shadows in which linger the secrets you *know* the other person has, even if you don't want to admit to it—and they're supposed to multiply there, until they ossify and become a twisted, ugly wedge. That would be normal, wouldn't it? Understandable. Rational. Toni thinks so, and that means it comes as a surprise that she didn't doubt Kel for a minute. Whatever he's done, or not done, he did it because he had to, because he had no other choice. Toni believes that, and there's no need for Kel to say a word.

More than that, even if Toni didn't believe it, it wouldn't matter. That's the strange thing to find out. Even if Kel had done it for the money, and beat the fucker to death with a bedside lamp, it wouldn't change a single thing. She'd still love him, still stand by him, and nothing could make that any different.

It's pure, clean knowledge, like a bright star that marks out what they have as special, as blessed. The things Danielle said echo across it, a stain on a comet's shining tail, ugly in Toni's memory.

I told you something would go wrong sooner or later. Didn't I say that?

Yeah, she'd said it. Many times. Never about anything this serious, but Danielle's always thought that, the way she so often put it, "a little break" would do them good. It frustrated Toni to hear it, over and over, the constant and irritating drip of words. It was just the same today, but the drip became a torrent, and Danielle seemed to take such pleasure in it. Guarded, concealed pleasure, maybe, but Toni saw it.

I'm not saying I told you so, honey. But you should stay out of this. Tell him to go away for a few days, see what the fallout's gonna be. You never know, it might do you both good. Not just this, but... well, you know what I mean. Right?

Toni took an ignoble satisfaction in telling Danielle exactly what they were going to do, and how they would do it together. Her expression hardened, the line of her jaw stiffened, and Toni had to hide a grin.

It felt good. It felt... liberating.

Besides, Danielle might not have liked it, but she still drove out there, went to see what was going on. She still tucked a few bills into Toni's hand before she went, and paused one last time, at the door, to smile.

Be careful.

They will be. The bags are packed and everything's ready. Danielle said she'd keep an eye on the apartment while they're gone, and tell anyone who asks that they've been planning a trip for weeks. Toni taps her foot, watching the toe of her ankle boot brush up and down against the black nylon backpack. Two backpacks. Well, one's a gym bag. The boot makes a soft scratching sound on the fabric, and it seems loud in the eerie not-quite-quiet. It's not silence, it's too busy for that. There's a TV on the wall in the corner, but it seems to be stuck on sitcom reruns. A guy with a wide broom is making lazy passes between the banks of benches, sweeping up little mounds of dust and debris and—though there are "no smoking" signs all over the place—cigarette ends. Toni really wants a cigarette right now, so she gropes in her pocket for the pack of nicotine gum she's started carrying more often.

The bus station is cold, though the days have all been so warm. A chilly draft is slicing through from somewhere, and Toni shivers against it as she pops the gum and offers a piece to Kel. He blinks, roused from whatever he was thinking about, and looks at Toni with a strange softness in his face.

"Thanks."

Toni lifts a shoulder, the gesture both acknowledging and brushing away whatever it is Kel wants to communicate. He still smiles, though. It's just a little smile, but it's there all the same. Toni's lips curl out a shy, hidden companion for it, and then he turns away, mixed up by the way he feels. Vulnerable, right now. That's a key point. Sitting here, wearing tight jeans and ankle boots and feeling ugly, clumsy, and more masculine than the average quarterback. Not like that really matters right now. Not against everything else, all the more important things.

People have been looking. When Kel bought the tickets, the guy behind the glass partition—with his ill-fitting black sweater and his bored expression—sat up and stared so hard Toni thought his eyes would melt or something. Kel just slipped an arm around her shoulders and glared back at the guy, the way he does when he's being that deliciously protective. Like he dares the words to be said, just so he can... fight them, Toni supposes, and that thought lingers uncomfortably. He's not a violent person. Not like that. That's not who he is, or the way he thinks. It never has been.

Even when things were at their worst, Kel never set out to hurt anybody. Any time he slipped, any time that happened... he didn't mean it, and he didn't want to be that guy. Neither of them did. They didn't want to be the people they were, so bound up in those places, those coarse chains of habit and need and desperate repetition.

They had that in common—fuck, they still do—and that's why they cling so tight to each other. Kel was his anchor, and he was Kel's, and together they climbed out of the abyss, each holding on to the other.

Toni sneaks another look at him. He's relaxed back into that crumpled-up slouch, trying to keep the world at bay, as if it could really just run off his shoulders and pool in the gutter, not touching or staining either of them. Toni watches him, and the seconds slip by. Kel doesn't turn or glance around. The dimness of the faltering electric light dances through the air between them, picking out every mote of dust, every discolored, tarnished echo.

They're heading for Chicago. That's the way the bus goes, anyway. Toni's never been there before. It has been a dream, for a while. Not the place itself, but just the fact that it's *a* place. A place they're going to go to, a place they mean to head toward. Somewhere to aim at. Toni's always dreamed of them going away somewhere together. The dreams used to be filled with white sand, and maybe drinks that come in coconut shells. Maui, or Fiji, or somewhere like that. Right now, those places are more of a world than ever away, but that doesn't really matter. They weren't ever real.

Toni reaches across and takes Kel's hand. He blinks, tensing for the quarter of a second before he realizes it's her, and then the corner of his mouth twitches into a hesitant, veiled smile. There aren't words to it, but it says a lot, and Kel threads his fingers through Toni's.

Time to go soon.

IT'S A good plan, as plans go. Toni was packing for the both of them, as it turns out, and so Kel didn't much care what happened after that, too caught up in the maelstrom of relief and confusion. He let Toni push him through the whole thing, and it seemed to move around him like clockwork. His head still feels sore and achy, as if his skull is a half size too small and his eyeballs have been lightly curried, but there's no nausea to speak of, so he supposes there's no massive damage.

He wanted to call Michael, but Toni went nuts at that. He wouldn't listen to reason, wouldn't see that it's the simplest way of trying to straighten things out. Just kept going on about Kel not linking himself to the scene, not leaving trails. It would have sounded stupid—it did sound stupid, like he's been watching way too much TV—but Kel can see what he was shooting for. If the worst does come to the worst, it'd be good to have as much of a head start as possible when it comes to connecting him to any crime that may have been committed. Toni has him thinking like that now, somewhere in the midst of all this craziness… yet it still seems so unreal, so impossible.

It's probably for the best. And taking some time off is a good idea. It's… well, it's a plan. A good plan. Kel just wishes he could stop seeing things flash behind his eyes, when he doesn't even really know how many of the pictures are real.

A news bulletin comes at the top of the hour, breaking through the sitcom reruns, though the volume is too low and the sound too tinny to make it possible to hear from where they're sitting. Kel blinks, trying to make out what's going on in the world. There are some national stories, and eventually some local things. The old railway embankment flashes up, just like Toni said, but there are no discernible details, nothing that puts an identity to it. All Kel sees, all he feels, is this horrible cold rush of dread. They show a digitized version of the dead guy's face—the way he'd look if he was still breathing—and it only flashes up for a little while, but it's long enough for Kel to put the pieces together.

His name was Julio, and somebody was missing him.

Kel looks away, a frown pulling at his brow. It's not like he can call in a tip, tell anyone what he does or doesn't know. He didn't bother to write down the john's license plate, and he shouldn't feel guilty for that, even though he does. It's not fair, but it's not his fault. Instinctively, he glances over at Toni and catches sight of the look on her face as she stares at the TV. It's only the fleeting glimpse of recognition, but it brings back to Kel the way she was earlier, streaming with tears, and all the awful, cruel coincidences of today come fighting back inside him. It's been a bitch of a twenty-four hours, hasn't it? Kel squeezes his honey's hand, and Toni turns to look at him. Kel can see him biting back on everything, trying to look calm and brave. It could almost be funny, the fact that he doesn't know how fucking brave he is.

It's almost time. Kel tears his gaze from Toni and glances at the white plastic clock, high on the wall. It's a relic of a predigital age, a blank face dulled with years and segmented by big, black numbers. Kel wonders about the fact the very light in here seems to be tinged depressing greenish-beige. It reminds him of hospitals, or maybe like being on the bottom of a fishbowl, cocooned by water and kept static by the weight of it pressing down, endless and all-consuming.

Kel shakes his head. The way his mind's been working lately is seriously freaking him out. He doesn't have time to mull it over, though, because the bus is here. Toni looks at him—those dark eyes staring out at him from the cautious, folded petals of a pale, nervous face—and stands up, hefts the bags and then glances toward the door. He doesn't resist when Kel takes the backpack from him. He could take both bags, not allow Toni to carry this stuff, but that doesn't seem like the right thing to do. Toni can carry what Toni can carry. Everything else, they can split.

They make their way out there and climb onboard the bus, all grimy metal and the dull, scratching growl of its engine. Crackly announcements echo off the concrete, and there's a scramble of other people boarding, even at this late hour. It's a ragged crowd, a mix of different types. Two foreign students, perhaps British or Australian, are wrapped up in canvas jackets and each other, giggling about their grand adventure. An elderly black man with a short, white beard wheezes as he mounts the steps, and his thin frame seems unusually bony beneath his woolen sweater. A white woman with pale-red hair and a rumpled black skirt suit tows a small suitcase on wheels, and has the harassed kind of look about her that suggests a missed or canceled flight and hastily arranged alternative transport. And then there's them. Kel sneaks a look at Toni. His face is sallow, shadows and the glancing colors of neon and electric light dancing over his skin. His mouth is a tight line, his eyes huge and dark. Kel thinks of all the times he's thought about doing this—just running, heading to the first place he ends up, escaping into the night. He's glad he didn't.

They sit at the back, and get comfortable on the well-padded upholstery. It's not that crowded, and the few people here are all hunched up on their own seats, cramped into their own spaces and their own problems. There's a low buzz of chatter, and the old man coughs with a deep, rattling burr.

Toni sits close, cuddles up against Kel. He finds that unexpectedly soothing, and it's easy to put his arm around his honey and hold on tight. As the bus starts to move, he turns his head and presses his face to Toni's temple and the soft, greasy curls of his hair, just breathing in his scent.

They're not going all the way to the Chicago terminal. Tickets are surprisingly expensive when not bought in advance, not to mention the fact they'd need money when they got there, and Kel knows they have to stretch what they have as far as possible. It's an uneasy feeling, walking around with almost every cent they have on them in cash, but there wasn't time to do anything else.

It's not the first midnight flit Kel's ever done, but they don't get any easier.

He asked Toni where she wanted to go. She's mentioned Seattle before, or New York. Those lazy, pleasant times when they've been lying in bed, sharing a joint or something, Kel has half listened to his honey spin dreams for the future, talking shit about the places they'll go and the things they'll do. He used to just smile, because he never believed any of it, and he didn't think Toni did either.

They could have blown the majority of their money on tickets to Seattle. It would have meant a long trip with several changes and, for the price, they might as well have flown, but they could have done. They still could, Kel supposes. The bus begins to ease away into the darkness, and he realizes that, for the first time in a long while, he's looking at the future and not feeling numb, like it's an endless spool of days without change. There are possibilities there, which never seemed real before. It feels like the start of something big, though the journey is comparatively small. Kel's still thinking about Michael, still groping his way through the complex maze of recollections, memories, and impressions that he's sure must be his own, but somehow might not be. It's as if Kel's slightly adrift in an ocean he never set out to cross, but it's okay, because Toni seems to have everything under control, doesn't he?

That's the strangest thing. He's been calm about it, relatively, and the way he's shepherded Kel through everything—from redressing his hand after the shower to planning all this, finding somewhere to go, somewhere to stay—it's so much more than Kel's been used to giving him credit for. That isn't fair, Kel decides. All this time, and he's treated Toni like the fragile one, the one who can't cope with a crisis, who just craps out and dissolves into a puddle of panic... but he hasn't.

Not today. Kel wonders if there's something that's changed—some great realization Toni's come to about himself—or whether this is all just delayed reactions and, sometime later tonight, everything's going to hit in one great explosion, and he'll have to scoop Toni off the carpet and hold him tight until the shakes and the sweating stop.

Toni's almost dozing off now, his head on Kel's shoulder, hair tickling the side of his neck. The tension has started to leak from his body, all those hard lines and angles dropping out, leaving him folded softly against his lover, defenseless and weary. Kel wonders if it's wrong to feel so protective of someone who can not only take care of himself, but give so very much back.

He glances at his hand, resting on Toni's upper arm. Even with the wrapped layers of gauze his honey so tenderly reapplied, the bruising is showing through, and it's really hard to move his fingers now. Even the slightest flicker hurts, and Kel supposes this could make life difficult for a while. Opening jars, cans... peeing isn't so bad, but it looks like it's going to be southpaw jerking for a couple of weeks. It occurs to him that, of all the things that could happen in the coming days, that might not be the worst thing; that changing the way he habitually whacks off might not be the most severe consequence. The strange thing, maybe, is that Kel can't think beyond that. There's nothing that exists past sitting here, watching the darkened world flit by the grubby glass, and feeling the rhythm of Toni's breathing, but it's a weird kind of nothing. It's the thick, airless stillness of a long drop, or the kind of stagnant silence that follows glass shattering.

Kel leans his head back against the seat and lets his eyes start to close. He's not sleeping. Just resting. Just... taking a tiny little break.

THEIR STOP is an invisible one, almost. Nothing more than a barely marked place on the highway, hard to see in the dark. Toni nudges Kel awake and they disembark, the night surprisingly chilly after the heating on the bus. It isn't far to the motel. Toni has nothing on the place except a phone number, and that was via Danielle. She was trying to help, to just give them somewhere to go, somewhere to head for. It's open into the small hours, and by the time they've walked though all these strange, foreign silhouettes—different buildings, different concrete, the constant roar of traffic—they're both so stiff, sore, and bent out of shape from travel that even a hole in the ground would start to look good. All the same, it's probably a blessing they're seeing it for the first time in the dark.

The building is long, low, and looks as if it could have been standing in exactly the same spot since the 1940s. The scrubby trees that cling to the parched earth nearby seem nothing but vague reminders of nature, and the tarmac ocean of the parking lot—replete with crumpled newspapers, cigarette butts, and other far less savory pieces of debris—laps at the shadows, pulling the eye into its center like a vortex.

"Oh… my… *God*," Toni says and lets the bag drop to her feet.

It hits the asphalt with a small, dull thump, and she glances at Kel.

He grins, and Toni thinks it might be the first time she's seen him smile like that since he came home. As if, just for a moment, things are all right again. Toni shakes her head, stretches out her tired, stiff arms, and reaches down to pick up the bag again. It may not be the classiest suite in the world, but it's better than the bus, it's better than nothing, and above all, it's better than sitting around in the apartment, waiting to see if or when there's a knock on the door.

Kel gets them checked in, and he takes care of everything. Toni lets him do it. She doesn't mind. It's soothing, really. Comforting. Like he's acting more or less his old self again, not the way he was earlier today, when it was so easy to push him through things, and yet so hard to watch him stumbling around, numb and dead-eyed. They're standing in the poky, brown-carpeted manager's office, and there's an artificial cheese plant right next to Toni. It smells dusty and faintly damp. She suppresses a shiver. Kel's nodding and saying "A'ight" in that irritating way of his as the manager signs them in. Toni's not sure what name he's put on the register. Better ask him when they get to the room. A single light bulb glimmers dully above them, its pale-green paper shade crisscrossed by the lines of ill-swept cobwebs. Behind the manager's desk hangs a tired, faded print of a picture that Toni rather likes. It's a sunny, Mediterranean landscape, peopled by the pointed upright pillars of cypresses and painted in broad brushstrokes that are less depictions of what a thing looks like than evocations of how it feels.

If it wasn't so dark in here, and if the picture wasn't so soiled at the edges, looking at it would feel like standing in the warmth of a midday sun.

Kel picks up both bags in his good hand—as if he's taking charge, making sure she doesn't have to carry anything—and they head off to the room. He glances back at Toni over his shoulder, and she can't help the flush of warmth that streaks through her in the split second before she follows.

The room isn't bad. Cramped and pretty threadbare. There's a battered armchair, and a TV on a squat hardboard stand. A small double bed is flanked by two only slightly mismatched nightstands with two lamps standing on them. The bases are a kind of pearlescent pink color, and the shades a really terrible reddish brown. A door leads off to the right, to a bathroom probably only slightly smaller than the one they have at home. Other than that, there's a rickety closet and a chest of drawers on which stands a white plastic kettle, mugs, and a small jar full of teabags, sachets of instant coffee, creamer, and artificial sweetener. The walls are covered with an ugly, textured paper, its original off-white color faded and greased with stains, and when Toni clicks the dimmer switch on, electric light starts to wash across the surface.

At last, the door closes, and they're alone.

Kel drops the bags on the bed and lets out a long, deep breath. He rolls his head, cracks his neck from side to side, and Toni wants to go to him, wants to slide her arms around him, have that broad back pressed against her chest. She doesn't, though. Just watches him, watches the shape of his body and the way the light touches him. Even in this mean room, even with everything that's still hanging over them, still clouding things between them, being with him feels so right.

He turns and he smiles, but he looks so tired, so beaten down. Toni tries to smile back, though it feels as if it comes out twisted, a grimace that isn't the comfort, the assurance that she wants to give. Her hand drifts to the neckline of her T-shirt, worrying at the fabric and rolling it into a small twist between forefinger and thumb. The silence grows thick and unwieldy. Outside, a car engine turns over and over before it starts, and finally it passes away into the distance. It'll be heading toward dawn soon. Toni's exhausted. She hasn't given much thought to it for a while, but it's hard to ignore now. Gritty eyes, aching back, stiff neck and shoulders… even the motel bed looks inviting.

"Tired?" Kel asks.

His voice sounds husky and dry. Toni nods.

"Mm-hm."

"I'll unpack some of the… y'know." He blinks, a frown flitting over his brow. "Where are your pills?"

Toni is already heading for the bathroom. She plans on taking a piss, and maybe making a vague attempt at chewing toothpaste before hitting the pillows, if Kel doesn't find the toothbrushes in time.

"Leave 'em."

It's almost surprising to find herself thinking like that, but screw the schedule, just for tonight. She doesn't care about it. In fact, right now, Toni wouldn't care if there was never another pill ever again. These past months—all the deep thinking and the soul-wrenching, the big decisions that feel like they've swept the world out from underneath her—they could all be for nothing. Toni doesn't give a damn anymore. There's no feeling there, no sense that it's the right thing to do. At this moment, Toni isn't aware of fitting into guy mode, girl mode, or anything in between.

That happens sometimes.

All right, a lot of the time, and usually it feels bad. Usually, it feels like Toni's a freak, a nothing. A *thing*, who's only a half of anything and can't ever be either one or the other properly. Those are the days when she feels lumpy and bony, ugly and irredeemable, and Danielle always tries so hard to cheer her up, to fix the balance and make Toni feel like herself again.

The way she's supposed to feel, probably.

Right now, Toni isn't sure that's ever been the right thing. It's like being a teenager all over again, when nobody in the entire world could possibly understand the unique condition of the inside of Antonio Frescelli's head, and all he ever wanted them to do was fuck off and leave him alone, yet they never, ever did. All he wanted was just time, and silence, and for everything to make sense.

That was a mistake, though. Thinking it would all come together somehow, that Toni would wake up one day and feel comfortable in this body, feel like the person in the mirror was the same person who was watching the reflection. Thinking the small voice in the dark, the one that whispers "I am," would make itself known as more than just "I," and become something the rest of the world could see, and believe in.

That never happened, no matter what Toni did to make it. Trying to obliterate the world never helped, nor did running from it, or even trying to hurt it the way it had hurt him.

He's so tired right now he can barely stand up, but he realizes Kel's looking at him, face drawn tight with concern.

"You ought to take 'em. I'll get you some water."

It confuses Toni. Kel wants her to take the pills? He's already ferreting in the bags, and Toni nearly fumbles the wash bag he throws. Kel crumples his mouth into a small, affectionate smile, and Toni turns, feeling lucky to get into the bathroom before her face betrays what's going on behind her eyes.

Kel's as good as his word. He appears at the bathroom door, holding a grubby glass that he half fills with water from the faucet, and he's brought the pill bottles with him. Toni spits toothpaste into the sink, rinses her mouth out, and watches his face for any sign of resentment, any hint of discomfort. He's just looking at her, though, all calm and cool. He looks just as tired as Toni feels, but he's waiting for her. She drops the toothbrush from the wash bag on the back of the sink, wipes her hands on the seat of her pants, and starts uncapping bottles.

"You shouldn't skip 'em," Kel says softly. His voice hums through her, so warm and delicious. "Not just straight out like that. S'not s'posed to be good for you, gettin' spikes or whatever. The book says that. Plus, it'll make you cranky."

Toni pauses, mouth full of brackish faucet water, and Kel smiles. One corner of his mouth dents into a shallow dimple, and Toni swallows.

They hit the sheets just before the sun comes up. Kel mumbles something and reaches out, his fingertips gently skimming the point of Toni's shoulder. She rolls over partway, but his eyes are already closed, his breathing changing as he slips into the sleep he so badly needs.

Toni curls up to him and snuggles up tight. All the things that have colored the day, hovered over them like black clouds, seem to drift away, and there's a feeling of peace he didn't expect to find. Maybe it's just fatigue. The sheets smell different—different laundry detergent, different environment—to the ones Toni's used to, and the coverlet is thin. The whole bed feels different, but not necessarily in a bad way.

He yawns, settles closer to Kel, and lets it all close over him.

CHAPTER
THIRTEEN

THEY SLEEP late, the heavy, mindless sleep of complete exhaustion. Kel wakes first, and his immediate reaction is a sense of dislocated panic. He can't remember where he is, why or how he got here, but then he grows aware of Toni beside him, and the fuzzy shapes of memories start bumping back against his mind. He groans. His head still aches, his body is stiff and sore and—very gradually—Kel remembers how they got here.

Their room has one window, square and placed high on the wall, which faces out to the parking lot. From outside, there are sounds of cars passing and a slightly more distant thrum of traffic. Voices call out, but Kel doesn't identify the words. He pulls himself upright, then swings his legs out of bed and wriggles his toes into the carpet's sparse pile.

It could all have been worse.

He gets up and glances over his shoulder at Toni. He's still sleeping, burrowed down deep beneath the covers. Almost nothing of him is visible except for that tousled mop of curls and part of one shoulder, where Kel can make out the top half of his fleur-de-lis tattoo. His mind drifts back to yesterday, to Michael and the blur of chaos it all unleashed. Kel looks down at his hand, still bound and now properly bruised and swollen. It's not worth trying to move the fingers. Toni thinks he ought to put it in a sling or something, keep it steady. Kel doesn't much like the idea, but he supposes his honey could have a point.

The motel room doesn't look much better in daylight. Kel guesses it's past eleven, maybe after midday. He goes for a piss and looks dubiously at the ill-fitting plastic door to the shower cubicle beside the toilet. Mold and mildew creep up the tiles, and the small shaving mirror behind the sink is blotchy and smeared.

All of this is his fault. And that boy's dead. Kel dreamed about him, the Latino. What was it Dean said? That some friend of his showed up, said he hadn't been around for a few days.

Guy looked like he was gonna bawl. Started spoutin' off in Spanish.

A brother, maybe. A friend, a lover… who knows?

You're Latino, right?

Kel shakes his head, blinks back the memories. It could have been the same guy, but it might not have been. He could give a description, he supposes… what'd the fucker look like? Ugh, it's one thing to recognize a guy when you see him, but quite another to try to reconstruct the face from memory. Like staring at a blank piece of paper. He remembers the voice better than the face, anyway. Angry and insistent. Something that could have been satin panties, and a thin little prick, worn and slanted like an unsharpened pencil.

Julio's not here today?

I don't know no Julio.

Nobody ever knows people like Julio. Kel thinks of Dean, how dismissive he was, and how all of them are just as guilty. They're never comfortable opening up to strangers, never happy to share or to help. Nobody thinks outside of their own little box, or stops wrestling with their own shit long enough to look at anyone else. And even the things you're so used to, that you no longer even think about, can go really wrong. Kel sniffs, pulls back hard on the way his mind is heading. There's no use in what-ifs.

He flushes the toilet, sluices hands, teeth, and face, and goes to make a coffee before braving the shower. He's staring dumbly at the mismatched china mugs and the jar of cheap instant coffee, and at first he doesn't hear Toni moving. His soft footsteps are easy to miss, but then he's only a few feet behind Kel, and the shape of him—the way the air parts around him, and just the dim, electric glimmer of his presence—is enough to make Kel raise his head.

Toni closes the distance, touches his shoulders gently.

"Okay?"

At first, Kel doesn't know what he means. Is he saying that he's all right, or is it a simple question, or does he want to be told that everything's going to be okay? He's not sure, so he just turns and, awkwardly, pulls Toni into a hug. He holds on real tight, like he's honestly scared Kel's going to pull away, and that hurts. Kel presses his face to Toni's neck, breathes in the perfume of his skin. He smells musty and sleep-warm, and his scent is rich, with just a hint of spice. No flowers, no fake spritz of fragrance. Kel can't deny the effect it has on him. He wants Toni close, and he doesn't ever want to let go.

"I'm gonna go out for a while," he says, his words buzzing against Toni's neck.

"Nn-nn," Toni protests. "Don't...."

"Yeah. Get some food. You're hungry, aren't you?"

Toni shakes his head, and he's pressed so tight that his nose rubs the side of Kel's neck. It's the same kind of denial as a kid caught with their hand in the cookie jar, protesting innocence in spite of the chocolate all around their mouth. Kel can't help smiling. He gives his honey a reassuring squeeze and pulls back.

"I won't be long."

Toni pouts but turns his attention to Kel's hand instead of arguing. He reaches for the swollen, puffy digits that protrude from the layers of gauze, and a cloud passes over his eyes.

"That looks really—"

"Yeah, but it's okay. Promise."

Toni seems doubtful, and Kel would do anything right then just to see him smile. Trouble is, he has no idea where to start, so he just pecks Toni's cheek and breaks away, pulling on the almost-clean clothes from last night, even though they smell of buses and weary hours. He's careful not to look at Toni, though Kel can feel his gaze. He knows exactly how he looks too, without even turning around to see it. He's standing by the bathroom door, arms folded, wearing lace panties, an old T-shirt, and a very sullen expression. So many fights they've had start this way and, for a while, the air in the room does feel tense, but it seems to pass.

"Be careful," Toni says, as Kel leaves the room.

He nods and steps out into the daylight. It's harsh and bright after the dankness indoors, and it almost feels as if he's stepping back in time. Over the years, Kel's been in so many places like this. So many rooms, so many anonymous, fleeting nights. Days too. Days that just poured into each other, pooling in the greasy gutters of pointless months, all without change or end.

It's warm, and a stale breeze skitters across the lot, blowing torn, dry ends of debris before it. Kel gropes in his pockets for cigarettes and lighter, and he has to work hard to strike a flame from the little plastic cylinder. He cusses, shakes it, and finally manages to light his cigarette before stepping down to the cracked pavement and starting to look around for the nearest food outlet. There isn't much here, but across the street appears to be a small strip mall of sorts, and Kel guesses that's his best bet. He heads over, drawing deep on his cigarette and taking in the look of the place. More weathered concrete and flat tar-and-gravel roofs. Long, low buildings that look as if they just slithered off the back of a truck and stuck where they fell. It's a hole, but it's no different from the one he and Toni just climbed out of. There's a fried chicken place on the corner, and Kel blows a spool of smoke into the air before taking a deep breath. Yeah, he can smell oil that's probably been in the fryer for days, but it's colored over with the magic of heavy seasoning and hot, greasy meat. His stomach growls, and he leans up against the nearest wall to finish his smoke before heading in.

The peeling shreds of fliers in bright neon colors speak of bands and DJs that belong to where Kel and Toni are heading to, not where they've come from. Kel scans the names and wonders if they will go all the way. Just get up and go, the way he used to think about doing. It doesn't seem fair, considered in the mundanity of daylight.

Toni's probably on the phone to Danielle already, asking what's going on and telling her where they are, telling her how everything's going. It'd be wrong to take her away from the friends she has back home, the life and all the things she's used to. Damn it, she has another electrolysis appointment in just over a week. They had plans, didn't they? Normal ones. A life they were building, investing in.

Kel doesn't want to be responsible for uprooting that. Anyway, it's not even like they know Michael's dead. If there were gonna be cops, there'd have been cops by now, right? It stands to reason. Kel stubs his cigarette out on the grimy wall behind him, and pinches the butt between his fingers. He didn't do anything wrong. He just defended himself and, if Michael doesn't keep his mouth shut about it, he'll come out of the thing worse than Kel. They can prove shit like that now, right?

Obviously, if he's not dead, Michael's likely to be pretty pissed. There are any number of ways he could make life difficult without involving the cops, but nothing Kel couldn't work around. He supposes, if he thinks hard about it, this could be just the catalyst he needed, just the thing to kick-start him into making some changes for the better. Over the past few months, he and Toni have already made so many changes. They've worked so hard to make a brighter future; something cleaner, something better, no matter what it means giving up. That's the theory, isn't it?

They've tried. Kel's tried. He thought it was working, and now he goes and does something like this…. He feels stupid. Small, useless, and stupid. It's like they've never talked about anything, never really listened to each other. Just pulling back the way they have, into this strange little world—this tight cocoon they share and no one else can intrude on—it's not going to help. Not with the present predicament and, what's worse, it's probably not gonna help Toni.

That realization stings. Everything Kel's done, he's done for Toni. He's sure that's true. He turns a little, flicks the spent cigarette into the overflowing dumpster that stands in the narrow alley between the chicken place and a small, unprepossessing grocery store. They probably didn't even need to flit the way they did. It's just a precaution. Just a day or so, then they'll go home and everything will be like it was… and that's good, isn't it?

Kel takes a breath of spicy, smoggy, chicken-flavored air. Yeah, it's good. But he still feels like he's standing on a knife-edge, and he knows—he's one hundred percent completely, utterly sure—he's thinking about Toni as his top priority in all this, but it isn't Toni's face that keeps floating through his mind.

Kel glances along the sidewalk. Outside the grocery store, there's an old and battered pay phone. Graffiti runs up one side of the plastic shield that curves around it. He ambles over, looking up and down the shabby street.

It has always been about Toni. Everything he's done has been to keep her safe, comfortable, and, as far as it's actually possible, sane. Or at least no crazier than the little freak started out. Kel is sure that's true. It's what he's always told himself, what he's always believed. But is that just because he wanted to? Sure, it feels good to be needed, to be part of something so intense—like they're on their own in the eye of a storm that will only ever happen once—but, just maybe, it's been better for him than it has for Toni.

Kel stares at the pay phone. It's true, really. They only ever think of themselves. Not just people like Dean—or people like the man who Kel's been for more years than he cares to contemplate—but everybody. Each and every person, wrapped up in their own battles, their own lives, magnifying every tiny detail until it's refracted through the prism of its own unimportance and seems like the biggest thing in the world. So busy trying to filter themselves into the people they want to be that nobody ever stops to try and understand anyone else… to put them first and think about what they need, what they want, instead of how it can be given to them in the way that best suits the provider.

Kel swallows grimly. People are selfish fuckers. Especially him. Why did he never think even to note the plate? Why didn't it matter? It shouldn't have to take something like this—like any of this—before he sees his mistakes.

Fishing in his pocket for loose change, he unhooks the receiver. Usually, he'd have to look the number up, but he's been thinking so much about dialing it, and he's come so close in the moments Toni hasn't been looking, that the digits trip pretty easily off his fingers. It's difficult, and not a little painful, to hold the receiver against his ear with his busted hand, but he manages.

The ringing seems to go on for a long while. Kel holds his breath, poised to cut off the call the second any kind of answering machine kicks in. It occurs to him that, in the movies, cops need eight seconds or something to trace a call, but that could have changed. It probably has changed, hasn't it? So much new technology. Not that there's much likelihood of anybody tapping this particular line anyway, but you can never—

"Hello?"

Kel squeezes his eyes tight shut. His stomach is doing backflips, and his head is growing light, yet he has no idea what to say. It's never been anything like this good to hear Michael's voice.

It isn't a good line, but The Sherbet Pervert sounds muzzy and tired, like he's just woken up. There's an element of irritation to his voice when he repeats, "Hello? Who is this?"

Kel holds his breath. He doesn't know whether to reveal himself or not. He's got an unsettling urge to apologize, which is stupid, and he knows he ought to hang up, or at least mutter something about a wrong number, but he doesn't. A small red truck grumbles past, heading down toward the highway and, perhaps, to the sprawling metropolis that lies beyond it. There could be anything out there, Kel supposes.

Michael lets out a breath, and the sound crackles against his ear.

"Look, if this is you… I'm sorry. All right?"

Well, that's definitely not what he expected. Does he know it's Kel, or does he think it's the wife? Kel grips the side of phone booth hard, still not daring to speak. The way it seemed to him that she left, he doubts the former Mrs. Pervert would be calling, so Michael must know it's him, mustn't he?

"I-I wish to God the whole thing had never happened," Michael says, and it truly sounds like he means it.

The distasteful memory of his face folded into snotty threads of tears is still fresh in Kel's mind, and he wrinkles his nose.

"I want to forget it. All of it. I'm hanging up now." He sniffs, and there's a trace of the anger, the bitterness in his tone when he concludes, "Don't call again."

The connection severed, Kel is left staring blankly at the receiver. It's pretty good to know he's not a murderer, but this is still the weirdest feeling. He's barely hung up when the text alert bleeps on his phone, and he fumbles for it, still not used to carrying it in the opposite pocket to where it usually sits. There are only three words on the screen, and that oh so familiar number.

Keep the money.

Kel's not complaining.

TONI DRINKS the cheap, nasty coffee and sits on the cheap, nasty bed, waiting for Kel to come back. Everything does seem different in the daylight, and that's not to say it's better. It's just the difference between soft shapes and jagged outlines, things that are impossible to ignore, where before, he could close his eyes and pretend it was all okay.

Toni knows it's Danielle when his phone bleeps. She must have been sitting on her hands for hours, dying to send a message and find out what's going on. He blinks at the screen. It just reads: *Can you talk?*

Toni messages back yes, and before she could have counted to five, the phone rings.

"Danielle?"

The words come in a torrent, no spaces left for Toni to reply or reassure, and Danielle sounds genuinely panicky.

"Are you okay? Where are you? Is everything all right? Did you get—"

Toni suppresses a smile. It would be endearing if it didn't smack so much of Danielle not liking to lose control.

"We're fine. Got to the motel late last... well, early this morning. Kel's getting, uh, lunch," she corrects, glancing at the clock on the nightstand. "Everything's okay, I promise. It's nice, actually. Kinda. Always said we were gonna go away someplace."

Danielle's short burst of breath is not a chuckle, however much Toni would like to pretend that's what it was. He clears his throat.

"So, what's going on there? Have you, uh, heard anything?"

"Ye—well, not really. It's more a case of not hearing," Danielle says vaguely. "But, they've identified that guy from the embankment."

"Oh?"

Toni doesn't say anything else, not wanting to let on the fact Kel knew him. That much was obvious when they were waiting for the bus, when the TV flashed up the boy's image.... Toni had looked away, desperate to avoid remembering those awful minutes in the morgue, the dead flesh and the smell of bleach. But, in turning, she caught sight of the expression in Kel's eyes. He squelched it real fast, but it was there. That fleeting moment of recognition, of pain, and fear. She thought she knew then why he was afraid, but now she's not so sure.

"Yeah." Danielle's voice cuts through Toni's thoughts, derailing them and dragging her uncomfortably back to the present. "But the news people screwed up. He was Puerto Rican, I think they said, not black. Or half-Puerto Rican, or... I don't know. Julio Cordero, or something. Had his brother on, making an appeal for information. It was awful."

Numbed by that, Toni has trouble thinking of anything to say. It's all too easy to imagine what that must be like for the brother, for the family as a whole. She can't stop thinking about the body in the morgue; all those terrible, aching seconds that seemed to stretch out into boundless nothingness. Waiting, half-convinced it was going to be Kel under that sheet, yet refusing to believe it, too afraid to give in to the fear... too fucking angry to let it be true.

Danielle had really believed it would be him. It was one of the reasons Toni didn't want her in there. Like she believed so strongly, that belief could have changed things, made it so it really was Kel on the gurney.

Toni knows that's not true. It's a stupid thing to think, and it's not fair to Danielle.

"I bet it was," she says, though she still feels kind of numb.

Toni checks the clock again, eager for Kel to come back. He said he wouldn't be long. She doesn't want him to be long. She wants him home. Back. Whatever.

Danielle's asking questions now, about the room, the motel, about the journey, and about when Toni thinks they'll head home.

"I can call Karen for you before Tuesday and cover if you need it. Say you're sick or something. Unless you think you'll be back by then. D'you think...?"

"Don't know," Toni mumbles.

That's the problem. They didn't think this through. They just ran.

She'd do it again, of course. Anything, if Kel needed it. And, Toni has to admit, it does feel kind of invigorating to be somewhere totally new, somewhere outside of the rut of everyday life.

That's not fair, Toni knows. Life hasn't *all* been a rut. It's been good. Kel's done so much for her, and so has Danielle. Sure, things have changed, but they're changing for the better, aren't they?

"Well, you'll let me know, won't you?"

There's a wheedling note in Danielle's voice. Toni guesses she's getting nervous. She smiles, warmed by a flush of affection.

"Of course. It's all right. We're just gonna…. It's just a couple of days. It's all right. Actually, it could prolly be kind of nice. Just us."

"Hm. I guess."

Danielle seems doubtful, but that doesn't bother Toni. It's surprisingly easy, when there's tens of miles between them, for Danielle's opinions to fade into inconsequence, and that's a pretty pleasurable feeling. Toni smiles to herself, teeth pinching her lower lip.

"It's not going to be long. Don't worry. I mean, it's not like we're totally bailing on everything. There's the apartment, friends, work… we'll be back really soon. It's not—" Toni stops, suddenly not entirely sure who she's trying to convince. Things really do feel different this morning. She clears her throat. "So, uh, tell me more about what they're saying on TV. I haven't seen the news."

Danielle talks, relays everything that's happened. People have asked her about them, once or twice. Asked if Kel's okay, if they've heard about the Latino kid. Word is that there have been cops showing up at the bus station, asking questions and trying to trace Julio's last movements. People say it's completely wrecking business. No arrest has been made. She makes it seem like gossip, but Danielle still sounds a little stiff and angry to Toni. It's hard to know quite why.

Eventually—Toni having promised that they'll see her soon, and telling her not to worry—she hangs up. Toni sits there for a while, picking at the faded floral pattern on the bedspread with one idle finger. Thoughts curl all over the place, tendrils of confusion and misty indecision. He glances down, frowns at that thin-fingered bony hand of his. The gel nails need redoing. One is chipped, two loosened at the joins from all the carrying of bags and schlepping around the bus station.

He flexes both hands out in front of him, studies them as if it's the first time he's ever seen them. They're funny things. Possibly the only part of your own body it's acceptable to stare at in public, apart from feet, and those have nails too, right? Only nails aren't for staring at. They're for studying. That's the word. It's one of those words that has weight to it, weight and meaning. Toni thinks a lot about words like that, how one little collection of letters can represent so many different things to people, or can carry with it an entire lifetime of goals, responsibilities, expectations, and more.

Yeah, you *study* your nails. Women can acceptably file them, paint them... make this whole performance of changing the way their nails look, and do it in public, if they want. They can go to nail bars and make that kind of grooming a social event, a rite of status and shit like that, which men can't. Not in the same way.

Men's nails are supposed to be clean and square, broad and honest and well-groomed. A man is judged by his handshake. Toni remembers how his father used to say that. His father would shake another man's hand and clap him on the arm as he did it, smile and laugh, and he'd have this grip that could choke a kitten. Just nodding and smiling while he crushed your hand, like he knew he was hurting and he thought it was funny.

Toni blinks. He used to bite his nails when he was a boy. His mother nagged about it, said they'd be ugly and weak when he grew up if he didn't stop it. She used to paint this horrible stuff on them, worse than hot sauce, and it was supposed to make sure he left them alone but it never did. Toni would forget he'd got it on, and then he'd absently put a finger near his mouth and it would sting so bad he wanted to cry, scream, or throw up.

They weren't bad people, his parents. Sometimes, Toni wonders where they are now, but the flashes of interest don't tend to last long. They weren't bad people and, fuck, they probably did love him in their own way—at some point, at least—but they never understood him. They never understood, and they didn't want to try.

He remembers, when he was a little kid, his father getting mad at him. Mad because he was a sissy, because he didn't want to play baseball or something—something stupid that didn't matter—and somehow that got him mad at Toni's mom, as if it was *her* fault, and then they'd both be fighting over him. Yelling. Hitting.

He stayed out of it, and he just felt betrayed. He didn't know why it was wrong to feel like he did, or to like what he liked. When he played with girls, *that* was wrong too, and apparently it was also wrong to hang around with older boys... basically everything Toni ever did was wrong, and every attempt he ever made to be himself was an embarrassment.

They were like different species, him and his dad. And, after his mom faded into that vague fog of painkillers and depression, there was nobody to stand between them. It was like a war on the surface of an alien planet, first contact with disputes over the mineral rights. Toni was just a kid, and he didn't know what to say, how to explain. He couldn't talk about it, couldn't make the words make sense—couldn't put a kid's words to the things he didn't even understand himself—and so they came out messed up. They came out in the ways he acted up, acted out... got himself in trouble.

It's something he hasn't thought about, he supposes. Toni guesses it's a flaw, a crack in the plan, and he hasn't wanted to probe at any of those. Danielle says she never remembers a time that, as a child, she didn't feel as if there was something wrong. Once she worked out what it was, she used to say things like that all the time, even though no one ever listened. She was sent for all kinds of counseling, at first at the school and then by her parents, but none of the shrinks listened. Not the way people are starting to listen to kids now.

Toni doesn't remember having the words for it, or the feelings. He flexes his fingers again and stares at—and *studies*—those damaged nails.

He doesn't remember wanting to grow them long when he was a kid. Not to primp and polish and paint. The chili paint didn't stop him biting, and his father had said painting 'em would turn the kid into a fag, and then of course it blew up into an argument, the way things so often did.

He remembers putting some of his mother's nail polish on for the first time, though. Brick-red. Dark, dramatic, and bold. Sitting there, at her vanity table, looking at the mirror and the bottles. The big powder puff that smelled of sweet lavender, sitting atop its little china stand, with the tray of jewel-like lipsticks and polishes to the side. Toni took one, unscrewed the top, and sniffed that sharp, bittersweet odor. It was amazing, at the time, to find how thick the stuff was, how easily it went on. Thick, gloopy drops that spread across the surface of his brittle, fractured nails. Filling in the cracks, disguising the damage, and covering over all that pale imperfection with one glorious slash of color.

Bright, bold, blood red.

My, my. And don't we look pretty today?

Mom's nail polish and a tight pair of jeans. It's funny the things you remember.

Toni rises from the bed, snatches up the wash bag with the pink daisies on it from the nightstand, and stalks purposefully into the bathroom.

CHAPTER
FOURTEEN

KEL KNOCKS softly on the door of the room and thinks he hears Toni's muffled voice call out. He pushes the door open, bag of fried chicken clutched between his chest and his bad hand, and that deliciously spicy, greasy smell wafts up all around him.

He can't stop smiling.

The view from this little pool of habitation doesn't amount to much. There's nothing to see except the highway, the acres of road that, once, must have seemed new and exciting but now, like so many other good intentions, have grown cracked and dirty. In the far distance, the quills of tall buildings prickle at the horizon. From the air, the remnants of an industrial past long perished must be visible, a dozen sprawling towns and cities—very much like the one Kel and Toni have just left—strewn across a patchwork of what would once have been solely crops and pasture.

Now, there doesn't seem to be a great deal of difference between the towns and the routes that cut through them. Everything congeals at the feet of the metropolis beyond. Yet, for all that, the sun is warm and it colors the air gold, like honey. The sound of birds is audible behind the buzz of traffic and, occasionally, tiny airplanes chalk jet trails across a bright blue sky.

Kel's almost whistling as he comes into the room. He's cheerful beyond reason, buoyed up with the sense of having done a good thing. He isn't sure he ought to tell Toni about the calls he's made, but whatever Toni doesn't know won't hurt him, right?

"Hey," he calls, as the door catches behind him. "I got chicken. They had those spicy popcorn bits like you like, so I... Toni? Where you at, baby?"

There's movement in the bathroom doorway, and Kel glances up, the greasy paper bag still crumpled against his body, the food's aroma wrapping itself all around him. Spots of neon blue mar his vision, and the room is dark and faded after the bright sunlight outside. At first, he thinks his mind's playing tricks on him, but it's not that. It's real.

Strange and unexpected, but real.

"Good," Toni says, one hand on the chipped white paint of the bathroom doorframe. "I'm hungry."

"Oh, God," Kel murmurs, before he can stop himself.

He hasn't seen his honey look like this for a long while. His clothes are baggy sweats, the sleeves of one of Kel's shirts pushed up to his elbows and flopping over in loose folds. Though it obscures the lines of his body, it can't hide his elegance, the way he's leaning up on the jamb like Elizabeth Taylor in *BUtterfield 8*... one of those old flicks they've sat on the couch and watched together so many times. But the long nails are gone.

The ends of Toni's fingers look red and slightly pruned, and Kel supposes he must have had to work to get them off, which is weird, because usually Toni's all about eking out every last day she can get without having to fix or file or infill, all those little bottles of powder and paint that Kel doesn't understand. His nails—his real nails—are brittle and peeling, slightly yellowed, and very short. But they're not the strangest thing.

Kel's gaze travels up his lover's body, up the beat-up old shirt with the Atlanta logo on the front, letters peeling in green, and he meets such fierce determination in Toni's face.

He looks amazing. No makeup, no "little touch" of concealer to mask a zit or hide a late night, the way he so often starts the day, and the way that so often ends up in what seems to Kel like a half-inch layer of pancake. Toni's eyes are dark and shadowed, his mouth half-furled, and Kel sees in him all the sharpness, the hard edges and the angles that were there the first day they met. He just didn't expect the short hair. How the hell has he done it? It must have been nail scissors or something like that. Kel pictures him standing in front of the blotchy mirror, next to those mildewed tiles, lopping off curl after curl that he'd spent so long growing... what the fuck is this about?

He knows he's staring, but he can't look away, and he can't bring himself to ask the questions that bundle themselves so heavily on his tongue, tying it up in threads of confused apprehension.

It's not that Toni's hair doesn't suit him short. It stands out in rough spikes, fuzzy and tousled. What, worn long, are softly curled tresses have become barely tamed coils, roughly hacked and reshaped. Was it a spur of the moment thing, Kel wonders, some attempt to chop off everything that's gone wrong?

Paring it all away, cutting out all the rot.

It doesn't seem like that. Toni is too calm, too confident for that to have been why he did it. He just looks at Kel for a while, and neither of them speaks. Kel doesn't know what to say. The tightly formed curls naturally cluster at Toni's temples and forehead, giving him the air of some smoky-eyed Grecian prince or debauched Art Deco film star. The corner of his mouth twitches, and Kel takes a breath, like he's coming up for air. Maybe he did forget to breathe for a second there.

"It took you months to grow all that out," he says, and he knows it's kind of a pointless, useless comment to make.

"Yeah." Toni shrugs. "But it'll grow again."

"Why—"

Toni's gaze tracks over his face, and Kel shivers. He doesn't understand what's going on, but it's something big. Toni eases forward, takes the chicken from him, and heads over to the bed, already opening up the bag and peeking inside.

"Ooh! Popcorn chicken! Love you," he adds, looking over his shoulder and smiling.

It's a distracting image, but Kel blinks, determined not to be sidetracked.

"Toni, what—"

His honey sits on the edge of the bed, curly head bent over the bag, picking out pack after greasy card-and-paper pack with his shorn fingers and setting them down on the nightstand.

"I was thinking," Toni says, and he pauses to glance up at Kel, sucking his thumb clean. "After what's happened—you know how shit makes you think, right? I was thinking about the stuff you said. About… well, if you were never around to say it again."

He runs his tongue over his lower lip, and the pain is clear in his eyes. Kel exhales slowly, comes to sit beside Toni on the bed. His knees apart, Kel links his fingers and lets them dangle, arms propped on his thighs, shoulders hunched forward. He's all ready to duck and cover, like that's gonna be any defense against anything.

"Uh-huh?"

He knows what Toni's getting at. The past few months have been hard, a lot of the time. Harder than anybody should have to take. So often, he'd thought—hell, they'd *both* thought—that they were gonna hit the point where they couldn't go on, for one reason or another. And yet, twenty-four stupid little hours have turned everything upside down.

It's funny how shit does make you think.

Kel opens his mouth, wanting to assure Toni that he's always going to be here to say dumb things… even the unkind, thoughtless ones he shouldn't have said in the first place.

"I didn't mean that you should—"

"Lemme finish," Toni says, but he doesn't snap, the way he usually does when Kel interrupts. He sounds positively calm, which is weird. "You didn't make my mind up for me. Nobody has. I just got thinking, and I ended up thinking that maybe you had a point, when you said I wasn't—y'know. That maybe… maybe what I've been doing hasn't been right for me. That I rushed in. Remember how you tried to say that? Well, I guess I can see it now."

Kel nods slowly, unable to escape the feeling that he's being set up for something.

"Uh… huh?"

"You were right, baby," Toni says simply, and Kel would really like that in writing, because then he could frame it and hang it on the wall. "You were right. I'm not like Danielle. I'm not…. It's never gonna be the way it is with her for me."

That's a bombshell. Kel frowns, confused.

"What? So, you're saying, after all this time, all the pills, you don't think you wanna—?"

"No! No, not like that. Fuck…. I knew you'd make this difficult."
Toni shoots a breath across his teeth and shakes his head, staring down
at the carpet. "It's not like that. It's… it's more complicated. I probably
shouldn't have—"

"Nuh-uh."

Kel reaches out, and closes his left hand over Toni's knuckles.
His skin feels cool to the touch, though the room is warm to the point
of being stuffy. Kel doesn't turn his head, doesn't look at him, because
he knows how much harder it'll be on both of them if he does. He just
wants his honey to know he's here, and that it's all right to say
whatever needs to be said. He frowns again as he studies the grease
stains on the far wall.

"Go on," he adds, and he takes Toni's hand in his and gives it a
gentle squeeze.

The slender fingers flutter briefly in his grasp, but then they still,
like birds coming to rest.

"Thanks," Toni says, his voice low in his throat. He takes a
breath, and it seems to catch a little before he speaks again, as if the
words are hard to say. "It's just that… I feel like I'm not matching up
so much of the time, and I've been so used to thinking that's just *me*,
but then I thought: what if it's not? What if it's just because it's not
who I am?"

He exhales again, and Kel sneaks a sidelong look at his lover.
Toni seems tired, but not frightened, not beaten down. The slender stalk
of the first green shoot that forces its way through the snow—
regardless of whether spring is ready to come or not—cannot be so
easily trampled.

"Then you don't wanna go through with it…? I don't
understand."

"Nah." Toni shakes his head. "It still feels right. When I dress…
when I look like that, I feel right. I feel good. But it's not…. The
surgery and all that shit? I don't want it. I don't even think I wanna
stick with the hormones. I've been thinking—fuck, I thought I'd been
thinking before, but that was fucking *nothing*, baby…. I don't need it.
And it's about need, y'know? About needing to be who you are. And
I'm not…."

He stops short of actually saying it. Kel can't help smiling.

"A girl?"

Toni pulls a face, like a wince, and Kel worries for a moment, thinking he's caused yet more pain, but his honey just shakes her head.

"No. And yeah. You know? I… I'm *me*, baby. It's like… I can do girl mode, I can do guy mode, but every time I pick one I'm shuttin' something off. I… I don't know. It's really hard to explain…."

Toni's fingers twitch within his grasp again, and Kel holds on. He's always gonna hold on and, when Toni's shoulders shift slightly, like he's suppressing a shiver, Kel leans closer, just to share a little of his warmth with her. He turns his face to the side and, quietly, he leans his cheek on Toni's arm.

Toni takes a breath and holds it. For a moment, everything seems still, and Kel's pretty sure he can feel the maelstrom inside her. It's a little bit like when the bad panics come, and he's sat on so many floors, beds, and bathtubs, holding Toni's hand and counting him through deep breaths and unbearable fear, like the world's ending and he's gonna die, and everything around him isn't real. Kel's never known why him being there has helped, but Toni says it does. Maybe it helps now.

"My whole life," Toni says softly, "it was like I couldn't do it right. Being a guy. I wasn't what I was supposed to be, y'know?"

Kel nods, his mouth crumpled against the fabric of the sweatshirt Toni's wearing. That's pretty familiar territory for him. He remembers when his aunt and uncle threw him out, and how Aunt Gina blamed him for everything. How she made those awful noises when she cried, like an animal's bellows of rage.

"I feel the same as a girl," Toni says. "And it's, like… well, what if I'm not doing it wrong? Maybe it's about doing it *my* way. I mean, Danielle says—"

Kel doesn't tense up, or even smile at those words, but Toni breaks off anyway, and then he's the one who's chuckling gently and shaking his head.

"Hm, I know. I know. But it's true, all right? Danielle says, who says a girl can't have a short haircut, or a dick, or wear pants? There's no one way to be a person, no one way to do it right… because there isn't any *right*. And… and sayin' you don't wanna fit the way someone says you should be, that doesn't mean you've got to fit another... thing. Stereotype," he adds, mildly irritable as he waves his free hand at the air, like he's pulling the word out of it. "And I think, maybe, that's what I am. I'm not like Danielle, but I don't blame her for encouraging me, y'know? Because she thinks everything is so simple. She doesn't see all the... the gray areas between things."

Kel says nothing. He's often thought that the ice queen—for all her helpline volunteering and all the sage advice she thrusts down Toni's throat—has been too quick to judge, too quick to disparage anything that doesn't fit with the way she views the world. Toni squeezes his fingers gently, and his hand feels small and almost frail in Kel's grasp.

"She listened to me. When I said I wanted to be a woman, she accepted that completely and, you know, nobody has ever fucking listened to me like that before."

Toni's voice takes on a slightly harder edge then, and Kel keeps looking at the stains on the wall, aware that maybe he hasn't been the anchor he should have been for his honey. Toni doesn't seem to blame him, though, so that's something.

"But... maybe that wasn't what I needed," Toni says quietly. "Maybe I wanted it to be, because it's not like transitioning is *easy*, but fuck... maybe it would have been an answer. You know? But it hasn't felt like one. It's not... *I'm* not... I mean, I'm not like her. I... I'm *me*."

He hushes suddenly on the heels of those words, and it's probably the longest, most coherent thing Kel has ever heard him say about himself, about his gender, and about where he wants to be in the world. Toni lets out a small, short breath, and Kel feels his fingers curl in a little bit, like a crab tensing up inside its shell.

"So," Kel says, sitting up but not moving away, and sure as hell not letting go of his honey's hand, "you don't want to take the pills?"

Toni shrugs. "I don't know. Maybe. I... I think you were right."

Kel blinks in surprise because, holy shit, that's twice in one day Toni's said those words, and it must mean the apocalypse is coming.

"I think I was looking for answers instead of questions. I think I wanted those answers to be, I don't know, clear-cut or something. Like Danielle said... how she always knew what she needed to fix. But I don't think it's the same for me. I think... I think maybe I ought to talk to somebody," Toni admits, his voice dropping to a barely audible murmur. "Start from there. Take it slow, quit rushing. Quit expecting everything to make sense at once because, you know, things *don't* sometimes. And that's... that's okay."

He exhales slowly, and Kel's not sure there isn't some panic there. He nudges Toni's shoulder with his own.

"Hey. You can still be my girl, though, right?"

Toni blinks and looks at him in surprise. "Huh?"

"What?" Kel shrugs, smiling softly. "Yeah, I think of you like that. From time to time. You've always been my honey, and you're always gonna be beautiful to me. Whatever, man. Whatever you do. You're who you are, T.," he says, squeezing his hand tight to emphasize his meaning. "Isn't that all that matters? They're only words."

He knows it's trite, knows that oversimplistic way of putting it doesn't make anything any easier. Toni grins at him, though, and for a few seconds Kel thinks he's made an impact.

"You thought of me as your... really?"

"A'ight." Kel curls his lip. "Yeah, maybe a couple of times. It—I dunno. Look, you know what? I don't look at you and think of a guy or a girl. I think of you as *you*, stupid. Panties or whatever. It doesn't matter."

Toni's smile is infectious, laughter threatening to spill over both of them and wipe away the intensity of the seriousness. Kel tugs on the hand he still holds, pulls Toni close into an awkward, messy hug. His honey giggles, all the tension broken, and they're holding each other, a nest of arms and elbows.

"So, what's this mean, huh? With the pills? You're not gonna just stop 'em?"

Toni's warm against him, and it's so tempting to just agree with whatever he says, to let him get away with anything, so long as he doesn't move away. Toni shakes his head.

"You were the one who said hormone spikes aren't good for the body."

Kel busses the top of his honey's head, and those curls tickle his lips, the dry, blunt ends of hairs crisp on his mouth. "I did. Huh. But...."

"I'm going to find another doctor. Start reducing the schedule, come back down again, and find someone to talk to... like everybody kept bitchin' at me to do. But don't think it means I think you're all right," Toni adds, digging his fingers into Kel's thigh. "I'm not saying I don't want to do any of it, that none of it's me. Just that, maybe, I've rushed into a few things. *Maybe*."

Kel breathes deeply, inhales the smell of Toni's hair. There's no victory in it. Kel's just glad that he seems so bright, so happy, so... calm. It's still weird. Not a word—not an emotional state—that he associates with Toni.

It's true, though, isn't it? They're only words.

THEY TALK for a long while after that, cross-legged on the bed, eating fried chicken out of the little card boxes, and Toni scoops coleslaw up with his fingers, and feels so at ease with himself. In among the soul-baring and the confessions, Kel's tentative inquiries probe at the walls he's worked so hard to build. Toni answers as best he can, even when the questions rub at the raw seams of things he doesn't want to talk about.

It is true. Words are just words, but the meanings they carry, the way the world bends around them, that's what's complicated. It doesn't mean a woman can't have a dick, though. Sex and gender aren't the same thing, and there's no black-and-white binary line, no rule that says he has to pick a side because the other one doesn't want him.

It's a long, complicated road, but it's easier to walk down without all the labels.

As the day turns to evening, the summer heat rubbing off the brick and concrete outside, they take a walk. Just to stretch legs stiff from so long sitting, and to breathe air that isn't filtered through the motel room's dusty curtains. Kel has his arm crooked around Toni's neck, and Toni slips his hand into the back pocket of his lover's jeans. A car passes, heading down toward the slip road and the highway. It's full of college kids and beer cans, and one of the young guys rolls down his window and screams "Faggots!" as they drive past. An empty can is hurled from the car, and it clatters on the sidewalk, bouncing against the nearest brick wall. Those boys are terrible shots.

Toni's still wearing Kel's sloppy sweats and, for a moment, he stiffens, his mouth half-open to hurl back some choice invective. But the car flies past, and he just blows a kiss at its retreating tail lights. It doesn't need to matter. Not now. That doesn't make it right… but it doesn't make it important either. Fuck 'em. Fuck everybody.

Beside him, Kel seems proud. He kisses Toni's cheek. Toni knows what he's done; calling Michael, checking up on what Danielle said about how things looked okay at his place. They *are* okay, and Toni is so grateful for that, so fucking glad it isn't hanging over them, this crime of potential. They've been so lucky. Kel confessed he'd made the call—told the truth even though he thought Toni would be pissed he'd done it. That was probably brave, even if Toni can't really dredge up the anger anymore. Sure, he'd have been furious if Kel had made the call the night they left, when everything really seemed as if it could still kick off, as if there might be police there to trace numbers, hunt them down.

Maybe Toni just watches too many cop shows. Right now, in the mellowing evening light, it doesn't seem as if it was ever plausible. They'd probably never even needed to flit, but he's so fucking pleased they did. A weight seems to have lifted from Toni, and it feels good to know that, right now, there are no expectations. No demands, no pressures… nobody wants Toni to be anything other than Toni, whatever that actually ends up entailing.

There's plenty of time to address that issue. It doesn't usually feel like time is something they have that much of, but these few snatches of it, these furtive stolen days and hours, they ooze by at the speed of molasses, and that's good.

They don't have to go home yet. There's time. Toni doesn't have to show her face at the bookstore until Tuesday, and Kel has no pressing appointments. Danielle is likely to be furious. About the hair, about the pills… about a lot of things, Toni imagines, but that can all be dealt with later. Chances are, he's been listening to Danielle too much, despite everything he owes her. It's not her fault—and maybe the dying breath of the troll voice says it's what people get for taking him seriously, because he's too dumb to even know his own mind—but maybe she has been too quick to push him down the only road she thinks is right. They'll talk about it when Toni gets back. He hopes she won't be too mad.

All the same, as their feet echo tandem rhythms on the sidewalk, and the sun slips behind the concrete walls, Toni does miss girl mode. There's a certain confidence that comes with dressing that way which leaves a huge hole behind it when it isn't there. It's not like being naked, and it's not like Toni doesn't feel right without kitten heels and skinny-fit jeans, but it does leave him... vulnerable.

Toni thinks about it as they walk, heading back toward the motel now the evening's getting later. It's hard to remember actually making the decision, or seizing one single moment as the point where the process of change—or at least the pledge to do it—would start. Toni recalls all the other feelings that messed things up at the same time, and that had done so for years. Being so angry, so frustrated, so confused. It's hard to talk about what you want when you don't know what it is yourself, and you have no real way of learning.

Kel always says that's what mistakes are for.

The last streaks of sunlight flare over the tarmac and grit, and the shallow breeze that comes with passing cars and cooling air ruffles through Toni's shortened curls. It feels good.

The more Toni thinks about it, this whole deal has never been about being a guy thing or a girl thing. It's comfort, it's freedom, it's confidence... and why should that have to be split down the middle? Why should it have to be so that there's guys or girls, and you have to choose which side of the line you stand on? It makes no sense. It's like, there's only male or female, inside, and if you don't feel right one way then you must be the other.

Okay, maybe a lot of people *do* fit like that, but what if you don't? What if it's too complicated to say you're this, or you're that, and you're not the other? It's like there's no cushion, no soft place to fall along the line, and it's as if there's a tightrope that runs between the two.

You choose, or you're a freak.

That's tough. Toni reasons it shouldn't be easy, because important things rarely are, but it still sucks. It sucks to have everyone wanting you to pick a side, saying you're either lying or you're in denial somehow if you don't... the way Danielle has been known to talk about people who resist definition.

Nevertheless, Toni has to admit that it's worth taking the time to go back to the beginning, probably. Taking these lessons and not rushing with them... and that pisses him off, when it's what so many people have said before. That he ought to speak to somebody, that he ought to do this, or that. It's such shit. Toni always thought that. It wasn't right that they all just said the same stuff over and over again. They don't know him, they don't live in his head, so how would they know?

Toni hates accepting that anyone's right.

Yet, bitter as it is, admitting it is a relief, and it doesn't spoil tonight. Especially not when Kel unlocks the door to their room and—though neither of them speak—Toni feels the heat in his gaze. A year ago, back in the familiar alleyways, stairwells, and landings that marked their courtship, he'd have grabbed Kel or Kel would've grabbed on to him, and one of them would have found himself pressed up hard against a wall. There would have been lips, hands, tongues... rough skin and smooth skin, and it wouldn't have stopped until daybreak.

Right now, Kel leans in and kisses the end of Toni's nose.

"Hey. You're still my honey. You know that?"

"Mm-hm." Toni can't hold back a smile. "I know it."

Kel winks, and they head inside.

After taking his turn with the narrow, mildewed shower cubicle, and leaving Kel to the bathroom on his own, Toni slips into bed. He turns off the light and waits, watching the way shadows snake over things, curling their way into the corners and recesses.

At last, Kel comes in. Toni turns over when he hears him leave the bathroom, pulling the covers up to his chin and feigning sleep. Kel gets in, grunts with satisfaction. He smells of soap and warm cotton, and he makes all the bad things seem as inconsequential as flies.

He made another call on that pay phone. He didn't want to tell Toni about it while they were walking, but he did. He told her about how he thinks he knows who's responsible for the Latino kid. A dark-red Honda Accord, a guy with thinning, sandy hair and a sharp chin, and an ugly, sour voice that talks about hurting, about choking.

Toni didn't want to hear it. Kel never talks about tricks, but he did tonight. He says he's not going to do it anymore. Not the same way. When they get home, they're gonna take a serious look at everything, at every fucking aspect of their lives, and they're going to fix them all up. Because you can only get lucky so many times. There are only so many chances. And it's not forever. It was never meant to be forever.

You take that fucking dick, slut. Choke on that fucking cock, you piece of garbage. You're nothing. You hear me? You're filth.

Kel looked like he had tears in his eyes when he spoke of it, though it could just have been the way the sunset touched his face.

Maybe it'll help somebody. Who knows? Maybe the cops'll find the guy, and they'll make sure he doesn't hurt anybody else. Toni supposes that stranger things have happened. Maybe The Sherbet Pervert will find someone to fall in love with, or maybe he'll dig up some other woman to lie to, and some other boy in dirty gym socks to lighten his lonely hours.

Maybe....

Toni opens his eyes and stares at the dark wall. The cracks in it are softened by shadows. Just maybe, Danielle will understand. Because they're still there—all his tensions, his confusions, and the mess of things he knows he has to sort out, like the ends of twine and rubber bands left tangled in a drawer—bubbling away beneath the surface. But time is a wonderful thing. And distance. This quiet, islanded silence, empty but for the sound of his breathing, and Kel's, it makes so much seem clearer. Like a lens, distilling everything down to its most basic parts.

Toni's right there when Kel reaches for him. He stays soft and pliant, rolling over to meet his lover's body, tip to toe, when Kel pulls him close. Broad, hard fingers skim the blind paths of warm skin and soft flesh.

"You're not wearing a stitch," Kel murmurs, as if he's surprised.

He has an old T-shirt on, and boxers, in defiance of the night's warmth, but Toni is completely bare, completely smooth and naked.

"Nope." She slides her hand under Kel's shirt, seeking the dark nub of his nipple. "Saves on laundry, huh?"

"These sheets are probably filthy," Kel says doubtfully.

Toni can feel his eagerness to close the last little piece of distance between them. Kel's minty breath grazes his face ever closer, and Toni loves the way that little crux of flesh hardens beneath the gentle pinching of her insistent fingers.

"I can be filthier," she whispers, and lands a soft kiss on his lips.

The trace of a smile curves Kel's mouth, half-hidden in the shadows, but there's nothing dirty about it. His eyes seem to shine, and the flash of a car's headlamps in the parking lot pierces the thin drapes, dancing over his skin. For a moment, Toni thinks he's going to say he loves him, and he wants to say it back. He presses closer, as if the words can ease their way through the barriers of skin and imprint themselves right onto Kel's bones.

Kel doesn't say it, though. He catches Toni's lips against his, and then he mumbles words that are less expected into the dark, damp place between their mouths, where kisses wait to be birthed and promises are too easily made.

"Doesn't matter... y'know?"

"Hm?" Toni closes his eyes.

He both knows and doesn't know, wants to hear and does not want. Is and isn't.

It's a complicated place to be.

"Whatever you do," Kel murmurs, emphasizing the words with a comforting squeeze. "Whatever you decide. Whether you go all the way, or if you stop. Whatever you wanna do, however you wanna live... I'll be there. Always."

He means it, Toni realizes. And the things he says—the things he tries to express, in the dark and the quiet, where there's nothing to drown out for the first time in so long—are beautiful. It doesn't matter, he says, what form Toni's gender takes, or how it changes things. And it will. Their relationship will change, and he'll change too, but he's not gonna break. *They're* not gonna break. Toni can be whatever he damn well wants to be, and it's not going to change the stuff that really matters.

What's really real.

Toni can't listen to too much more of it. Kel's voice opens up small, aching places inside him, and leaves him so hungry, so desperate. He slides on top of Kel and straddles his lap, cleaving tight and trailing tiny kisses along his jaw, neck, chest.... With some difficulty, despite Kel's cooperation, Toni manages to pull the T-shirt off and he tries to get Kel's underwear down—which is easier started than finished. There's smothered laughter, clashing of noses, knees, and elbows, and it's an intimacy, a relief.

At last, Kel's naked enough to have Toni pressed completely against him, bare and warm. Toni rocks slowly, chafes their cocks together in an irresistible rhythm, his lips fastened to Kel's. He doesn't hold back on the vocals either, because he knows how hot they get Kel: that succession of little "unh" sounds that seem to break softly from his mouth as if he doesn't mean them to, as if he's just a little embarrassed at how much it all turns him on. It works, just like it always does, even if it's only a little bit true.

He's never been embarrassed at all.

Kel's fingers curl, just their very tips skimming over Toni's back and shoulders, tracing lines down his spine, circling his ass. He loves those featherlight touches, and quivers back against them, never once breaking pace.

IN THE grainy, shifting darkness, its edges pierced by the orange glow of the lights in the parking lot, they make love. Kel may not fully understand what's changed for Toni, but he supposes he has to accept it, and he can't pretend he dislikes it.

It's what he's been saying for so long, isn't it? That he'll support whatever choice his honey makes, but he doesn't believe—he's never believed—that Toni was headed down the right road. He has a journey ahead of him, Kel's sure, but maybe it's not that tight, linear program he talked so much about. There's more to who he is, where he's been, and the things that have fucked him up than what just a few short years of transition could change. It might be a part of the medicine, but it's sure as hell not the whole cure.

Kel supposes, if Toni follows through and actually does get his ass down to a therapist, they have a whole lot to look forward to on that score… but he can't devote too much thought to it right now. Not when each jar, each bump of their hardening flesh is knocking back through his body, and he can't think of anything else except the pleasure and the potential. Kel kind of wants to fuck Toni, hard, to just pin him down and do him until the sky bursts, but he wants everything else too. Every possibility, every permutation, all at once.

Toni sighs and rolls off him. Kel knows he hasn't come, so he's not sure what's going on for a second, until Toni props himself up on one elbow, looking down at him in the gloom. A knowing smile on his face, he licks a stripe down his palm, then reaches down. His hand fastens around Kel's shaft, and he strokes gently, that incredible grip molding itself to every available inch of cock. Kel draws a breath through his nostrils, closes his eyes… feels Toni's lips on his neck. It's a gift he doesn't mind accepting.

It goes real slow, because Toni's far too good at bringing him to the brink and then taking him back. It's like he knows Kel's body better than Kel does himself and—if he wasn't so focused on the way this feels—that might scare him. Equally, it might not. Right now, in the darkness, with just the occasional pale sweep of headlights from a car coming in or out of the parking lot to break the shadows, it doesn't seem like it could be frightening. It's comforting, in a way.

Toni touches something right at the pit of Kel's gut, and drags the feeling up through his body. Heat floods him, but it's not a heat of desperation. It's lazy, like sunbathing in July, and he can reach for Toni's jaw and pull him close, taste him. Caresses draw hot swirls across his balls, his inner thighs, and then back to his shaft. The head of his cock, wet with want, rubs Toni's palm in an exquisite friction that's over way too fast, because Toni wants to draw this out. Kel's hips twitch in needy, pleading movements, but he won't do it, he won't give in and just jack him hell-for-leather.

"Cocktease," Kel mumbles against his mouth.

Toni smiles. "You love it."

Kel moves to touch him, but Toni pushes his hand away.

"Nn-nn. This is about you."

Kel's not gonna argue with that. He lets his hand settle on Toni's waist, just between the jut of a hip and the slim valleys of ribs above it, barely padded with flesh.

Toni sets to work again, and now he seems determined, his grip tightening, his strokes ever firmer. Kel hears himself groan, suspects he may have begged. It doesn't matter. Toni knows just how he wants it, and that's what he gets. He walks the edge of the void, teetering between falling back and falling in, until he's thrusting into Toni's hand and breathing hard, his cock twitching impatiently. Toni kisses his neck and takes him past the brink, coaxing him through a climax that seems to last forever, catching on to the tail of every wisp of sensation and pushing it through, until Kel feels dizzy with it.

He doesn't stop there. His strokes just get slower, longer, slicker, and Kel slams his head back against the pillow, breathless and teeth gritted. It's more than he can take, pleasure that verges on pain, hypersensitive and overintense.

"Toni... quit it, baby."

Toni chuckles, teases a little more, touches a little more, not satisfied until he makes Kel squeak and flinch.

"Bastard," Kel mutters, pushes his hands away, hard, and rolls over, meaning to pin Toni beneath him.

He reaches down, wants to give Toni a taste of his own medicine, but he's not as hard as Kel would have expected. Toni looks guiltily at him in the half-light, lower lip drawn in and eyes wide. He looks like he wants to apologize, but Kel doesn't let him. He leans in, kisses that soft mouth, and closes his fingers around Toni's cock. It's easy to touch him, gentle and lazy, and to show him how much he means. Whoever he ends up being, however he wants to live his life, and whatever changes he may eventually decide it's right to make, Kel's determined his honey's going to make those choices knowing that he's safe, that he's loved, and that he isn't alone.

The pleasure Kel gives him is long, drawn-out and, eventually, messy. He holds Toni's gaze the whole time, one good hand working on his shaft and balls, knowing almost everything by touch. Toni's slim thighs close, open, and quake, and he rises up on his elbows, spine curved and head dropping back. The line of his throat—a beautiful arch bisected by the sharp angle of his Adam's apple—is colored amber by the reflections of the streetlamps outside, and his eyes start to close, lashes twin lines of sable on his cheek.

"Look at me," Kel says softly. "A'ight? Look at me, baby."

Toni does, and one of those wonderful noises breaks from his mouth. It's somewhere between an "oh" and an "unh" and, in among the supple planes of his waist, his neat, trim arms and the ribs that are still a little too obvious for Kel's liking, his honey has rarely seemed so feminine. It's a hungry, raw femininity, feral and powerful, but it's there all the same, right alongside his irrepressible maleness, that lithe energy that Kel loves so much.

Even his cock is pretty. So well-proportioned, so hard and heavy in his palm. It sits at that beautiful place between smooth and textured, strong and sleek, and the heat that blooms from it drives Kel crazy. He wants his mouth around it, but that would mean breaking away from where he is now, and that won't do. Especially when Toni reaches out a languid hand and cups his cheek, dark eyes half-hooded. He mumbles a curse, and his fingers tense on Kel's skin. Kel knows what he wants. He leans in. Lips meet, tongue slipping along tongue, and Toni's sighing into his mouth, smooth-skinned belly tightening, and then he's coming, his pleasure hot and wet between them. He's oddly vulnerable at that moment, in a way Kel's not seen for a long time. Toni holds on to him, face pressed close to his, breath rasping in small, panting gasps.

Kel holds him tight, whispers promises that don't make sense and can't possibly be fulfilled. He knows it's bull even as he says it. Nothing in life is ever perfect, and he can't make it that way, however hard he tries. All the same, Toni makes it worth trying, worth promising... worth working for.

They'll move on in the morning.

Oh, they could go anywhere. Just fucking go. All the way to Chicago, to Seattle, even. Anywhere his honey wants. They could do it—they have all they'll ever need to get by right here in this bed—and it could be a wonderful life.

Except, that wouldn't be right.

They can't just run from everything they have at home. Good things and bad, they need to be dealt with, changed by measured and decisive action. If he's learned anything from life, from the meetings he goes to, from everything Toni's put him through, Kel's learned that change comes slow. There's no point in fighting that, in trying to push through it fast and pretending it doesn't exist.

Change has to be worked for, built brick by brick.

Toni snuggles up close, his arm around Kel's neck, and sighs contentedly. Kel blinks, almost like he's forgotten Toni's there, turns his head, and buries his nose in those short-cropped curls. He smells so good. He strokes Toni's shoulder with lazy fingers, more than ready for sleep.

Yeah. In the morning, he'll hit the bus schedules, get tickets fixed up, and, when Toni's ready, they're gonna pack up again and they're gonna go home. Just fucking go.

Because, once you find home, you don't run from it.

Not ever again.

M. KING resides in a damp, verdant corner of southwest England, where she may usually be found behind a keyboard and a vat of coffee. Her work features flawed and fascinating characters, vibrant storytelling, and worlds to lose yourself in time and again, with titles ranging from horror to fantasy, humor to romance, erotica to tear-jerking drama... and more.

On the rare occasions she isn't writing, M. King enjoys taking long, muddy walks with her dogs—otherwise known as the hairy chaos monkeys—reading, dabbling in her herb garden, and falling off horses. Just not all at the same time.

Visit her website at http://www.thenakednib.com. You can contact her at mkingauthor@gmx.com.

Also from M. KING

BREAKING FAITH

M. KING

http://www.dreamspinnerpress.com

Also from M. KING

PASSING
SHADOWS

M. KING

http://www.dreamspinnerpress.com